MEASURE OF
PEACE
CAETHES FARON

ISBN-13: 978-0615850207
ISBN-10: 0615850200

The *Measure of Devotion* trilogy:

Measure of Devotion
Measure of Strength
Measure of Peace

MEASURE OF PEACE

CHAPTER ONE

The crunch of tires on gravel pulled Jason from the letter he was reading. A glance out the window confirmed that Kale's maroon and beige Killian S Model had turned off the road and was speeding up the long, tree-lined drive. The convertible, one of the newest cars on the market, was capable of a stunning seventy kilometers an hour. The thrill on Kale's face as he topped out with the top down made the car well worth the price. Jason folded up the letter and shoved it into his desk drawer. Its troubling contents could wait until later.

Jason hurried downstairs. Kale had been at the art gallery all day, and Jason's skin crawled with the need to see him. Jason could have accompanied Kale into Calea, but he liked to encourage Kale's independence, even if Jason would have preferred to spend the rest of time by his side. Jason wasn't needed at the gallery, so he'd left Kale to it.

"Jason, I'm home." Kale's voice boomed through their modest house.

Jason hopped down from the third stair to the floor and ran into Kale's strong arms. "Welcome back, love."

Kale chuckled. "I was gone for what, seven hours? No need to get this excited."

"I can't help it. I missed you."

"Aww. Isn't that sweet? I missed you too. You could have come along, you know."

"Yes, but this is your opening. I didn't want to be in the way. You want to go for a walk and tell me about it?"

Kale's smile lit up his face, and Jason marveled at how much lighter he looked. He'd retained the glow of freedom ever since the day they'd crossed the border into Naiara two years ago, making Kale a free man. He still bore the scars of slavery on his body and mind, but there was now a luminous quality to him. From his sandy hair to his pale green eyes to his honey-toned skin, there was an undeniable glow about him.

"Sure." Kale tossed his satchel onto the hall table and reached for Jason's hand in a familiar gesture. Their affection had become more relaxed and habitual, without the need to hide or temper their feelings. Naiara had freed more than just Kale's body.

The sun heated Jason's skin, and he unfastened his cufflinks to roll up his sleeves. He wished he had thought to remove his vest. Even at home, Jason dressed more formally than Kale, who preferred a tunic-style shirt like the one he presently wore and simple cotton or wool trousers.

They meandered through the gardens along the cobblestone path Kale had laid with his own hands. The light fragrance of the dozen or so varieties of flowers that Kale had planted sweetened the air. The summer sun was still high in the sky despite the evening hour. Birds twittered to each other in the grove of trees past the gardens. It was their own little slice of paradise outside the old city walls. The eight acres was more than enough for the vegetable garden Kale tended, the flowers, an orange grove, and a pond that straddled the back of their property line.

Jason steered them over to some shrubs. "I groomed these bushes earlier today. I hope I didn't ruin anything. There were some stray stems." With all the work Kale was doing for his art show, he didn't get to spend as much time in

2

the garden as Jason knew he would have liked. Jason tried to help out when he could in the yard, but it was Kale's domain.

Kale knelt and inspected the bushes in question. "You did great." He stood and pulled Jason in for a quick kiss. "Thanks for taking care of them for me. This show has taken more of my time than I realized it would." Kale took Jason's hand, and they continued their stroll.

"It's my pleasure. I like to feel useful."

"Yeah, because earning all the money to keep us in our current lifestyle isn't useful at all."

"You know what I mean." The truth was that nobody would have guessed Jason was a steel magnate from the way they lived. The one real external indicator of Jason's wealth, besides their car, was their complete use of the new electrical appliances, even in the kitchen. Outside of the city, it had been impossible to find a house completely wired with electricity, so Jason had simply paid for the lines to be extended to their dream home. And by dream home, he meant their small, two-story cottage with pale yellow siding and dark red shutters. "Is everything ready for tomorrow?"

"Everything except for me. Josie had to shoo me out of the gallery. Every picture has been framed and hung perfectly. She and Carmichael really know their stuff. Do you know they redo the lighting for every show to make sure each piece is perfectly accentuated?"

"It doesn't surprise me, especially from a gallery of their caliber."

"I mean, I knew they did that for big artists who come in, but I didn't expect they'd do it for me."

Jason squeezed Kale's hand. In the year and a half since they'd moved to their new home, Kale had become a renowned artist. He even earned enough off his art and commissions to cover their living expenses. The art studio on the second floor of their house overlooked the back garden and was well used, though Kale still preferred to draw outside when the weather permitted. "I don't know when you're going to realize that you are a big artist. How many people do you think ever make a living from their art? Tomorrow's opening is a big deal for Carmichael's. They're going to make a lot of money on your show."

"I hope so. I'd hate to think they're wasting all their efforts. They're only doing it because we're friends with Josie."

"And as I recall, we're friends with Josie because she was so enamored with your drawing of that homeless woman she saw you working on in the park. I had to keep my hands all over you for her to finally get the message that only your art was available."

Kale chuckled. Jason had always loved the sound and look of Kale laughing, the way his eyes crinkled at the edges, forming lines that crisscrossed those still etched in his skin from the years he'd spent laying rail in the sun. "Well, you know if you ever got really worried, you could steal me back across the border to Arine, make me your slave again."

The joke hung uncomfortably in the air. While Jason was happy Kale could make light of his past in Arine, he still hated that those thoughts were in Kale's mind.

"Hey." Kale stopped and turned Jason toward him. "I'm only joking. I love you, Jason. I know I don't say it enough, but my gods, there's no one else I'd rather spend my life with." Kale's lips descended, brushing lightly against Jason's. He pushed further, his tongue delving into Jason's mouth. When Kale retreated, the bitter taste of coffee lingered.

"Hmm. Did you stop by Beans and Books on the way home?"

"I picked up a new novel. We were running out of reading material. I also ran into Lisa. She's a ball of nerves about the lecture day after tomorrow. Trumbly Hall is the biggest venue she's ever spoken in."

"She has no need to worry. She's an excellent public speaker. I swear, if any change for the better comes to Naiara, it's going to be with her leading the charge."

"I told her we'd attend."

"Good. What's her subject matter to be?"

"The lack of a strong social net for the poor."

"Not women's rights?"

"No. She's going to argue that women's rights make little difference when so many women are trapped by poverty."

"Clever. It should be interesting." They had reached the end of the stone path near a stack of boards. Kale had plans to build a gazebo as soon as he wasn't needed in the city so much. This art show was the first time Kale had been exclusively showcased, and he was putting as much time as he could into ensuring it was a success for the gallery owners.

"Neissa's probably here already. We should head in so we're not late for dinner. It also wouldn't hurt to get some weeding in before the sun sets."

"Don't worry about it. I weeded the vegetable patch after you left this morning. I'm sure there's plenty left for you to do, but it will wait until later. You don't need to be famous artist, horticulture expert, and lover extraordinaire all at once. It makes us mere mortals feel inadequate." Jason wrapped his arm around Kale's waist and squeezed him close, smiling as he kissed Kale's neck.

"I know. I've been slacking. Why do you think I've let you top every time for the last few weeks?"

Jason felt heat rise in his cheeks. After all this time, he should be used to Kale's teasing. Kale lifted Jason's hand that wasn't around his waist to his smiling lips and kissed it before holding it to his heart. He still wasn't one for flowery words, but he had become much less inhibited in his physical affection.

"I appreciate all your help, Jason. I know you have your own work to do with the business. Your support means a lot to me."

"You're welcome. You know you're worth it. Besides, Martin has the business running so smoothly, I'm hardly needed anymore."

"Don't be so modest. I know you could have been busy with more than a dozen charities these last few weeks, but you decided to take care of things here so I wouldn't have to."

"Then you should thank Neissa as well. She's been a great help."

"I intend to. I know how lucky I am."

Neissa was the lady they'd hired to cook dinners for them, since neither Jason nor Kale could cook more than the basics. They managed breakfast on their own, and Neissa usually had leftovers or something light arranged for lunch. Once a week, she spent a day cleaning. Other than that, Jason and Kale took care of the house themselves. Living simply let them focus on the important things in life: each other, friends, and causes that were close to their hearts.

While Kale freshened up for dinner, Jason went back to his office to go over Martin's letter again. The actual message from Martin was quite short, just a small paragraph stating that he had received the accompanying letter from Mr. Smithson, Jason's attorney in Perdana. Rumors had reached him of Robert Wadsworth's declining health. Jason didn't know what to make of it. A part of him knew he should care about his father's condition, but he couldn't muster the will. Down the hall, the bedroom door closed, and Jason hid the letter away before joining Kale in the dining room.

Throughout dinner, Jason couldn't keep his mind from wandering up to the letter in his desk. He didn't want it to affect him.

"Jason? Jason? Did you even hear what I asked?" Kale stared at him, brows creased with worry.

"Sorry, what was that?" Jason picked up a roll to try to hide his distraction.

"Nothing important. What's on your mind?"

"Nothing."

"Don't, Jason. Is something going on that I should know about? You don't need to shoulder everything yourself just because of this show. Tell me." Kale reached over and placed his hand on Jason's arm.

"I'm just thinking about some correspondence from Martin, wondering how I'm going to reply. There's nothing wrong." It was true enough, and there was no reason to burden Kale.

"All right. But if you need help with anything, or just to talk something through, let me know."

"Of course." The rest of the meal passed in the comfortable silence of two people perfectly at home with each other.

When they were done, they went up to the bedroom. Once they were both undressed, Kale retrieved the new book from his satchel and began to read *The Grisly Tale of Hunter Humphreys*. It was their nightly ritual. Jason would curl up against Kale's firm body, and Kale would read, his voice rich, strong, and warm. Jason felt relieved that they had a new book to hold Kale's attention until he was too tired to keep reading. Jason didn't think he'd be able to be physical tonight, not when his thoughts kept wandering back to that letter.

CHAPTER TWO

Kale ran. The sound of the whip snapping against bare flesh again and again thundered in the air. Torrential rain obscured his vision in the already dark night. Up ahead, he could just make out the outline of the overseer as the man pulled his arm back for yet another strike. The light of the torches and a flash of lightning formed a ghostly silhouette.

The muscles of Kale's legs burned as he trudged up the hill, feet slipping on the slick mud. The smell of wet earth nearly masked the torch smoke. A clap of thunder, a crack of the whip, and the shriek of a scream. The thunder nearly drowned out the screams, but they still pierced Kale's ears.

He crested the hill and saw his brother's face twist with agony, his back laid open, rain carrying his blood to pool in the mud below.

"My baby!" Kale's mother sobbed a few meters away.

He ran to throw his body between the whip and his small, twelve-year-old brother, but a man nearly twice his size intercepted him, pushing him back. Kale struggled against the weight, arms burning with the effort. The man stumbled, but it was a short-lived victory as the man's arm swung and hit Kale square in the jaw, sending him to the ground.

Kale's mother was by his side. She slapped him and spat on his face. Her saliva burned his skin. "This is all your fault!

You left us!"

The pain in Kale's chest was so fierce he wished the overseer would whip him instead. It would hurt less, and Kale was ready to die. His mother's face morphed into his brother's. "Why, Kale? Why'd you leave us? Don't you love us anymore?"

Once again, the face changed, and Jason's brown eyes peered down at him. "Kale, wake up. Wake up, Kale."

Kale shot up, dislodging Jason's hands that had been shaking his shoulders. His lungs burned with the oxygen he gulped in as quickly as his body allowed. Shivers overtook him as the air hit the sweat that drenched his body.

"Shh. It's all right, Kale. I'm here. It was just a dream. A nightmare." Jason rubbed soothing circles on Kale's back. His touch was incongruent with the dream images.

"I'll go sleep in the guest room." Before Kale could swing his legs off the side of the bed, he was flat on his back again, with Jason on top of him. The weight momentarily constricted Kale's breathing.

Jason entwined his legs around Kale's. It would be impossible to break free without a struggle, and there was no fight left in Kale. "No, you're staying right here. You're not bothering me, and I won't let you be alone."

The words comforted Kale, and he worked to relax his body, to remind his skin and muscles that the man on top of him loved him, had given him freedom. The man on top of him would not hurt him, wasn't his slave-master. The pressure was the familiar weight of his lover, nothing more. Shoulder muscles relaxed first, and the rest of Kale's body followed.

"What happened?" Jason's voice was soft and tender.

"I don't remember." Kale avoided Jason's eyes, knowing he'd see hurt there like there was every time. Kale hated lying, and not just because a part of him ached to confide in Jason. There was nothing Jason could do to fix the problem. He would only feel guilty. It was Kale's job to protect Jason, and he wouldn't burden him with the horrors that assaulted him every night.

"Well, if you ever do remember, or just want to talk, you know I'm here. There's nothing you could say that would change the way I feel about you. Whatever dark and ugly things haunt you, you can share them. They won't scare me." Worry tinged Jason's voice.

How could Kale divulge his nightmares to such a sweet man who worried so much over him? Jason's mind wasn't capable of imagining the things Kale dreamed about. If Kale shared, worry would turn to panic. Jason would feel guilty until he could fix it, and there was no fixing Kale. Nightmares were the price for his sins.

"I know, Jason. Let's just go to sleep. I have a busy day ahead of me." Kale wondered if Jason would pursue his line of questioning. A moment passed before Kale felt Jason nod and then relax on top of him. A minute later, a snore ruffled his chest hair.

Thoughts and images raced so fast through Kale's mind that sleep was an impossibility. The backdrop to all these thoughts was an oppressive guilt binding his soul. Shame washed over him, threatening to drown him. Had he so quickly forgotten the true meaning of oppression? The woman who gave him life was back in Arine, the property of a man. The thought turned his stomach. Whether he was disgusted at the thought of his mother still living as a slave or at himself for so easily leaving her there, he didn't know. Both.

In a matter of hours, Kale would attend the opening of his art showcase. People would mill about, looking at his drawings and paintings. They would toast him, the brother and son who had abandoned his family. While Thomas and Mama worked long days, Kale fiddled with his pastels and charcoal, tended a garden that was his to do with as he pleased, and called it work. They suffered while he built a life with a man who adored him.

That man was still curled around Kale tight enough that any escape attempt would wake him. Instead of fleeing to the spare bedroom, Kale ran his fingers through Jason's thick brown hair. A feather soft moan escaped Jason's mouth as he stirred before settling into the touch. It would be the epitome of ungratefulness for Kale to share his nightmares. Jason had freed him and given him a life that was more ideal than anything Kale could ever deserve. How could he even hint that it wasn't enough? It would be cruel to unburden himself onto his partner who would try so very hard to understand but would fall short through no fault of his own. Jason couldn't understand. No free man could.

Moonlight drifted in through a crack in the drapes and illuminated a black and white photograph on Jason's bedside table. It had been taken by a photographer friend the day they'd bought the house. Kale smiled at the memory, though it paled in comparison to the smiles caught on film that day. Their arms were draped around each other and their faces alight with the possibilities of their new life. Jason snuggled in closer to Kale. His hot breath on Kale's chest was so familiar that, on the occasions when Kale had been able to escape to the guest bedroom, his sleep was restless without it.

Kale closed his eyes and tried to sleep. He would need to be up in a few hours, and people were counting on him. He couldn't let them down, despite how easily he had let down his own family. As drowsiness overtook him, his thoughts drifted with anticipation to the activities of the day. A brief moment of honesty before he drifted off, because it wasn't his guilt or wretchedness that really bothered him. What he hated most was how damn happy he was. He had no right to it, but he felt it just the same.

CHAPTER THREE

Jason elbowed his way through the crowd, careful not to jostle the two champagne flutes he carried. When he reached Kale, he stood back while a reporter from the Calea Gazette snapped a photograph of Kale with one of his pieces. The reporter tried to coax a smile out of Kale, but all he got was an expression that most resembled a grimace. When it was apparent Kale wasn't going to get any more comfortable in front of the camera, the reporter shook his hand and thanked him for his time.

"You might want to try not looking like you're in quite so much pain." Jason handed Kale the champagne.

"I just don't understand what they want a picture of me for or why they want an interview. I drew some pictures and painted some others. It's not like I have a plan to solve childhood hunger."

"No, you don't, but you may inspire someone who does. This is amazing, Kale. I've never seen a crowd like this for an art show. I overheard them turning people away at the door. You've really hit a nerve."

"They've all come to see the ex-slave who can draw. I'm an oddity to them."

"You're an inspiration."

Before Kale could reply, another reporter approached

with some questions. Jason stayed close, but also took the opportunity to look at some of the pieces. Kale had always been shy about letting Jason see his work. Jason was convinced that the only reason Kale even let his work be displayed publicly was because he felt an obligation to bring in an income. That obligation was solely in his head, but Jason didn't mind it being there if it pushed Kale to live up to his potential.

The show was entitled "Forgotten Faces," and it was a collection of candid portraits of the poor and homeless throughout Calea. As the capital of Naiara, it had a considerable amount of poverty juxtaposed against the wealth that ran the country. Jason admired a painting of a beggar woman on the steps of the opera house. Theatre goers dressed in their finery scurried by. The opera house was adorned with gold leafing on the columns flanking the entrance. Yet somehow, Kale had made the drab colors of the woman the focal point. Kale was exceptional at using contrasting images to make a point. A glance at one of Kale's pictures revealed more to Jason than an hour of conversation with his lover.

"They leave you speechless, don't they?" Jason turned to see Lisa standing next to him.

"Yeah, they do." Jason looked at the picture for a moment longer. "Thanks for coming. I know Kale appreciates the support."

Lisa shook her head. "I didn't come for him, Jason. Don't get me wrong, I support him and would show up anywhere for him, but I came because there was no way I was going to miss this. These pictures were the inspiration for the lecture I'm giving tomorrow. I needed to see them again to remind me why I'm doing it and to calm my nerves."

"Wait, how did you get to see them? I wasn't even allowed to see a lot of these ahead of time."

Lisa's mouth quirked to the side. "Josie showed me. She knew I was interested in the subject matter and thought I should see them all." Her lips straightened into a firm line. "These images stay with you. I see them at the strangest times. It's like they've become a part of my consciousness. I can't imagine what it must be like to live with that sort of genius."

Jason's heart swelled with pride, and he glanced at Kale, who still looked supremely uncomfortable with the attention focused on him. "It's amazing. What's even more remarkable is that he really doesn't know how great he is. I'm still waiting for him to figure it out." Times like this made Jason marvel at his good fortune. There were days when he thought for sure Kale would realize just how extraordinary he was and decide that he didn't need Jason anymore.

"Wipe that look off your face. I've never seen a man more in love than Kale. Besides, you're the key to all this. You'd have a revolt on your hands if you two ever left each other."

"No, I have very little to do with this." Jason went back to admiring the picture.

"That's not what Kale says. According to him, he couldn't draw when you were apart. He says you gave him the security to be vulnerable enough to put himself on the canvas."

Jason's head jerked around to Lisa. "Really? When did he say all that?"

"Oh, just here and there."

"Hmm." Jason let the moment pass. He didn't know Kale talked about him to other people. "I knew he was becoming more popular, but I really didn't expect this. I don't know how Carmichael filled this place so quickly. It's not because of Kale's past, is it?" Jason wasn't ashamed of Kale's history as a slave, but he knew Kale was eager to make his way on his own merits, not as the subject of morbid curiosity. Jason hated to think that the interest in Kale's art came from anything but the art itself.

"Are you kidding? I doubt most people here even know his history, and they certainly wouldn't be this interested

15

based on the novelty. The gallery didn't need to do much more than announce the show. People are here from all over Naiara. Everyone's worried it will sell out."

"It's a four-week show."

Lisa laughed. "Not the show, silly, the art. I know Kale's dense enough to think that there isn't a demand for his original pieces, but I didn't expect you to be so obtuse. The only reason he's not selling more is because he's not producing more. When word got out that there was going to be a show full of his originals, people clamored to be the first to get their picks."

Jason had no idea. He knew Kale was making a name for himself throughout the country—it was an advantage to living in the capital and having a broad network of influential friends—but this frenzy was more than Jason had imagined. The normally hushed gallery was so loud Jason couldn't hear the string quartet in the corner.

Lisa rested her hand on Jason's arm. "I've got to go say hello to some people. You and Kale are going to come out with us afterward, right? We all want to celebrate with him somewhere a little more intimate."

"Of course. Thanks, Lisa. I'll see you later."

Lisa nodded and made her way to the other side of the room. Jason was eager to be near Kale, who still seemed to be in the midst of an interview. Jason suspected he hated every minute of it. Jason didn't want to encroach on or curtail the interview, but he wanted Kale to know that he was there should he need him. He positioned himself within Kale's line of sight, but far enough off to the side that Kale wouldn't feel like he was hovering.

As soon as Jason made eye contact with him, Kale sighed and started to smile. He looked back at the reporter, nodded, shook the man's hand, and advanced toward Jason.

"Save me, please."

Jason chuckled. "Is fame not all it's cracked up to be?"

"I don't know why I even need to be here. The art looks

the same whether I'm in the room or not."

"People like to walk amongst genius, myself included. You don't have to ask me twice to hang on your arm. Why don't you give me a tour? I haven't gotten to see them all yet. You can pretend we're back home, and it's just us."

"I think I can manage that." Kale took Jason's arm and led him around the exhibit.

Jason tried to discuss each piece objectively, as if they were at someone else's show. Kale responded well. He was still uneasy talking about his own work, but at least it was in a context he could manage. Over time, Jason noticed people following them, straining to hear Kale's commentary. Jason gradually raised his voice, and Kale subconsciously mirrored his volume. When they reached the end, the group following them broke into applause, startling Kale into finally looking around.

"Were they there the entire time?"

"Yes, you dolt. They love you." Jason couldn't resist the bewildered look on Kale's face and kissed him. "I'm so proud of you. Thank you for being mine."

This was Jason's life. Here in this gallery—in the man in front of him—was everything important to him. Nothing else mattered; not whatever was happening in Arine, and certainly not the letter buried in his desk.

CHAPTER FOUR

"We must demand abolishment. It's time we force Arine out of barbarism and into modern times." Harry slammed his fist on the glass top of the wrought iron table, rattling the empty wine bottles in the middle.

"It's not practical." Jason's voice was steady. Kale's lover was one of the more sober people around the table. The six of them sat outside the Lady Lion, a cafe they frequented often for its late hours. The opening had ended three hours before, and Kale's friends had brought him here for a private celebration. Thankfully, the conversation had turned from Kale to politics.

"No, no. If we're going to have this discussion, we're going to have it properly. Margaret!" Daniel bellowed for the waitress. "Bring us all some coffee, nice and strong. And clear these bottles and glasses away."

Margaret reached for Kale's whiskey. "No, thank you. I'll keep mine." As always, Kale didn't get drunk. While his friends were trying to sober up for a debate, Kale wanted the soothing comfort of his drink. He would likely need it.

"This is the time to act. With our trade treaty up for renewal this year, we finally have some leverage with Arine. I say we don't let the government ratify the treaty as long as slavery is legal in Arine." Jessica was the daughter of a

Member of Parliament. Not only did Kale's friends have the desire for change, they were actually in a position to affect it. Sometimes, Kale felt out of place among such principled people. He was active in politics and wanted change, but he was a simple man who liked to draw and spend lazy afternoons with his lover.

"You two could really help the movement. You'd be the perfect spokespeople for it." Lisa took a sip of her newly arrived coffee.

"Hmph, because I'm so good at public speaking?" Kale had barely been able to handle the interviews at the gallery. He couldn't inspire people with words. Jason could, though. If he wanted to.

"Words aren't how you communicate best. Your exhibit tonight did more for bringing awareness to the problems of the poor in Calea than a dozen lectures ever could. If you could do a similar show with pictures from your memories as a slave, it would go a long way." Kale envied the fire in Lisa's eye.

"Kale draws what he wants, Lisa. His memories aren't your personal political playground." Jason's voice held a dangerous edge. Kale placed a hand on his arm. At Kale's touch, Jason met his eyes. Kale could see exactly which memories Jason was thinking of: the ones still imprinted on the flesh of Kale's back.

"Perhaps you don't want the law to change. You make quite a profit off of slaves in your steel mills." Daniel's eyes were cool, all trace of the warm wine gone.

"Watch yourself." Kale didn't mind a debate, but accusations were another matter.

"It doesn't matter to my business either way. I do enough domestic business that, if a trade treaty didn't pass because of a requirement to ban slavery, we wouldn't go under. And if slavery was abolished, we'd be able to absorb the costs of hiring free workers just fine."

"Then why don't you do it? Why use slaves? It's wrong."

The pleading in Jessica's voice removed any sting of accusation. Hope shone in her face as she leaned forward.

"You don't think I've struggled with that? But Kale and I have talked it over. The truth of the matter is, if I didn't hire those slaves, they'd be working in much worse conditions."

"Hire?" Jessica sat back in her chair.

"Yes. I hire a labor firm that provides the slaves."

"Oh, isn't that great? So not only do you get cheap labor, these firms get to pocket the money that should go to the laborers." Daniel's sneer was beginning to wear on Kale's nerves.

"You don't know what you're talking about. Jason's right. The way he runs his mill is heaven compared to what else those slaves would be doing."

Harry leaned his elbows on the table, finally joining the conversation after finishing his coffee. "But it's not right."

"No, it's not. Every man deserves to be free. I won't argue with you on that point, but we're not discussing a perfect world." It was nice to hear Jason speak pragmatically. He'd once been as idealistic as their friends. Kale wondered if his jaded cynicism was affecting Jason. "Arinians see owning slaves as their birthright as conquerors. They won't give it up easily. Their society isn't ready to. Even if they did ban slavery, what would happen to all the slaves? They wouldn't be able to get work. The stigma would be too strong. They're not trained for the workforce. Their lives would be better only in that they would die free."

"Better to die free than live a slave!" Daniel pontificated.

Kale grunted. None of these children had a fucking clue what they were talking about. Daniel shot a look his way, but Lisa spoke before he could.

"What do you think, Kale? You must have a strong perspective on this. It's really your opinion we should be asking for."

Kale pursed his lips, considering whether he should answer or brush off the question. Lisa was a gentle girl with a good heart. She didn't want to hear his truth—she only thought she did.

"Yes, Kale. Tell us what you think. What was it like living as a slave to your lover?" Sharp looks from Harry and Lisa met Daniel's obnoxious tone.

Kale toyed with his glass and then met Daniel's eyes. "What do I think? I think you don't know what it's like to live a life where you spend eighteen hours a day on your feet, where you'd give anything just for a moment to sit, but you don't dare take a chance because you know the pain of getting caught far outweighs the pain of working. Sitting here drinking coffee and wine, you can't possibly understand what it means to thirst, to want a drop of water so badly the thought crosses your mind to drink your own piss, except you realize you haven't pissed all day because there's no moisture left in your body. It's for the best anyway, because you don't get bathroom breaks. You don't know what it's like to forget what anything tastes like except for stale, moldy bread, to finally taste butter on your lips and think that you must have been transported to the heavens because nothing could possibly taste so good. You've never collapsed at the end of the day and been thankful for the bed bugs biting your skin because at least that means you've got a straw mattress under you instead of the hard floor. None of you has a damn idea what you're talking about." Kale tried to distance himself from these conversations as much as he could, but with every word, he knew his mother and brother suffered through the same, maybe worse, maybe a little better.

Kale didn't bother voicing the real horrors. There was no way to make his friends understand what it meant to realize as a boy that a slave was not a man, that by virtue of his birth, he was less than, different, substandard. The truth was, not all slaves had it physically bad. Kale certainly hadn't while he'd belonged to Jason. The other slaves Kale had known in Perdana could even be said to have lived a life of moderate comfort. Compared to the lower classes of Arine, upper-class slaves had a better physical existence. The true torture took place in the realm of the mind. Physical pain faded and healed, but not the mental. There was no way to convey it accurately to people who had never lived through it, who had never once doubted that they were people. Simpler for all involved to restrict it to the bodily harm of being a slave.

Jason met Kale's eyes. He was the one man who could comprehend the depths of the mental agony. "Kale's right." Jason turned to the group. "You don't understand, and until you at least try to, you won't get anywhere. You need to approach this from the right angle." Jason didn't seem to be upset by Kale's diatribe.

"And let this opportunity pass us by?" Jessica shook her head, clearly not willing to take a passive role.

"No, certainly not. I'm saying the exact opposite: don't waste it. There's a real chance here for change, but it needs to be change that people who haven't been afforded the same privileges as you can accept. It's a privilege to not have to live in a slave society. Don't take it for granted. Reforms are more peaceful and long-lasting than violent revolutions."

"Jason's right." Harry nodded. "We need to push for reforms that will help the lives of the slaves. Prepare the road for abolition."

"Yes, like regulations and controls on the trade." Lisa pushed her coffee mug out of the way so she could lean further onto the table.

"The greedy Arinians," Daniel said, "won't like anything that cuts into their profits."

"Actually, I can help with that. We've done studies on the issue and have found that humane treatment of slaves yields better quality work and results in a net profit. I can have my business associate, Martin, send over the findings for you to study." Jason was actually an authority on this issue. Couple that with his close friendship with the prime minister, and he could do more than merely help the cause.

Lisa clapped her hands. "That would be perfect, Jason.

We need to show Arine that it's in everybody's best interest to enact real change."

On and on, they went around the table, trying to find the optimal balance of reform and idealism. All around, Kale saw bright eyes despite the late hour. Fierce passion filled the air. These people, who had never even seen a real slave, who had never witnessed the horrors of dehumanization, were spending their free time working to make the world better. Meanwhile, Kale had left his own family behind and was too much of a coward to even talk to Jason about it. So great was his fear of being owned that he couldn't even give voice to thoughts that might threaten to disrupt his happiness.

Whiskey slid down his throat, leaving a pleasant burn in its wake. He ached for his family, and he ached for the fire of his friends to light his soul. If it burned brightly enough, it just might banish the dark shadows that paralyzed him.

CHAPTER FIVE

The absence of Kale's warmth in the bed forced Jason's eyes open. It wasn't uncommon for Kale to wake before him, but he was usually next to him in bed, reading or sketching, when Jason woke.

After a stretch that made his muscles feel like rubber, Jason sat up against the headboard. His internal clock said it was time to be up, but they hadn't gotten home until after two o'clock in the morning, and Jason's body and mind protested. It took a moment for his blurry eyes to focus on a scowling Kale sitting on the sofa fully dressed. Another moment, and Jason saw the letter clasped in his hand. The sight banished the fog of drowsiness, and Jason sighed. This was not how he wanted to start the morning.

"Do you have anything to say for yourself?" Kale's cool, green eyes penetrated Jason's, and Jason had to look away. It wasn't fair, Kale ambushing him like this so early in the day. They were on decidedly unequal footing.

"No. Should I? It's a private letter. Do you have anything to say for yourself, going through my things?"

"Don't give me that, Jason." The downside to Kale finally using his name was that Jason occasionally had to hear it in the tense tone that made Jason feel like an errant child being scolded by his parents. "When were you planning on telling me about this?"

Jason swung his legs over the edge of the bed and braced himself to rise. He needed coffee and a splash of cold water on his face. "Never. It's not relevant." Jason stood and wrapped his robe around himself.

"Your father is dying, and you weren't even going to tell me?" The hurt in Kale's voice arrested Jason. Kale's anger he could rebuff until he was more prepared for this conversation. Hurt, however, required his immediate attention.

Jason sat on the sofa next to Kale and wasn't too surprised when Kale moved away. "Look, I didn't want to bother you with it. It's inconsequential. We've never been close. You know that better than most. I didn't want you thinking that my decision to stay away had something to do with you, because it doesn't."

"You're not even planning on going?"

"What, you thought I would go without telling you?"

"I thought you might under the cover of business."

"And leave you? After I had to work so hard to get you? Not likely." Jason reached out to caress Kale's face, but Kale sat back, out of reach, appearing to skim the letter. "I don't understand why this bothers you. I don't bore you with the details of every letter that crosses my desk."

"We don't keep secrets."

"Like you don't keep secrets about what wakes you up screaming in the middle of the night?" Jason's voice came dangerously close to a yell.

Kale looked as if he'd been slapped. His mouth formed a firm line, but his voice was whisper soft. "You withheld it to lie to me. That's why I'm upset."

Jason settled into the cushions with his arm across the back of the sofa. "All right, that's partly true. I don't want to go, and I didn't want you feeling bad about it. I know you think my falling out with him was your fault, but it wasn't. We argued about a whole litany of things for years before we argued about you."

"He's your father, Jason." At least this time his name was said more gently. "Regardless of the cause, you need to go to him and mend this rift."

"What?" Jason leaned forward. "Why? That man has never approved of me. He disowned me."

"And took you back when you married Renee."

"Yes, I'm sure he's thrilled that my wife lives in Arine while I'm here playing house with my slave. You know that's how he sees us. I'm dead to that man, and pretty soon, he'll be dead to me." Jason's resolve wavered on the last words. It was the first time he had spoken them out loud.

"Jason, you can't fool me. You may like to pretend that he's nothing to you, but I know better. You've always wanted his approval. If he is really nothing to you, why do you care what he thinks?"

"Going to him won't change what he thinks of me, so why go? So I can get more of the same from him? One last jab at me from his deathbed?" Jason didn't even realize that's what bothered him until the words came out. There was no taking them back. Kale would know they were true.

"If you don't go, you'll always wonder. It could turn out better than you think. You could make peace with him. And if he chooses to be an ass, at least you'll know. You won't have to wonder and torture yourself with guilt, which we both know you excel at."

"I'm willing to take the chance."

A glimmer of distress passed over Kale's face, a brief widening of the eyes as the muscles of his cheeks tensed. At one time, Jason had believed Kale was the picture of equanimity. That was before he'd trained his eyes to search for the signs. Kale wasn't a calm pool; he was the ocean that only appeared tranquil from a distance. "Why do you have to be so stubborn?"

"Why do you want me to go so badly?" Jason narrowed his eyes, alert to any change in Kale's demeanor in case the other man wouldn't be forthcoming. "We don't keep secrets from each other, remember? Why do you want me to go?"

"Because you have a chance at peace with your father."

"And why does that matter to you? Because you never met your father?"

"What? Don't make this about me. I've told you before that I've never had a father, so there's never been one for me to miss."

Jason had missed the mark, but there was something there. Kale had been more defensive than normal. "Yes, but you do have a mother and a brother. Is this about them?"

"No, it's about you and your father." Kale's voice was steady, but his breathing had increased, his chest rising and falling in shallow waves. Jason had seen it before.

"Kale, what are your nightmares about?" Jason scooted closer to him on the sofa but didn't touch, worried at this point that it might provoke a negative reaction.

Kale's face was stricken. His skin blanched, turmoil swirling in his eyes. For a moment, Jason wanted to take the question back and hold Kale in his arms, anything to make that look go away. "Nothing."

Jason grasped Kale's head between his hands, forcing eye contact while he pressed his body against Kale's, letting his weight settle against him without pinning him. "What is this really about, Kale?"

Tears pooled in Kale's beautiful, pale green eyes, magnifying the amber flakes in his irises. Kale rarely cried. Jason could only think of a few instances in the years they had been together. He had let this go on too long. He should have pushed for the truth about the night terrors long ago.

"They're still there, Jason. They're my family, and I left them there so I could live this perfect life with you. I don't know if they're even alive. You have a chance for closure. It's important. I know because I live every day without it." The tears broke free from his lashes and spilled down his cheeks. "Please take it."

"Oh, Kale." Jason pulled Kale into a hug. "Why didn't you tell me about this sooner?"

"I didn't want to burden you or make you think anything was wrong or that I was ungrateful. I'm so happy here with you, Jason. I really am. But that just makes it harder, knowing how happy I am. What right do I have?"

"Every right. It's not your fault they're slaves."

"Maybe not." Kale leaned back on the sofa. "But I should have tried. I shouldn't have run away without even a backward glance. They're my family. I need to go back and try to find them. After last night—seeing how everyone cares so much for the slaves in Arine they've never met, and here I am with family still enslaved not doing half as much as they are —I decided it's time to act. I was rummaging through your things because I was looking for your appointment book. I wanted to see if there was a time that might be good for a visit to Arine."

"We'll make time. We can leave as soon as you like— today if you want."

"Thank you. But I want you to make a real effort with your father. I can't bear the thought of the regret you'll feel if you don't at least try."

Jason nodded. He would do anything for Kale. "Of course. I promise I'll try."

"Good." Kale stood, placing Martin's crumpled letter on the side table. "We promised Lisa we'd go to her lecture. Today should be about her, but I'm anxious to leave as soon as we can be ready."

Jason nodded. Kale could always be counted on to keep his commitments to his friends. Jason couldn't imagine the feelings of disloyalty eating away at Kale for leaving his family in Arine. It would take more than words to assuage his guilt. Jason only hoped that Kale would be able to find the peace he so wanted for those around him.

CHAPTER SIX

Kale felt an itch deep inside. Ever since the decision had been made to travel back to Malar County, he'd felt out of place. While Jason had been willing to leave right away, Kale insisted they attend to practical matters first. The trip would be easier if there weren't things back home occupying their thoughts. Even though every minute of his day was spent preparing, Kale still felt as if he should do more. His blood tingled with the urge to move, to walk out the door and keep going until he reached Arine.

Kale folded the last of Jason's trousers and placed them in his trunk. Keeping his hands busy helped calm some of his anxiety. It took a little maneuvering, but Kale situated everything and closed the trunk. The soft click of the clasps removed one more item from his mental checklist.

"I just got off the phone with Donald in the prime minister's office." Jason walked through the open bedroom door. "He assures me that Gerald will place the full weight of the government behind us if we run into any problems while we're in Arine."

"That's nice to know." Kale scanned his closet, trying to decide what to bring.

"You're not worried are you? The Arinian government is already concerned they're going to have to make some concessions on the issue of slavery in order to get the trade treaty signed. There's enormous international pressure. They're not going to inflame the situation by making an issue over a legal Naiaran citizen who used to be a slave."

"I'm aware. It's not the government I'm worried about." Kale turned from the closet to give Jason his full attention. "I have no fears of being made a slave again. You've made sure of that. It's one of the many things you've given me, and you don't have to worry. I promise. I'm much more concerned with the local trouble we may run into." There wouldn't be too many people happy with the thought of a former slave returning to buy back his family. There was no legal way for a slave to be freed in Arine, so the circumstances were more than taboo—they were anathema. Only Naiara's willingness to grant Kale citizenship had saved him from legal entanglements.

"I've packed all your documents in my valise that I'll be carrying with me on the train. Your title is in there along with our passports and the articles of incorporation, just in case." It was wise on Jason's part, but Kale had mixed feelings about his title. On one hand, it was a reminder that Kale had been merchandise that could switch hands. On the other, it was the closest thing he would ever have to emancipation. Jason had established a corporation owned by Kale and had transferred Kale's title into the corporation. Holding his own title was the closest Kale could come to freedom while the law still viewed him as a slave. "I hope we won't need them. Do you really think there's a chance you'll be recognized?"

"Not by most people, but the Cartwrights will recognize me. I haven't changed that much since your father bought me from them to give to you. They'll take issue with me being back as a free man. My only other concern is your father."

"We don't have to stay in his home, Kale. We don't even have to see him."

"Yes, we do. Or at least you do."

"I'm not going to let you stay by yourself."

"Exactly. Staying there is the best situation. I can find my family, and you can take the time you need with your father. Beyond that, there are practicalities. Once your father passes, you'll need to be there to handle the estate."

"That's what attorneys are for."

"We can't move forward while our past is still clinging to us. If it doesn't work out, we can always go to a hotel. I'm not asking you to do anything against your conscience. I'm just asking you to take a chance, to know that you did your best so that, when he passes, we'll be free of him in heart and mind as well as body."

"I hate it when you make sense. Out of all the men in the world, I have to fall for the one who's always right."

"I can think of a few times I've been wrong. At least when you've been wrong, lives haven't been destroyed in the fallout."

"Not destroyed, strengthened."

Their eyes met and held. Kale was once again stunned that Jason held no animosity toward him for all the hell he had put him through, the hell he had put both of them through. Jason believed the words he said. Kale cupped Jason's neck and kissed him hard. Kale was the luckiest bastard in the world. For some unknown reason, the gods had smiled down on him.

When they broke apart, Jason was flushed, but there wasn't time to pursue him further, so Kale went back to the closet.

"Did you pack a set of tails?" Jason moved toward his trunk.

"Don't open that. Yours is all done. Yes, I packed tails, though I don't know when you think you'll have cause to use them." This was what was making Kale's packing so difficult. If it was up to him, he'd throw a few shirts and a few pair of trousers in a bag and be good, but Jason wanted them to pack their finest clothes. It was a sad attempt to impress his father. It amazed Kale that Jason knew so little about his own father after growing up with the man. Kale had spent less than three days in Robert Wadsworth's home and knew that fancy clothes were more likely to decrease Robert's opinion of his son than to increase it.

"I don't want to be caught unprepared."

"Then prepare yourself to see your father differently than you ever have. That letter made it sound as if he's pretty bad off." Kale pulled some shirts from their hangers and threw them on the bed to fold.

"Don't worry about me. Is there anything I can do to help?"

"Did you get the tickets arranged?"

"Yes, they're waiting for us at will call in three hours. I also have a space in freight reserved for the car."

Kale smiled his thanks. It would be nice to have that bit of freedom and familiarity, but he had been too frugal to ask that they take it.

"There was no way I was going to listen to you pine for it the entire time. I've called Martin and let him know we're coming. He says he shouldn't need me for any business matters. Since you've already packed my things, I don't see that there's anything else for me to do. What do you have left?"

"Just to pack my trunk. It shouldn't take long. We'll drop off that painting in the corner at the gallery on our way to the station. I don't have any other commissions that can't wait until we get back. Are you sure you don't want to call your father?"

"I don't even know if he has a telephone. He's never been one to keep up with technology."

"You could write or send a telegram if that's really the issue."

"No. I don't want him to know we're coming. I want to see his reaction. If he doesn't want us staying there, I don't want him to have time to spread rumors about us and make things more difficult. It's better this way."

"Fine, if you say so. I'll be ready in a half hour."

Jason nodded and took his valise downstairs. Kale turned back to the closet and grabbed a stack of trousers. He made sure he had some nice clothes to match Jason's so he wouldn't embarrass him, but other than that, he didn't care. Ten minutes later, he hefted their trunks into the car.

CHAPTER SEVEN

Jason sat across from Kale, watching him gaze absently out the window. The ride to the station had been filled with empty chatter, confirming that everything was ready. There had been an undercurrent of excitement, but it was comfortable. As soon as they'd boarded the train, the chatter stopped. Kale sat and looked out the window as the train pulled away and hadn't moved in the three hours since. He didn't even seem to be aware of Jason watching him.

If they found Kale's family and purchased them, the family would be entitled to Naiaran citizenship as refugees, the same as Kale had been. Jason had never thought of Kale as a refugee, but he supposed it was accurate. While Jason had freely made the decision to move to Naiara with Kale, Kale had come under completely different circumstances, fleeing a government that saw him as nothing more than property. Jason had done everything he could to help Kale feel like a free man, but how could he erase a lifetime of training? Kale would always retain the memories of being sold away from his mother and brother. While most men remembered with fondness the day they'd met the loves of their lives, for Kale that memory was of a rope changing hands as he was passed from one spoiled brat to another like a nursery room toy. Jason hoped this trip would give some closure to that part of

Kale's life and somehow make up for those memories.

A crease appeared and vanished just as quickly between Kale's eyes. Jason yearned for some sign of what he was thinking. The whole trip had him uneasy. He hoped for the best, but there were so many ways this could end in disaster. If Kale's family had been sold, they might not even be able to find them. There was no requirement for slave titles to be officially registered, and they often weren't in rural areas. Even if they did find Kale's family, they didn't have the power to force their owners to sell. Kale had told him before that the worst part was not knowing, but Jason didn't believe it. If Kale found them and couldn't purchase them, it would be so much worse. Jason didn't know how he'd be able to convince Kale to walk away. No amount of legal connections would protect them from charges of theft if Kale stole his family. Even if he smuggled them over the border, the law would force the return of the "stolen merchandise" if they were ever caught.

Then there was the other scenario. Jason didn't want to think about it. He didn't know which would be worse: finding Kale's family and not being able to save them, or finding out they were dead.

Jason shook the thought from his head. He needed to stay positive for Kale's sake. In all likelihood, everything would work out fine. In a few days, he would meet Kale's mother and brother. Would he see parts of Kale in them? Were Kale's intriguing eyes a gift from his mother? Would his brother emulate Kale's quiet steadiness?

A few days was all it would it take. Then they would be headed back home. With his family in tow, Kale would see the urgency in leaving and would forget his silly notion that Jason and his father should reconcile. With any luck, he would be in and out of Malar County without having to exchange more than a few words with the man.

CHAPTER EIGHT

The car bounced down the rough dirt road. Kale had only been to Robert Wadsworth's ranch a couple of times, but it wasn't hard to remember the way. He had never thought he'd be driving his own car down this road as a free man. Hell, the last time he had been to the ranch he'd barely even known what a car was. Automobiles had been introduced much later in Arine than in Naiara.

"You'll turn right up here." Jason pointed, and Kale nodded his understanding. His mind was too cluttered to make room for conversation. All Kale's thoughts were about a life far removed from the one he shared with his companion. It wasn't that Kale didn't think Jason would understand. He knew Jason would make an effort and wouldn't presume to understand when he really didn't. It was just that life with Jason really was perfect. Even the little imperfections made their domestic bliss that much sweeter. Kale couldn't ask for more. He didn't want to drag Jason into unpleasant memories of a past that neither of them could change. If he opened his mouth and brought Jason into his thoughts, it would only taint what they had.

The ranch house came into view, and the sound of a gasp focused Kale's attention. Next to him, Jason practically vibrated, his hand gripping the door handle until his knuckles whitened. Kale cursed himself for being so selfish. He should have been more attentive to Jason. He reached over and grabbed Jason's hand, giving him a smile.

The sprawling house would have looked inviting had Kale not had a history with it. Thick, red cedar logs formed a palatial, two-story structure. Large stone chimneys littered the roof. Rocking chairs and wicker sofas lounged on the porch. Dainty pink and yellow flowers poured out of clay pots. Dark green shutters framed the windows. From a distance, the place looked almost quaint. Only when Kale pulled into the massive driveway did it feel as if the house towered above them. It was that perfect mix of wealth and rural style that made Robert Wadsworth so respected throughout Malar County.

Kale parked the car. "Are you ready for this?"

Jason nodded. "As ready as I can be to face a man who hates me. At least this time I have you firmly by my side."

Kale kissed him on the lips. After a moment, when Jason didn't relax, Kale pulled back. "Hey, my offer still stands. Say the word, and I'll greet dear old Dad with a bear hug."

Jason smiled and then chuckled. "Finish him off with the shock?"

"Anything for you."

"Thanks. I really couldn't do this without you. You know you're the only reason I'm even here."

"I know, but save some of the sweet talk for your father." Kale got out of the car, and he and Jason walked to the door together. After Jason lightly knocked, he grabbed Kale's hand in a crushing grip. Kale didn't see the point in antagonizing Robert by flaunting their relationship, but he wasn't going to leave Jason without support.

A nondescript slave answered the door and ushered them to wait in the sitting room. Neither of them sat. Kale didn't think Jason would release his hand if he made a move toward one of the chairs. Standing was a welcome change after sitting in the car anyway. Sweat pooled on Kale's palm even though Jason's hand felt unpleasantly cool.

"Mr. Wadsworth will see you now." The slave didn't wait for any acknowledgement before turning and leading the way to Robert's study.

The study was alight with the orange glow of a few gas lamps and the setting sun. Kale had never been in the room, but it exuded Robert. Well-worn brown leather furniture clustered in front of the fireplace, a large walnut desk sat in the back under the window, and hunting trophies decorated the walls. Pungent cigar smoke filled the air. At the center of the haze was Robert, propped up with cushions in a large armchair. His cheeks and eyes were sunken, and it appeared he had lost a good bit of weight, though it was hard to tell with a blanket covering his legs. Instead of its usual perpetual tan, Robert's skin had a gray pallor.

Jason's hand slipped from Kale's. His lips parted as he stepped forward, his brown eyes wide. He moved as if all the breath had left his body. Across the room, Kale caught a longing in Robert's identical brown eyes. It was brief, and Kale wasn't sure whether he longed for the son he had or the son he wanted. Robert looked down as he tapped the ash from his cigar into the waiting glass tray. When the cigar reached his lips, his eyes shot to Kale with familiar cold hatred. It was chilling coming from eyes that looked so like Jason's. Kale felt his knees weaken as he fought the urge to retreat to the sanctuary of the kitchen. He reminded himself that he was no longer a slave. It had been more than a year since he'd had to remind himself of that fact.

"Son." Robert's voice was hoarse. He took another puff from his cigar. Jason didn't appear inclined to answer him. "I see you've come to await my death and your inheritance. You're in luck. The doctors say it will only be a few days now before the mass in my lungs kills me."

Tense silence.

"You don't have anything to say? I see you've brought your slave with you."

"He's not my slave."

"Ah, I thought that would loosen your tongue. You're not in Naiara anymore, boy. Here, he's a slave."

"He's a Naiaran citizen."

"I don't give a damn. While he's in my house, he'll conduct himself as a slave."

Kale honestly didn't care. Acting like a slave would no more make him one than acting free had made him so back when he was Jason's valet. Jason would never see it that way. This was about him demanding respect from his father. It was difficult to demean one of the wealthiest men on the continent, but the quickest way to hurt Jason was to hurt those close to him.

"He'll conduct himself as my lover and companion."

"At least keep it a secret that he's free. There will be an insurrection if word gets out."

"This isn't a negotiation, Father. You accept me as I am—and that includes Kale—or we'll leave."

Both men stared each other down. Neither flinched. When Kale thought he would have to intervene, Jason turned for the door. Robert's face cracked. After only two of Jason's steps, Robert spoke.

"Wait. I suppose not many people will even realize he was a slave. I suppose that will have to do."

Jason turned again. For a minute, Kale wondered if he would still refuse. "Very well. We'll stay here then, as long as things remain civil."

"Demetri." Blond-haired, blue-eyed Demetri stepped forward. Kale had been so absorbed in the drama unfolding before him that he hadn't even seen him. Had he really grown so far removed from his past that he no longer noticed slaves? "Go have Master Jason's room prepared, and arrange for dinner to be served."

Demetri bowed and left, but not before shooting Kale a look seething with contempt. Some things never changed.

"If you had shown some simple courtesy, we would have

had your room ready for you."

"Well, I didn't want to waste any time when I heard of your failing health."

"No, wouldn't want to miss the big event, would you? I've already eaten. I'll see you tomorrow." Robert puffed his cigar and lifted a book that lay abandoned on his lap.

After a hurried dinner, Kale followed Jason up to his room. It looked exactly as it had the last time they'd visited. They both divested themselves of their clothing and collapsed into bed.

"How is it we were basically sitting all day, yet I'm exhausted?" Jason rolled over and flung his arm across Kale's chest.

"I'm tired after just watching you and your father. I imagine it was emotionally draining."

"I suppose. I don't understand why he can't find it in himself to be agreeable. Did he really think I would concede? He's never managed to understand that I'll choose you over him every time."

"You know it's not about me. Not personally."

"And that's supposed to make it better?"

"To him, I'm a slave. Nothing more. You can't judge your father by your own standards. It's not fair. I was just a slave to you for far longer than I've been just a slave to him." A twinge of hurt flashed in Jason's eyes. "I don't mind, Jason. It's the simple truth of the matter. You've nothing to be sorry for. You treated me like what I was. You need to stop expecting more from your father."

"I suppose I can try. It's just that whenever I see him, I remember the terror he caused you last time."

"That was as much my fault as it was his."

"You're too forgiving and much too understanding of men who mistreat you."

"There's no point in tossing blame on a dying man. It won't change anything. You have little enough time left as it is."

"I know. I'll try. That's all I can promise. I'll try for you."

"Thank you. I don't want you living with regret. It's a weight no one should have to bear."

Jason propped his chin on the hand that rested on Kale's chest and stared straight at him. "How are you feeling about tomorrow?"

Kale shifted his weight. "Nervous. I haven't been back there since I was fourteen."

"How long of a drive is it?"

"I'd guess about three hours."

"Are you sure you don't want me to go?"

Kale's feelings changed from minute to minute. The desire for Jason's company, his support, wrestled with something deeper that insisted this was something he needed to do on his own. "I'm sure, though you're sweet to offer. I'll be fine. You need to spend time with your father."

Jason's eyes were wary. If he looked hard enough, he would find the doubt he sought. Kale rolled him over and kissed him. Distraction turned to passion, and Kale shifted his pelvis against Jason's. Lust chased the wariness from Jason's eyes. It was a quick, rough fuck, and for a few glorious minutes, the tension fled from Kale's body. As soon as he rolled off Jason and pulled his lover toward him, it crept back into first his thoughts and then his muscles.

"If you change your mind, just let me know." A yawn swallowed the last words.

Kale kissed Jason's mop of brown hair. "I will. I'm planning on leaving early. Do you want me to wake you before I go?"

"'Course." Jason snuggled closer.

Satisfaction poured through Kale. The man in his arms needed him, and Kale had reached the point where he could admit that he filled Jason's need. If only he could fill his family's.

CHAPTER NINE

Jason gazed out the bay windows to the softly rolling hills. The clock in the corner stood eerily silent. Dust coated every surface of the small corner room at the back of the house. The pink cushion he sat on in the window seat had delicate tassels hanging off every corner. It was a room suspended in time. When he closed his eyes, Jason swore the smell of Lena's sweet lilac perfume drifted by, as if carried on a draft. It was the smell of a hundred hugs, the scent of countless smiles. In the suffocating silence, he imagined her light laughter banishing the heavy air. Remnants of his mother.

After she had died trying to bring a baby into the world, Jason's father had forbidden him to enter this room. The few portraits of her that hung in the house were removed. She was never to be spoken of. When the fights with his father had grown particularly painful, or when the loneliness threatened to swallow him whole, he had retreated here in the ultimate act of defiance his eight-year-old mind could conceive. It was the only place in the house where he felt comforted, embraced by the only person who had ever loved him. This corner of the house had always been her domain, where she came to sew or read when she'd wanted solitude.

Thick trees clustered in the distance around the watering hole. In the quiet of the room, Jason could just hear the bass notes of the cattle, though he couldn't see any. Everything in his field of vision would be his soon, and he didn't want any of it. All he wanted was the little sewing room in the corner with the bay windows.

A tear fell on his hand, and Jason looked down at the spot, mystified that he hadn't even known he was crying. The evidence of his emotional crack widened the rupture, and his face crumpled at the sting behind his eyes and nose. Tears poured with a force that shook his chest. Placing his feet on the window seat, he wrapped his arms around his knees and sobbed. His heart longed for the warmth of his mother, but he couldn't have her. With a stab of shame, he admitted that he could barely even remember what she looked like. What kind of son forgot his own mother?

Kale. He needed Kale. Except he had left early in the morning. True to his word, he'd woken Jason. Once more, Jason had asked if Kale wanted him to go with him. Kale had answered with a resolute no and a gentle kiss. Kale had always been the strong one. Here Jason was falling apart without him, while Kale went off to find the mother and brother he hadn't seen in well over a decade.

A restless mind hounded Jason as soon as Kale left. After breakfast, he had searched for peace in this little room. There wasn't much else to do, and this house hadn't been his home in years. It hadn't really felt like home since his mother had died. All his happy childhood memories centered around her. Even his father had seemed different while she lived.

Jason cried until his eyes burned dry and the pressure in his head threatened to burst. It seemed strange that one house could feel both familiar and foreign to him at the same time. The place reminded him of everything he hated in life: ignorance, his father, and Kale's oppression. Kale was the only person who could have convinced him to return. Jason wasn't interested in what would happen to the ranch. It could burn for all he cared.

Unfurling himself from the window seat, he wiped his

eyes and sat at his mother's writing desk. As a child, he had been too shy to poke through her things, still in awe of the woman whom he held in the same esteem as the saints. Pulling on the ornate brass handle, he had to jiggle the first drawer to open it. Inside were some old letters from his aunt and grandparents. All dead now. He had only seen Aunt Estelle once when his mother took him to Perdana the year before she died. Actually, he supposed Estelle must have been at his mother's funeral. The whole day was a blur in his mind, one he was content to have remain locked away in his memory. Estelle and his grandmother had both died a few years after his mother, Estelle from a fever and Grandmother from natural causes, though Jason suspected it was from a broken heart. His grandfather had died when Jason was a toddler, and after Estelle was gone, his dear grandmother had no one left. She and his father had never gotten along.

The drawer slid closed more easily than it had opened, and Jason moved to the other side of the desk. An identical drawer opened to reveal two leather-bound books. Jason opened the first, a date and address book. There, in his mother's fluid, loopy penmanship were notes about the local quilting group's charity sale, the summer bazaar, a friend's birthday. Jason pushed the book aside. If that was her datebook, then he had an idea what the next book was. He saw the word "Journal" embossed on the cover.

A light knocking on the door startled Jason, and he shoved both books back in the drawer.

"Sir?" Demetri's decorous voice penetrated the wood.

"Yes?" Jason hoped his face wasn't red and splotchy.

The door opened, and Demetri stood primly in the entryway. "I was wondering if you'd like me to serve your lunch in here or if you'd prefer to take it in the dining room, sir."

"How did you know I was here?"

"I used to see you sneak in here as a child. When you weren't in your room, I figured this was where you'd be, sir."

It was easy to forget how long Demetri had been a part of his life. For the longest time, Jason had admired his father's slave. Demetri had always talked to Jason as if he were a grown-up, which, to a child, was the utmost compliment. Jason shook his head when he thought how different his life would have been if his father had given him Demetri as Jason had asked. Denying him was the nicest thing his father had ever done for him. Not only would Jason not have Kale in his life, but he would have been fundamentally different. Kale was more than a companion and lover; he had touched Jason's soul and irrevocably altered it.

"Sir?"

Jason wanted to know where his father was having lunch, but it didn't seem appropriate to ask. He hadn't even realized he was hungry and could have spent the rest of the day wrapped in the memory of his mother. However, it probably wasn't healthy. He didn't want Kale coming back to find him in a state that would prompt concern. "I'll eat in the dining room. I'll be along in a moment. Thank you."

Demetri nodded and left, closing the door behind him. Jason reached for the drawer and stopped himself, curling his hand into a fist. Better to wait for when he had the time to read his mother's words. A wave of dizziness overcame him as he stood. The crying and lack of food left him lightheaded. With any luck, Kale would return soon, and Jason could avoid toppling into another emotional abyss.

CHAPTER TEN

If Jason were with him, he would be holding Kale's hand. Jason wouldn't let him stew or doubt or be haunted by thoughts of every possible scenario. But Jason wasn't with Kale, and it had been Kale's choice, so he needed to live with it. The least he could do was try to rein in his thoughts the way Jason would want him to. There was no point wondering what was going to happen when a little patience would answer the question for him.

Once he got to the other side of the county, it had been more difficult to find Monroe's farm than Kale had anticipated. Why he'd thought he'd be able to find it was a mystery. He'd been born on the farm and had only left a handful of times. When he'd left for the final time, it had been too traumatic for him to remember anything other than the feeling that his chest had been hollowed out with a wooden spoon. It had taken all of his energy not to lose his mind on the ride from Monroe's. He certainly hadn't been enjoying the scenery.

Peeking over the trees in the distance was some manmade object. It looked like rusty pipes jutting into the air. Kale squinted and leaned forward. As he crested a hill, he got a better view and whistled. That damn old water tower was still standing. He was about to enter Cedar City, the closest town to Monroe's farm. When the town had erected the water tower, there had been a big to-do about it. To celebrate, someone had gotten it into his head to decorate it with a wrought iron statue of a cedar tree standing proudly on top of the tank. The result was a tangle of metal protruding into the air like an iron weed that could be seen for kilometers. All the slaves at Monroe's had made fun of it. Kale wasn't as lost as he'd thought.

Fifteen minutes later, he turned onto the road leading to Monroe's house. Only a few more minutes. The car flew over a large rock, and Kale glanced at the speedometer. It was nearly topped out at seventy kilometers an hour. Jason would kill him if he got in an accident. With some effort, he lightened his foot on the gas pedal. The car slowed and then sped as he worked to keep his weight off the gas. It felt as if his foot was a stone his leg had to lift off the pedal. Kale's fingers tapped the steering wheel, and he adjusted his weight, not able to settle in one spot.

On the left, a break in the trees revealed a driveway. Kale guessed it was the one. Nerves tightened in his stomach. The imminent reunion with his family was only part of the cause. Being in Arine was stressful in itself, and the sooner he got his family, the sooner he could leave. There was a nagging fear in his gut that he would be caught and dragged to the auction block in chains. It was completely absurd. But if something did happen, Jason wasn't even there to help. Kale could disappear and Jason would never know. Kale took a deep breath, squashing his fear as his chest constricted, attempting to push it down far enough to not bother him.

The road bent to the left, and Kale's heart dropped. Maybe he had gotten it wrong. The porch was covered in weeds and vines. The once white house was now a greenish, brownish, gray mess. One of the second story windows was broken. Kale parked the car and got out. The crunch of his shoes on gravel as he approached drew his attention to the abnormal silence. Farms bustled with noise in the daytime. A window on the side of the house revealed that there wasn't much left inside: a few odd knickknacks, worn-down furniture, and spider webs. Buzzing drew his gaze upward to a hornet's nest. Of all the scenarios he had played out in his mind, this hadn't been one of them.

The house was surrounded by a barrier of trees, secluding it from the farm. Kale explored the rest of the property, looking for remnants of the childhood he had spent there. The fields were overgrown. Wheat, corn, peanuts, soybeans, had all been grown on this farm at one time or another. Now there was nothing but brush. It was hard to imagine this place had ever teemed with life. To his right were the rows of huts that had housed the slaves. It was easy to spot the one he had lived in. His mother had worked in the kitchens, so they'd had a hut on the end closest to the house.

Kale entered the building where he had been born, watching for rotted wood. The small, one-room structure was unremarkable. He didn't know what he had expected. There was no sign that anyone had ever lived there. The rough brick of the fireplace didn't feel familiar beneath his hand. Closing his eyes, he dredged up his memories of this room. The earliest were of his mama telling him and Thomas stories of the gods in front of the fire while his brother was still a toddler. When Thomas learned how to talk, he would ask "Ale" to tell the stories. Kale embellished the familiar tales with dramatic arm gestures and theatrical voices in an effort to win Thomas's dimples and gurgling laugh. Their little family had been happy.

The hut had been too small for the eight people who lived there, so Kale had spent much of his time outside when he wasn't working. The only time he had ever slept indoors was when it had been too cold. Behind the hut, he walked until he found the pond. It was small and infested with mosquitos, but it had been heaven to a young boy. It was here he had taught Thomas how to catch bullfrogs and fish.

Kale sat, not caring about the dirt on his trousers. There

were more painful lessons he had passed on to his brother. This was where he had taught him that slaves were less than free, that slaves didn't get to have fathers the way free boys did. His mama had taught him, and he had taught Thomas. It wasn't something a person was born knowing. This was where he had learned the futility of hope.

Kale should have been put to work in the fields. He had the build for it, but his mama was adamant that he wouldn't become a field slave. The only time he had ever spent in the fields was dragging the water bucket around. It was his mother's doing. Andrew, the master's valet, had taken a liking to her. Kale hadn't understood it as a young boy, but as he got older, it wasn't hard to figure out why he and his brother were always sent away when Andrew came by.

Anger seethed in his chest. He hated his mother for it. Not for the act, but for grooming him from birth to be sold, to be ripped away from her and everything he knew. She'd always told him to pay attention to the house slaves. He wasn't even allowed to play with the field hands. Never mimic a free a person, she had said. That led to trouble. But she had insisted that he behave like Andrew and Garrison, the butler. Any time he slipped into lazy speech, or did something that would have gotten him in trouble with a free person, she had cuffed him upside the head. Kale chuckled. His mother had hit him more frequently than any master had. He sobered. It was precisely because she'd cuffed him that he hadn't felt the whip more than he had.

His dear, sweet mother wanted the best for him. She had to have known that there was no way their master would keep him. He had no need for another valet. Andrew had whispered in the master's ear about the young slave boy who was worth more than the mending and washing Kale did. It made more financial sense for his master to sell him as a valet and buy two sorely needed labor slaves to help on such a large farm.

Kale dug his fingers into the ground, digging in the dirt

to relieve his frustrations. He hated the master, Andrew, his mama, even Thomas. He hated them all. He should have stayed. He should have been allowed to see Thomas grow up, to take care of his mother as she aged. All choice had been stripped from him. It wasn't really his mother and Thomas he hated—it was himself for leaving.

A hard surface blocked the path of his finger in the ground. Kale uncovered the flat stone and threw it across the pond out of habit, watching it skip on the water. The master's groom—Kale couldn't remember his name—had taught him how to skip stones. Kale had loved showing Thomas the trick. There had been pride in being able to do something his brother couldn't and then teach it to him. Thomas hadn't been as quick to learn and had begged Kale to teach him every night, even when Kale was bone tired from working. Wide green eyes had stared up at him over a freckled nose and a bottom lip that jutted out. No matter how tired Kale was, he always mustered the energy to give Thomas whatever he wanted. He would have done anything for that kid. He still would.

Anger wasn't going to help him. If Kale hadn't been sold, he wouldn't have ended up as Jason's. The horror of returning to life before Jason had freed him was unspeakable. It had all been for the best for him, and now he needed to make it the same for his family. Where had they gone? Where had his childhood disappeared to? It hadn't been ideal, but it was the only life he had. Kale lay down in the grass and closed his eyes, allowing himself to mourn his childhood, the childhood that had ended too soon, and the childhood that had never been.

Kale had no idea how much time passed. Eventually, he opened his eyes and stood. A part of him wanted to stay there forever, in the last place he had been with his family. That life was gone. He no longer had a place there. He never really had.

Back at the car, he was careful not to look behind him.

The roar of the engine brought him back to his life, the nearly perfect life with Jason. The farther from the house he drove, the more he grounded himself in reality and left nostalgia behind. Yes, there were good memories there filled with his mother and brother, with boisterous songs and late, star-gazing nights telling tall tales. But that was also where he had received his first beating, where he had learned that he and the family he loved so much were less human than free people. That was where he had learned that, for a slave, there was no such thing as family, that a slave could be sold away from everything he knew and loved, and no one even cared. That place was where he had learned a slave shouldn't love. They had been hard lessons to unlearn, and they had almost prevented him from allowing Jason to save him. Kale didn't ever want to see that place again.

A growling in his stomach reminded him that it had been a while since his last meal. He would need to stop somewhere to eat. He passed a small restaurant and felt queasy. For some inexplicable reason, he felt shame. The thought of walking into a pub or restaurant and eating among men and women who had been free all their lives was unbearable. He could eat when he got back to the ranch.

Once out of the city, Kale let his foot loose and accelerated. The wind whipped through his hair. He needed to find his family, and in order to do that, he needed to get home to Jason.

CHAPTER ELEVEN

Lunch had been a good idea. Jason's father had taken his meal elsewhere, and Jason hadn't even had to see him. Refreshed, he headed back to his mother's nook to read her journal. It was either that or sit at one of the front windows, worried about Kale and watching for his return. It would have been one shade under miraculous for him to be back already, so there was no reason to worry. Jason couldn't help it, though. He hated that Kale was where Jason couldn't protect him or at least offer support, and Kale had been deluding himself when he'd said he didn't need it.

No matter. There was nothing he could do until Kale returned. Until then, it was best to keep busy. Jason sat at the delicate, feminine desk and withdrew the journal. The leather binding was the most masculine thing in the room. Logic dictated he start at the beginning, but he fanned the pages, looking for the place where her handwriting stopped. It was a little past the halfway mark.

The last date was two days before she'd died. Was there any hint that she knew what was coming? This was the last thing she had written. It was the closest he had been to her life since he had been shooed from her bedroom when the labor pains had grown too much. At the time, he'd had no idea he would never see his mother alive again. He had seen her at the viewing, looking asleep in her coffin, surrounded by flowers. He hadn't understood why she didn't get up and join the family. Moms didn't die; it just didn't happen. None of it had made sense. All these years later, he didn't know if it made any more sense now than it had then. He had never even seen the baby's body. He didn't even remember a coffin. It was as if Baby Wadsworth had never existed. Jason had never even known the gender.

Jason's eyes focused on the page. The handwriting was familiar, the phrases, her manner, but something was missing. Jason couldn't quite picture her, remember her voice. The familiar sting of tears threatened his eyes, and he shoved them away. There had been too much crying already. He tried to remember the day this was written. His mother described him running about, playing with a sailboat, pleading with her to come to the pond and watch him sail it. She had been too tired but had let him sail it in the bathtub while she looked on. Jason thought he remembered it but feared it could just as easily have been an invented memory.

Further on, the entry turned to her thoughts and feelings. She complained about the discomfort and fatigue of pregnancy, anxious for it to be over. There was nervous excitement over the coming birth, plans of what she would do with her new baby. He saw a fear that she seemed hesitant to explore, telling herself it was just the usual apprehension over childbirth. Then it just stopped. The next day, she would have been in labor and unable to write. The day after that, she was dead.

Jason flipped to the front of the journal. The first entry was a couple of months into her pregnancy. He wanted more. He wanted his mother before the pregnancy, wanted her mundane, everyday writings. There had to be more of these little journals somewhere. As a child, he had seen her writing in them. Jason closed the book and brushed the cover with his hand, the cool leather soft beneath his skin. It was likely that the additional journals would be somewhere in this room. There was nothing anywhere else in the house that even hinted a woman had once lived there.

Jason noticed a tall cupboard in the wall to the right of the writing desk. His heart quickened as he strode to it. When opened, it revealed knickknacks in a general storage space for items that didn't belong anywhere else. Jason sighed. There was nowhere else in the room they could be. He had already gone through every drawer in the desk. None of them were big enough to house a lifetime of journals.

After Lena's death, his father had shut up every reminder of her. It was one of the many things Jason hated him for. Jason had struggled to keep her alive while Robert tried to pretend she never existed. There was a chance his father had destroyed the journals. It would explain why Jason had never seen them. The only room in the house Jason didn't enter was his father's bedroom, and it wasn't likely he kept them there when he had eschewed all other remnants of her life. The thought of all those pages of writing lost raised Jason's heart rate. He stood before the window, trying to calm himself. He was being ridiculous. The most likely place for the journals to be stored would be the attic. It was easier to think the worst of his father than to think of having to trudge through the crates in storage. It could take days. Jason kicked the window seat in frustration and turned to leave.

Something wasn't right. He felt a discrepancy. The sound. When his foot hit the window seat, it didn't sound as it should. Appraising the seat, he realized that it wasn't built into the home; it was a separate piece of cedar furniture fitted into the bay window. He'd never really thought about it before. Sweeping the cushion to the floor, Jason saw what he was looking for: hinges. The metal squealed in protest as he lifted the lid. The smell of the cedar wafted out, and inside, in neat stacks, were dozens of little journals.

CHAPTER TWELVE

"Jason?" Kale's muffled voice floated to Jason from the sitting room on the other side of the sewing room door. He had been so absorbed in his task that he hadn't even heard the car.

"I'm in here, Kale." Jason jumped up from the floor, knocking over a stack of journals from the circle around him where he'd placed them as he removed them from the chest, trying to arrange them in chronological order.

The door swung open before Jason could reach it. He stopped short when he saw Kale was alone. If Kale had been successful, he would have his mother and brother with him. There was no way he would leave them in the care of Robert's slaves, people he barely knew.

"What have you been doing?" Kale eyed the books strewn across the floor.

"Some reading." Kale arched his eyebrows and gave him a dry stare. "They're my mother's journals. I was just organizing them."

"Quite the system you have."

"Let me put them away, and we'll talk." Kale nodded, and Jason began to stack them back in the chest, this time in the order he wanted to read them. He kept the earliest journal to take to his room.

In their bedroom, Jason set the book down on his bedside table then wrapped his arms around Kale. "Why don't you tell me what happened?"

"They weren't there."

"I gathered that. Did Mr. Monroe tell you where they are?"

"No. No one's there. The entire place was abandoned. It looked like no one had been there for years."

Jason pulled Kale down to sit on the bed with him. "That must have been difficult. Are you all right?"

Kale nodded.

"Really?" Jason could see Kale working to hold himself together. He wasn't sure whether he wanted to push Kale to the breaking point or let him be. Letting Kale keep everything to himself, the way he was wont to do, could lead to problems. After everything they had been through together, Jason had promised himself he would never let Kale get lost in his own darkness again.

"No. I should have let you come."

Jason massaged Kale's shoulder with one hand while he held Kale's hand with the other. "I understand your reasons for not wanting me to come, and I admire them. I'm still here for you. This isn't the end. We'll find them."

"Thanks, Jason. I had hoped this would be easier. How was your day? Did you spend much time with your father?"

Jason's hand dropped to the bed. "No. I spent all day in my mother's sewing room. I feel her so strongly there. It was nice to be close to her again." Kale's face tightened as if he was trying to keep pain from showing. "But we don't need to talk about it. Whatever you need tonight, I'm here."

"I need a drink."

"All right. Let's go to a bar in town. We'll get a drink and ask around, see if anyone knows what happened to the Monroes."

◆ ◆ ◆

Jason had never stepped foot in Carson's bar in his life. He'd a made a point of avoiding it when he lived in Malar. At the time, he'd thought it below him. Now bars were all too familiar. For nearly three years between the time he'd sold Kale and the time he was reunited with him, Jason had drowned in bars. The dark lighting, stale stench, and littered floors had provided the perfect environment in which to let the whiskey do its work. Fighting off the power alcohol held over him had been one of the most difficult battles of his life. He had only taken up drinking again when he and Kale had achieved security in their lives and relationship, with nothing left to drown. Since moving to Naiara, he and Kale often spent evenings downing a pint with friends.

The temperature inside was noticeably higher than outside. The stench of sweat and alcohol was as thick as the bodies crammed into the small building. Kale went to the bar to place their order while Jason tried to find a place to sit. A few minutes later, Kale came over with a whiskey for himself and a beer for Jason. There wasn't an empty seat in the place, so they stood against the wall with their drinks.

"I asked the bartender if he knew of the Monroes. Said he hadn't heard of them."

"There's plenty more people to talk to tonight. Someone must know something. It seemed when I lived here that everyone knew everyone else's business."

"Yeah, but they did live on the other side of the county. I'm not sure anyone here will know them."

"It's better than sitting in the house. Don't worry, Kale. Even if we don't find anything tonight, we can still have a decent time, get our minds off things."

The beer was refreshing and a nice distraction from the heat. Kale quietly sipped his whiskey. Jason knew Kale wouldn't get drunk. He never did. That was Jason's specialty, which was why he typically avoided hard liquor and stuck with beer. He'd developed quite a taste for it. Most wealthy people were wine connoisseurs, but not Jason. The complexities of beer, such a common drink, intrigued him. The beer Kale had bought him was a smooth, light wheat beer. He thought he detected some honey and maybe a dash of apple. If they were in the country much longer, perhaps he could visit some breweries. It would be a nice distraction if Kale decided to go off by himself again.

"You fellas want a seat?" Jason turned toward the deep voice on his right. A neatly dressed man sat by himself at a table for four.

"Thank you." Jason stretched his hand across the table as he and Kale sat. "My name's Jason, and this is Kale."

"George. Nice to meet you." The man's grip was firm without being crushing. "I own the leather shop down the street. You both new in town?" George shook Kale's hand.

"No, just visiting. Looking for someone, actually."

"Oh?" There was a note of suspicion in the lilt of George's voice.

"Nothing bad. I'm wondering where I can find Jedediah Monroe. I went out to his place today, and it was deserted. There were some slaves he had when I was younger, and I was hoping I could buy them off him." Jason was horrible at lying to Kale, but with anyone else, he had no problem saying what was needed to get what he wanted.

"Seems a lot of trouble to go to for some slaves."

Jason smiled. "You caught me. It's not really about some slaves. It's actually about one. There was a girl who used to serve there. Now that I have some money, I wanted to make some of my boyhood dreams come true, if you know what I mean." Jason's stomach roiled at the insinuation, but he didn't let it show on his face.

George laughed. "Ah, I see." Disgusting that looking for a slave to buy for sex was understandable here. Of course, Jason hadn't had qualms about it either, years ago. "Yeah, I've heard of the Monroes. Didn't really know them personally, but I buy hides out in that area and hear plenty. From what I understand, they fell on some hard times. Ended up selling most of their slaves and carted the rest out to their family's place. Last I heard, they were living in a cousin's guest house."

"Why not sell the farm? Why abandon it and let it fall into disrepair?"

"That land has been in the Monroe family for more than two hundred years. Maybe they don't want someone else owning it. Maybe they're hoping to return someday. Who knows?"

"Well, thanks for the information. Any idea where this cousin lives?"

"Not around here. I don't think they're in Malar County. I seem to remember hearing something about them moving northeast of here, but I'm not sure."

Jason raised his beer to George. "Thanks again."

"My pleasure. Does your friend ever talk?" George tilted his head toward Kale.

Normally, Kale was the one who could charm anyone into anything, but he didn't look predisposed to speak. Jason couldn't blame him. "Bad day."

"Thank you for your help." Kale looked George directly in the eye. "I appreciate it."

"You're welcome." George focused back on Jason. "So, you say you grew up here. Who's your family?"

Jason shifted in his seat. It would be rude not to answer, especially after George had been so helpful. "I'm a Wadsworth."

George's face lit up. "You're Robert's boy? Well, damn, I'll be. His cattle have some of the best hides in the country. You in the cattle business too?"

"No. My business is steel."

George nodded. "That's right, I had heard you married into the Arlington steel empire. Seems I remember something else about you moving to Naiara." George looked from Kale, to Jason, and then back to Kale. "Wait a minute. Kale, you said your name was?"

Jason could sense as much as see Kale tense beside him.

Kale gave a curt nod, and George's eyes went wide.

George eyed Jason. "That's what it was. Rumor had it you fell in with your personal slave and took him across the border to free him."

"Yes. Is that a problem?" Jason's voice was cool. He dared George to take issue with them.

George shook his head. "No, no problem. Never heard something so bizarre in my life. I don't like meddling in other people's business though. As long as you mean me no harm, we got no problem."

"I'm glad to hear it." Jason let warmth seep back into his tone.

"I suppose you're not really looking for a—"

"Well, well, looky who's here, boys: my old slave, Kale." Jason whipped his head around to see Carter Cartwright standing behind him with a couple of his friends. Kale froze, keeping his eyes lowered to his drink. He was so still that Jason wondered if he was even breathing.

"I don't believe you have business with us, Carter."

"Oh, I believe a slave impersonating a free man is everyone's business, seeing as it's illegal."

Kale remained disturbingly still. This had been his worst fear about returning to Arine. Jason had promised himself and Kale there wouldn't be any problems. It was time to live up to his word. "I don't see any slaves here, Carter. You should get your facts straight before you throw around accusations."

"You know damn well what I'm talking about, Jason. That there is Kale, the slave your father bought from mine for you. Just 'cause you took him across the border doesn't mean he's free when he comes back here." Carter took a menacing step forward. He glowered down at Jason, fists clenched, itching for a fight.

Jason deliberately stood, not giving up a centimeter of space, even though it meant being nearly nose to nose with Carter. It took immense willpower to stand his ground when Carter's foul breath assaulted his nostrils. Carter easily had fifty pounds on him plus a lifetime of experience in barroom brawling.

Jason kept his voice calm. "You're mistaken, Carter. Kale is a free citizen of Naiara with diplomatic status. If you stir trouble with him, you'd instigate an international incident. I'd hate to have to tell your daddy that you were arrested and brought before the prime minister and the king for assaulting a Naiaran agent under the protection of the government. Have you ever met the king? Nice fellow, although he does hate it when he's made to look foolish to the Naiarans." Anger flared in Carter's eyes, and they darted from side to side, as if searching for the truth. "I know I said a lot of big words just now. If any of them confused you, I'd be happy to clarify."

Carter's eyes narrowed, and he stepped backward, jabbing a finger in Jason's direction. "You'd best leave this county as quick as you came. No wonder your daddy's dyin'. Mine'd rather be dead than see me shame myself like you have." Before Jason could respond, Carter turned on his heel and motioned for his friends to follow. "Let's go. This place has gotten too trashy."

It wasn't worth following and taking a swing at him. Jason had wanted to avert trouble, and he had done it. Surrendering to his anger would give Carter exactly what he wanted. Jason lowered himself to his seat and registered the surprise on George's face. Of greater concern to him was Kale, who breathed deeply, eyes still fixated on the drink clasped in his hands. Jason gently rubbed his back. "It's all right."

"Thank you."

"I told you there wouldn't be any trouble."

"You shouldn't have to fight my battles for me."

"That's what I'm here for, to fight when you can't. It

wasn't cowardice, Kale. You didn't know if he would accept that you're free. There was tremendous risk for you in acting and none for me. You were always the wise one of us, and that's why you sat there and kept your mouth shut even though I'm sure you had an earful for him."

Kale's breathing was returning to normal, and his body slouched into a more natural posture, his grip on the glass relaxing. Jason knew Kale had been scared. More than that, he had been terrified, and with good reason. However, despite all that was at stake, it wasn't cowardice that had stilled Kale. It was shame, his hurt pride at being viewed as a slave, and probably at having family who were still slaves despite his efforts. Jason would do anything to protect Kale's pride. Kale could keep his fear under control, but without his pride, he was nothing.

It was a familiar situation. A picture of Kale standing broken before him when Jason had discovered that—in an ironic twist of fate—Kale had ended up working for a labor firm at one of Jason's steel mills flashed before him. Without his pride, Kale had shriveled into a shell of a man. Seeing Kale stripped of the one thing that mattered to him had been the worst moment of Jason's life. Worse than the moment when Renee had told him he would have to sell Kale or lose her. Far worse than when Kale had told him he had never loved Jason, so that Jason would sell him in order to live happily ever after with Renee.

Jason's hand shot out and grabbed Kale's drink. He downed the whiskey in a single gulp to chase away the images. Jason couldn't let Kale turn into that broken man again, even for a moment. "You're fine, Kale. I've got you. You never have to hang your head. And if you want to go find Carter and beat the shit out of him, I'll be right there with you. Gods know he deserves it."

"No. You're right. I'm fine."

"Sorry to interrupt, but you're diplomats?" George's face looked as if he didn't know how to process what had just happened.

"Yes, I was wondering that myself." Kale faced Jason with a hint of his usual good humor glinting in his eyes.

"Well, I'm sure he's not smart enough to figure it out."

George laughed and shook his head. "You sure are smooth, Jason."

Kale ordered another drink, and the three of them relaxed into comfortable banter. Jason had the information they needed to find Monroe. It was time to enjoy the respite from his father's home and the ghosts that lingered there.

CHAPTER THIRTEEN

"Martin, it's Kale." Despite Jason's insistence that his father was opposed to scientific progress, there was actually a telephone in the house.

"Kale, what can I do for you?" Martin's tone was as formal as ever, but Kale detected a trace of warmth in his voice.

"I was hoping you could look into something for me." Martin had been Jason's secretary until Jason and Kale decided to move to Naiara. Now, he served as president of Arlington Steel. He was their go-to man, and they both trusted him implicitly.

"Certainly, let me just get a piece of paper." There was some rummaging on the line, and Martin returned. "All right, Kale, go ahead."

"Jedediah Monroe. I want you to see if there's any record of court proceedings regarding his estate, creditors, bankruptcy, that sort of thing. It would be in Malar County. Also, see if you can find anything about a cousin he might be staying with. We don't know where they live, but we don't think it's in Malar. Any information you can dig up about what kind of people they are would be helpful in addition to their whereabouts."

"I'll telephone Mr. Smithson, and we'll start searching

immediately. I take it the search hasn't gone well if you're needing my help." Mr. Smithson was one of Jason's attorneys.

"No, there've been a few bumps."

"Well, don't worry. We'll find them." The earnest words comforted Kale. He and Jason weren't alone. "I don't mean to pry, but was this Mr. Monroe your original owner?"

"I figured you would have known that already from my title."

"I've never seen your title. Jason wouldn't let anyone handle it but him and his attorneys when it became necessary." There was some commotion: a female voice and the clink of a tea cup and saucer. "Sophie's here and wants to say hello."

"Kale, it's been too long. How are you? How's Mr. Wadsworth holding up? You'd better be taking care of each other at a time like this."

Kale chuckled. Just the sound of her voice cheered him, such a stark contrast to the gloom of recent days. "We're doing all right, Sophie. Don't worry about us."

"I do, and I will, and you should be used to it. Don't lie to me. If everything was all right, you wouldn't be needing Martin's help."

"We came across a little obstacle is all." Kale hesitated to say more, but he knew Sophie would pull it out of him. "My family wasn't where I thought they'd be. I went out to the farm where I was raised, and the place was abandoned. I knew there was good chance they wouldn't still be there."

"Oh, hon, I'm sorry. But don't be getting down. It's just a delay is all. You know Martin won't sleep 'til he finds out what you need. I'll make sure of it."

"Thanks, Sophie. How's that beau of yours doing?" Sophie had been their cook-cum-housekeeper and had stayed on to keep up the Perdana house with Martin. While Kale didn't want to see her leave their odd little family, he wanted her to live her own life and be happy. She was young and pretty and should be out having a good time.

"Martin had no right telling you and Mr. Wadsworth about Max. He's just fine. Now, I have to be getting back to my chores."

"Sure you do, Sophie."

"Oh shush. A girl's allowed to have some private things. Give my love to Mr. Wadsworth, and be good."

"I will, Sophie." The call disconnected. Kale hung up the hand piece and leaned against the wall. He was glad he'd made the call himself. Jason offered, but Kale had already let Jason do too much. That scene in the bar the previous night had been ridiculous. Kale could stand up for himself.

Jason was reading one of his mother's journals when Kale reached their room. "Sophie sends her love."

"Thanks. Did you get any more information out of her about her gentleman caller?"

"No, she ended the conversation pretty quickly after I brought him up."

"You know, I always wanted her and Martin to end up together. Wishful thinking."

"They would make a good pair. I admit I've thought the same. They already act like an old married couple." Kale sat on the stuffed chair next to the fireplace. There wasn't a sofa in the room, just a desk and chair Jason currently inhabited. "Martin and Mr. Smithson are going to see what they can find and call us back."

"Good. They'll find something. Do you want to head down to breakfast? Demetri said it would be served at nine."

"Oh, well if Demetri said…" Kale drew out the words as he stood.

"Stop. He's not that bad. You can't blame him for my stupidity in wanting him as my valet. He was the only slave I knew. Besides, can you imagine where I'd be right now if I'd gotten my wish?"

Yes, Kale could. Jason would probably be happily married with a few children. Instead of avoiding his dying father, he'd probably be gathered with his family around him, letting the grandkids spend as much time as they could with their grandfather while the wife tutted and fussed, making sure Robert was comfortable. Domestic bliss, that's what Jason would have right now had his father given him Demetri, the habitually well-behaved slave who would have never entered into a personal relationship with his master.

Jason's arms wrapped around Kale. His weight pressed against Kale in a comfortable and familiar way. Sometimes, Kale felt more like himself with Jason's body pressed against his than without it. "Stop. I should know better than to mention it, even in jest. How many years do you think it'll take until you'll realize there's no one I'll ever want more than you?"

"I do know it. I just question your judgment every now and then. I want the best for you."

"You are the best for me." Jason tilted his head up and closed his eyes. It was impossible for Kale to resist Jason's lips. It was amazing how even simple kisses still ignited something inside him. There had been thousands over the years, and every one felt like the first.

"Well, now that that's settled, let's go eat." Kale couldn't resist lightly swatting Jason's ass before he let him go. It was unsettling how much Jason's presence affected him.

When they reached the dining room, Kale was surprised to see Robert sitting at the head of the table. After their arrival, Kale hadn't seen Robert at all. Instead of one of the normal dining room chairs, Robert was tucked into an armchair pushed up to the table. Hopefully, this was a sign he was willing to work on reconciliation.

Robert nodded to Jason, and Jason responded in kind. A place was set on each side of Robert, and Jason sat on his father's left, leaving Kale with the right. Once they were seated, Kale and Jason were served plates heaping with eggs, sausage, ham, tomatoes, and toast. Robert received a bowl of tomato soup.

"I heard you had a confrontation with Carter Cartwright

last night." Robert didn't look up from his spoon. "I don't want you causing trouble here. I'd prefer you not tarnish my name in my home." Apparently, he hadn't made the effort to join them for a reconciliation, but for a scolding.

"How did you hear about that?" Jason asked.

"It doesn't matter. Don't change the subject. You're always trying to avoid taking responsibility."

Kale couldn't abide Robert's condescending tone. "Carter started it. Jason handled himself well. He ended it before Carter could resort to blows."

"I don't recall asking for your opinion. I understand you were the cause of the problem."

"He was defending me, yes."

"Kale wasn't the cause. Carter just wanted to cause problems." Jason interjected.

"Yes, as well he should when one of his former slaves comes traipsing into his bar."

"It's not his bar, Father."

"It's more his than yours."

"You should be proud of Jason for not rising to the bait. He's always been good at diplomacy."

"I'm aware of my son's talent for talking his way out of problems."

Silence hung thick in the air. Kale concentrated on eating his eggs. There was nothing he could say to a man who had already determined to hate him no matter the circumstance.

"What, you don't have anything more to say? My son defends you, and you can't be bothered?"

"What would you like me to say, sir? You raised a fine man. Whether you choose to see that or not is up to you." Kale held Robert's gaze. He wouldn't look away again. He had played the same game the last time he'd been in this dining room with Robert, except this time he was free to see it through to the end. Kale thought he saw a softening in Robert's eyes before he succumbed to a coughing fit. Once it had passed, they all returned to eating.

"What do you boys have planned for today?"

Jason exchanged looks with Kale. They hadn't discussed it. There wasn't much to do until they heard back from Martin, and that likely wouldn't be until tomorrow. Kale knew Jason wanted to continue reading his mother's journals, but he certainly wasn't going to tell Robert that. The idea of Jason cooped up inside all day dredging up the past didn't sit well with Kale. They needed to be active. "I was hoping to tour the ranch. A man we met last night said your cattle have the best hides in the country."

Robert paused and lifted his eyebrows. "You must mean George."

"Yes, sir. Thought it'd be nice to see what all the fuss is about. He isn't the first person who's told me Wadsworth cattle are the best. I thought Jason and I could saddle up some horses and go for a ride."

"That sounds like a good idea," Jason said, "but I don't even know where the property line is. Do you think we could have someone show us around, Father?"

"Hmph. That's the problem with you: you don't even know what you have, what I worked so hard for. John will be in from his morning rounds soon. You can have him take you out."

"Thank you, sir." Kale knew Jason wasn't about to thank him.

Jason didn't seem embarrassed at all by his ignorance. It was part of the fundamental problem between father and son. They didn't value the same things, and they each took it as a sign of disrespect and lack of love. Neither recognized that they felt exactly the same.

Chapter Fourteen

An hour later, Kale was astride a mare, riding with Jason and John—the free man who managed the ranch—sandwiches tucked away in their saddlebags for lunch. "We'll go down to the creek first and follow it around. It's the lifeblood of this place." On the way, John pointed out all the different facilities: the storehouse, the barn, the corrals. He pointed to the hay fields in the distance. They all studiously avoided the family burial plot behind the house.

They followed the creek's path through the land. John pointed out spots where some of the cows liked to hide when they knew their calving time was approaching. He showed them all the different places they rotated the cattle to for grazing.

"Where's the property line?" Kale asked John as they emerged from a wooded patch. Land stretched for kilometers in each direction, and Kale supposed they must be getting close to the boundary.

John laughed. "I don't have time to show you today."

"Mr. Wadsworth implied he wanted Jason to learn where the line is."

"Robert was pulling your leg. If he wanted me to take you all the way to the back line, he would have had me pack some provisions."

"Provisions?"

"Yeah, you can't reach the back of the property and get back to the house in one day."

"Just how big is the ranch?"

"Right around fourteen thousand acres."

"What? How many cattle are there?"

"We have a little over sixteen hundred head right now."

"Surely you don't need all that acreage for that many cattle?" Jason turned to John.

John looked at Jason like he was missing something fundamental. "Robert just likes to buy up land. He says it's the only thing they're not making any more of."

Kale liked the simple sensibility of that. Seeing the ranch, he found a lot to admire about the senior Wadsworth. For a brief moment, Kale wondered how they would have gotten along had Kale been born free and entered Robert's life under different circumstances.

After lunch, John showed them around for a few more hours. It was refreshing to be outside on a horse again. Kale found being surrounded by nothing but living, breathing things peaceful, and peace was something Kale needed. They scaled a hill and beheld a panoramic view of the countryside.

"You see the house down there?" John pointed to their right. The cabin was a tiny speck in the distance.

"Yes, sir." Kale replied.

"Good. Don't get lost. I've got some work to do. You should head back so you're not late for dinner."

"Thank you for your time." Kale reached out his hand. John didn't seem to have much of a problem with Kale despite his boss's prejudice. Or perhaps it was just that he saw more in common between himself and Kale than with Jason, even though he'd been a free man from birth.

"Not a problem. You ever have any questions and see me around, just ask." John nodded and rode off in a direction slightly to the left of home.

Jason and Kale stayed at the top of the hill, enjoying the

view. The sun lowered in the sky, and the landscape was awash in her red hues. Perfect lighting for a painting.

"This is all going to be yours soon. Any idea what you're going to do with it?"

Jason shrugged. "Never considered it for an instant. I never thought I would inherit it, and we don't even know if I will. There's no telling if my father reinstated me in the will after I married Renee."

"Who else is he going to leave it to?"

"John."

"No."

"He likes him. He's like family."

"But he's not blood. All your father's ever wanted is for you to take pride in what he built for you."

"He didn't do this for me."

"Maybe not, but he wanted to live on through it. How do you think he feels knowing his son has no interest in his life's work? Or in remembering him through it when he's gone?"

"He's the one who decided to push me out of his life."

"You were already out of his life before he disowned you."

"Why are you taking his side all of a sudden?" Jason's forehead crinkled in irritation rather than hurt.

"I'm not taking his side, Jason. I can just see it differently than you do. I want you and your father to be at peace. There's no reason not to be."

"He's made no secret of the fact that he despises me."

"You can decide to continue being mad at him, or you can try to understand him. You're not going to change your father's mind by holding onto your hurt and anger. It's not an endurance test. You both make a lot of assumptions about each other. It's almost funny how alike you are."

"I am not like him." Jason scoffed.

"Oh, yes you are. The fact that you can't see it should make you pause and listen to me. It's us all over again. You made an awful lot of assumptions about me in the beginning, but once you decided to get to know me, those barriers came down. He doesn't have much time left. Try thinking less about yourself and more about him. You're going to regret it if you don't."

"No, I won't."

"You're a fool if you believe that. I know you better than you know yourself, and once it sinks in that he's gone and he's never coming back, you are going to break down and hate yourself for not taking advantage of this time."

Jason sighed. "I'll try, Kale."

"I've heard that before."

"I mean it."

"Trying does not include reading your mother's journals all day. They'll still be here after he's gone."

"You don't understand. I need to feel close to her. I miss her so damn much."

Kale took a deep breath before he spoke, controlling his voice. "I don't understand what it's like to want to feel close to your mother? You can feel close to yours anytime you want. I have nothing to tie me to mine. Even if I find her, there's nothing I can do to make the man who owns her give her to me. I'm sorry if I can't find a tear to shed for the boy who wants to use his dead mother as an excuse to piss away his last chance at a relationship with his father. I suppose I'm the lucky one since I never knew mine."

Jason's eyes widened, and his face fell. "I'm so sorry, Kale. I didn't mean it. I'm being a selfish prick. You're right."

The distress on Jason's face pinched Kale's chest. It was easy to forget how tenderhearted Jason really was. "I just want what's best for you. You don't need to apologize, just realize this time is precious, and you're never getting it back. You might want to try talking about what you have in common."

"We don't have anything in common besides our hair and eye color."

"Yes you do. You both have your love for your mother."

A shadow of hurt passed across Jason's face. "I'm not sure we have a lot of common ground there."

Kale heaved a sigh. Jason always had a blind spot when it came to anything dealing with his heart. "Or you could just try not being rude to the man."

"He's the one who's rude."

"We're guests in his house, and he's your father. Show some respect. If nothing else, be the bigger man."

"All right, Kale. I will be."

"Good. Now let's go to dinner. You can show me what a grown-up you are." Kale smiled at Jason and set off at a gallop, leaving the tense atmosphere behind. An instant later, he heard Jason following on his heels.

Chapter Fifteen

Jason dunked his head under the water and scrubbed the dirt from his hair. Kale had suggested they take a dip in the creek before dinner, but Jason didn't like the idea. For one, there could be fish or other slimy tendrils in the creek that would brush up against him and scare him witless. He'd always been afraid of such things, but had thus far kept it a secret from Kale. He didn't want to expose his ridiculous childhood fear in what he was sure would be an embarrassing moment. Not only that, but he wanted some time alone to think. Kale's words at the top of the hill had stung, and Jason wanted to examine them further.

There was no doubt that Kale didn't speak out of malice or a desire to hurt Jason, so the question remained, why did his words hurt? Why did Jason hold on to this hatred of his father when Kale, who had arguably more reason to hate Robert, had so easily relinquished it? For as long as Jason could remember, he had hated his father. At this point, it was as much habit as anything else.

No, that wasn't true. As a child, he hadn't had much reason to hate his father other than the fact that he wasn't his mother. As an adult, he'd found actual reasons for his dislike. Robert's treatment of him since he had left home and made his own choices was abominable. Robert had never been able to respect him as a man. Jason merely reciprocated.

Still, Kale wanted him to try, so he would. After the years they had spent together, Jason knew that Kale possessed a wisdom that eluded Jason. It was one of the many reasons Jason had fallen in love with him and refused to let go. At dinner, he would try his best to at least be respectful and put forth an effort. Jason didn't think for a moment that he would ever experience the fatherly love from Robert that other people experienced in their families, but maybe Robert could depart this world with his son's respect and good will.

Jason's fingers pruned, and the water was tepid. He could waste no more time in the bath. He quickly dried off and opened the door to the bedroom. Kale was there, already dressed with Jason's clothes laid out on the bed.

"How is it I went to the creek to bathe and still beat you?" Kale's hair was wet, the ends curling slightly.

Jason shrugged. "The bath was a nice change to sitting on a horse all day. Besides—"

"You like to think in the bath. I know. How being covered in water makes it easier to think, I'll never know."

"And I'll never understand how putting a charcoal pencil to paper can help you think."

"Fair point."

"At least yours has such beautiful results. All I get are pruney fingers."

"Oh, I think the result is plenty pretty." Kale raised Jason's hand to his lips and kissed the tip of each finger. Jason's cheeks warmed, and Kale chuckled. It was worth the embarrassing blush to hear Kale so happy. "Now get dressed or we'll be late for dinner."

◆ ◆ ◆

The table was set as before, with Jason's father at the head and one place set on either side of him. Remembering his promise to put forth some effort, Jason smiled as he took his seat. "Good evening, Father. How was your day?" Jason looked at his father expectantly after he had arranged his napkin on his lap.

There was a pause before his father spoke, as if Robert was trying to figure out what had caused this change in his son and if it was good or bad. "Fine. The doctors have me taking some nasty-tasting stuff that makes me sleep most of the day away. I haven't been this idle since I learned to crawl."

"I'm sorry to hear that. I suppose it must make you more comfortable, though?"

Robert coughed into his napkin. The rattle in his throat echoed the way his entire body shook. Jason was tempted to reach across and pat his back, but he was worried he might hurt his father's fragile frame. He was at a loss. All his life, he had seen his father as tougher than old leather and stronger than the bulls they raised. Jason had never realized that it was part admiration for the man who raised him. He had always taken his father's invulnerability for granted. Until recently, Jason had been convinced the mean old cuss would outlive them all.

Robert's coughing settled, and he drank some water. The glass shook in his hand. "I've never had the obsession with comfort that you have. I'd rather be up doing than in bed. If I'm going to die anyway, at least let me go doing what I love."

Typical. Robert couldn't accept Jason's efforts. Jason didn't know why he let his father's jabs affect him. Time should have made him immune to them. Kale was right; he had always been seeking his father's approval. Any evidence that he didn't have it hurt.

"I'm sorry. If there's anything I can do, please let me know."

"You think you can learn how to run a ranch, so I can die knowing my life's work won't be run into shambles within the year? If not, there's nothing you can do."

"John showed us around today."

"I know. I know everything that happens on this ranch."

Jason continued, ignoring the interruption. "It's impressive. I never knew how massive it all was."

"Of course not. You could never be bothered to care."

Jason focused on his soup. There was nothing more he could think to say. How did Kale expect him to make this work?

The rest of the soup course passed in silence. After his bowl was cleared away, a plate with a thick steak, potatoes, and green beans was placed in front of Jason, standard fare at the ranch. Beef had been served every night that Jason could remember. In front of his father sat an identical plate, except the steak was already cut into tiny, bite-sized pieces. Jason guessed it was to lessen his father's chance of choking. As a child, Jason had been mortified by his father's table manners. Robert always took such big bites of meat that he resembled the cows chewing cud. Darlene, their cook, must have been worried that one of those large bites would get lodged in his throat should he cough.

Robert grimaced when he saw the plate and banged his fist on the table. It used to be he could shake the whole table with that fist. Now it barely made a sound. "Demetri, have Darlene come here, please."

"Yes, Master." Demetri bowed and scuttled into the kitchen.

A few minutes later, Darlene, looking as formidable as she had to Jason as a child, stood before Robert.

"Darlene, we have had this conversation before. I do not need my food cut for me like I'm a damn child."

"Yes, Master."

Jason tried to hide his smile. Darlene was the same as she had ever been. Robert glared at her. "Was that a 'yes you're right, Master' or a 'yes you need your food cut, Master'?"

"You know you tear off pieces of your steak bigger than your mouth. The doctor says you shouldn't even be eating meat, sir, but you command me to fix it for you, so I do. And after you nearly choked that time, I'm going to keep cutting it up for you until you're better. If you don't like it, there are potatoes and beans on that plate that'd be better for you anyway, sir. I won't have you choking to death on my cooking and ruining my good reputation, Master."

Robert sat stone still. Jason couldn't see the expression on his face, and he cringed to think what he would do. Darlene stood proudly before him, not backing down. If anyone could get away with talking to his father that way, it was she. The woman had been with the family as long as Jason could remember. It was impossible to think of home without picturing Darlene in the kitchen.

After a tense minute, Robert chuckled and then laughed outright. "Go get back to your kitchen, Darlene."

Darlene bobbed her head and left.

"I thought you beat slaves who talked to you like that." Jason said when the meal resumed.

"Darlene knows her place. I only beat slaves who forget." Robert eyed Kale before stabbing a piece of steak with his fork. "That woman has kept me fed for more than twenty years." Robert chewed his bite slowly before he swallowed. "She has a right to protect her reputation." Robert chuckled again. "What kind of slave would she be if it turned out I choked to death on her food?"

So many of Jason's feelings toward his father would've been resolved if Robert had treated Kale the same way he treated Darlene. It baffled Jason that it was too much to ask that his father treat the love of his life with the same level of courtesy with which he treated his cook.

Jason caught some movement out of the corner of his eye and saw that Kale was shaking his head at him. His feelings must have shown on his face. Jason supposed he could keep his thoughts to himself and talk them through with Kale later. No doubt his lover would have some annoyingly simple way to make Robert's behavior make sense. However, if he wasn't going to give voice to his feelings, he would have to stay silent. He had no more patience for his father.

The only sound in the dining room was the clink of silverware on plates and the occasional hacking cough from Robert. It was awkward, but Jason guessed it was preferable to heated argument.

"If you don't mind me asking, sir—" Jason and Robert both looked at Kale, stunned by the intrusion into their silence, "—how did you build all this? From what I understand, you didn't inherit any of it. To go from nothing to the biggest cattle operation in the country in one generation, it's unheard of. I'd love to hear how you managed it, if it's not too much trouble, sir." Kale's eyes were earnest, and he leaned toward Robert, eager for his response. Even Jason couldn't tell if it was an act.

Robert wiped his mouth with his napkin. "I bought this land when I was twenty years old. I was an orphan and had been working since I was nine. I saved everything I earned. This bit of land had been for sale for a while. It was raw and wild, and no one wanted to put the effort into taming it. I convinced the owner to sell it to me a piece at a time. I still don't know why he agreed to it. I fenced some land down by the creek and bought five head of cattle and a horse.

"I still worked any labor jobs I could find. Those first couple of years, I lived in a tent perched right where this house stands. There was too much work to be done for me to build a cabin. The first thing I built here was the stable for Trudy, my horse. I spent every minute of the day working until I was so tired that sleeping on the cold ground seemed luxurious."

Robert shook his head. "I couldn't do that now. It's amazing the things a young body can withstand. I don't know if I would have ever got around to building a cabin if I hadn't met Lena. I remember the first time I saw her. I was shearing sheep, and she was visiting with the boss's daughter. That night, I went home and knew I had to build a cabin. I couldn't very well go ask to court her without a home." A rattling cough swallowed his chuckle.

"So I built this cabin. It wasn't nearly so big. We added on to it as the years went by, and I could afford to put some money into it. I don't know what possessed me to think that having a plain cabin and a ranch that hadn't yet turned a profit qualified me to go courtin', but I did. To this day, I don't know what Lena saw in me. She could have married anyone, and she loved the city and pretty things. I couldn't give her any of that. I could only give her four walls and roof and the promise that I would love her 'til all the breath was out of my body.

"When we married, she didn't know a thing about cattle, and she could only ride sidesaddle. I hated to see her work, but she insisted, and it really helped. I don't know if I could have held on long enough to see my first profit if it hadn't been for her."

"How did you go from five cattle to this?" Kale was wide-eyed.

"Discipline. Everything we earned went back into the business. I couldn't afford a decent bull, so we used the best stud we could afford. I knew we'd start earning faster if we invested in the best quality rather than raise subpar cattle and try to break out of it into higher quality later. Lena milked the cows and sold the dairy. We even sold their dung as manure. Once I was able to quit working for other people, we started growing our own hay and used the dung ourselves. Around that time, I purchased our first slaves. It was a relief to have more hands.

"Lena and I had been trying for children, but there were difficulties. It worked out for the best. By the time Jason was on the way, we were a full operation. We profited off of every bit of the cattle. We made money off their milk, their hides, their meat. We didn't take the easy road and just raise 'em and sell 'em so someone else could make the money."

"So that's where Jason gets his love of efficiency." Kale

smiled at father and son.

Jason had never thought of it before. His father had never sat him down and explained the concept of efficiency to him, but his example had planted the lesson. Robert didn't waste anything, and Jason knew from an early age that no part of the cattle was allowed to pass through their ranch without leaving them money.

"Huh?"

"Well, that's how he's become so successful, sir. Arlington Steel was only a fraction of the size it is now when he inherited it from his father-in-law. He's always said efficiency is the quickest and easiest way to increase profits."

"Quick and easy. That sounds like my son. What we do here is certainly not quick or easy."

"Absolutely. I'm sorry if I implied otherwise, sir. I guess I didn't explain myself well. Jason's an expert at looking at the operation and maximizing productivity. His mills produce more than any others, and that increase has allowed him to expand the business and build more mills in strategic locations. I can only assume that he learned it from you."

Their dinner plates were carted away, and slices of apple pie were brought to the table. Jason couldn't remember ever hearing his father talk this much. Every word Robert spoke was news to him. All he had ever heard from his father was that he had built this place from nothing. Until now, Jason hadn't really known what that meant.

"Hmph. I suppose some of his old man might've rubbed off on him, despite his efforts to the contrary. We certainly didn't expand our business until we knew we could. I've seen too many folks be lured in by the promise of a bright future and get themselves entangled in debt. We operate on a strictly cash basis. That's why it took so long for us to add on to the house. As soon as Lena told me I was going to be a daddy, I knew I couldn't raise my son in the little old cabin Lena and I were living in. I wanted to build a whole new home. We could have afforded it, but Lena was sentimental. She didn't want to abandon the house I had built her. So instead, we added on." Robert smiled. "I was determined to prove to her that I could provide as good a life as she could have had with anyone else, so I made sure this would be the house of her dreams. All the modern appliances went into it, a private bathroom for every bedroom, the best gas lighting and fixtures. I wanted to make sure when her parents came to visit after the birth they would be impressed by how I took care of their little girl. It doesn't even really resemble the original cabin, but Lena loved the sentiment."

"So that's where Jason gets it from."

Jason snorted. "I'm the sentimental one? I'm not the man who carried a lock of his lover's hair around for three years."

"A moment of weakness on my part. You have always been sentimental."

"I have to agree with Kale. You are entirely too attached to sentiment. I think Kale's all the proof we need of that." The mild tone of his father's voice made the words seem almost nice.

Robert yawned, and Jason noticed that his eyes drooped. By his own admission, Robert had slept much of the day. When Jason was a child, his father had been up with the sun and worked until late into the night. It was strange to think that a simple meal and conversation was enough to tire him.

"Dinner was delightful, Father. Thank you."

Robert nodded. "Yes, I suppose it was."

Robert made no move to stand, signaling the end of dinner. It occurred to Jason that he hadn't seen his father stand the entire time he had been home. Given his father's state and the way he was constantly propped up with pillows, Jason realized that Demetri must be carrying him. Robert wouldn't want his son to see him carted around like an invalid. "May Kale and I be excused? It's getting late."

"Yes, of course. Have a nice night." Robert genuinely smiled and nodded at both Jason and Kale.

In the hall, Jason put his arm around Kale's waist and

kissed his cheek. "Thank you."

"I figured someone had to nudge the two of you along."

"Yes, and you did beautifully."

Chapter Sixteen

In bed, Jason rolled around this new image of his father as he laid on his back, staring in the darkness. It was easy to get wrapped up in the warm spell cast by the story his father had told, but he just couldn't reconcile his conflicting images of the man.

"What are you thinking about?" Kale was on his side with his back to Jason.

"How do you know I'm thinking about anything?"

"Because you think too loud. You might as well tell me what it is. I'm not going to be able to sleep until you stop."

Jason smiled. Being known so well never ceased to amaze him. It was an entirely comfortable feeling. "I just don't know what to make of my father."

"Then don't make anything of him. Just love him, respect him, and be content."

"But I can't make sense of him."

"Yes, no use being content when you can fret instead." Jason felt Kale roll over to face him.

"He's such an enigma."

"Only to you. He's quite a simple man. I believe that used to be your complaint about him."

"You're telling me you understand him? You understand how he could allow Darlene to speak to him like that, but he couldn't tolerate the love of my life being far more respectful?"

"That's precisely the problem. You treated me like a lover, and I treated you the same. That's what your father had issue with. He's actually a very fair man when it comes to his slaves. That's his reputation. If he were a tyrant, I would have heard about it back when I belonged to Carter."

"But he treats Darlene like family, why can't you be treated as family?"

"For one, Darlene has earned her place in this household. She's loyal and hardworking. Second, I'll concede that she is part of the family, but the same way a dog or pet is. You love your dog, but you won't hesitate to shoot him if he turns vicious."

"He should have treated you better."

"You need to see it from his point of view. I was way out of line with you and you with me. We were lovers for gods' sakes. He was right when he said that you weren't merely fucking me. You cared about me more than you should have, and you let me get away with everything. I had forgotten my place, and he took it upon himself to correct me. It wasn't his right since he didn't own me, but you can hardly blame him for it."

"Oh, I think I can."

"In a way, he was trying to protect you. I was dancing dangerously close to the line of impersonating a free man. Had I crossed that line, you would have lost me forever. Someone would have reported us."

"Him, most likely."

"No, if he'd wanted to, he would have. He could have, but he didn't. From an objective viewpoint, he did us a favor."

Jason's mouth tasted bitter. "How can you defend him?"

"You've put me in a position where I have to. I don't like it, so if you could just get past it, I'd appreciate it."

"I know I should be able to, especially since you have, and

you're the one he slapped and threatened to beat." Jason sighed, trying to release all his negative feelings with his breath. As soon as he was done, a yawn overtook him.

Kale threw his arm over Jason and pulled him in tight. Being surrounded by Kale, his scent, his touch, the steady rhythm of his breathing, soothed him. Jason's body reacted to it as if this was the place he was meant to be, his natural habitat, protected from the outside world.

"Tonight was nice. There could be more nice moments with your father if you'd only allow it."

Kale's breath tickled his ear, the advice sounding even more practical in Kale's strong, smooth voice than it already did. "You're right. You're always right. It's rather annoying. I'll try to let the past be."

"Good. Now stop talking, so I can get some sleep."

Kale's lips brushed the rim of Jason's ear. If nothing else, Jason should love his father for giving him the best man Jason had ever known.

CHAPTER SEVENTEEN

It was easy for Kale to find the hilltop where he and Jason had spoken the previous day. Martin wasn't likely to call until the evening if he even found anything today. Kale hoped for a call either way. Waiting inside the house would be unbearable, and he wanted Jason to have some time alone with his father. Once they had news from Martin, Kale intended to ask Jason to accompany him. For all the talk he spouted about Jason needing to spend time with his father, he was selfish enough to take Jason with him when the time came. After what he'd experienced at Monroe's, Kale knew he couldn't go through something like that again without Jason's support.

After breakfast, he had saddled a horse and sought out the hill with the panoramic view, a sketchpad and pastels in his saddlebags. Kale hobbled the horse and sat to draw. It was nice to work on his art again. He should have done so sooner. With a light hand, he sketched the area and then filled in the color. It wasn't anything he'd show publicly, but he wanted to unleash himself on the page and produce something, whether or not it was good. Closing his eyes, he pictured the way the scenery had been lit the day before. Taking some reds and oranges, he attempted to recreate the image. The result was a little off—the shadows didn't fall correctly—but Kale was satisfied.

Flipping the page, Kale began drawing the mare grazing a few paces away. It was an easy subject that he had drawn countless times. His pencil flew across the page. No need for pastels—he had only wanted those for the sunlit landscape. Within minutes, the horse took shape. A sense of satisfaction overcame him when images came into focus on the page. There was always a moment when he looked at his incomplete work and thought that it could really go either way. He could either make something great, or it could all fall apart. It always amazed him at how simple and small the touches were that made it come alive. A curve here, a shadow there, adding the eyes to a face. Such little things, but without them, the picture fell flat.

Jason had asked him once how he knew when he was done. Kale still didn't know. It was always a wild guess how far he would take a picture. Over time, especially since he had been afforded the luxury of pursuing art, he had developed the gut instinct that told him when one more shadow would be too much, when a detail should be left obscured. There was no explaining it, it just was. Kale smirked. This was exactly why he had never accepted the offer to teach an art class. What would he say? Just keep drawing until it feels right?

The horse on the page was complete, or as complete as Kale was going to make her. It was good. If he'd been in a different mood, he might have spent more time emphasizing her musculature, but he didn't have the patience for it at the moment. Another flip of the page, and fresh emptiness stared at him.

Kale looked around for inspiration. A tree would be nice, but there were none interesting enough or in the shapes he wanted. Perhaps he could draw an image from his own mind. Closing his eyes, Kale tried to empty his head so inspiration could come. What flashed before him was the picture of his mother mending his brother's trousers while Thomas sat at her feet. Kale pushed the image away. There was too much pain and longing in his chest to draw such a thing.

His hand began to glide across the pad. The pain and longing were exactly why he needed to release the image onto the page. Arms and legs took shape. A chair, the fireplace, a crackling fire, feet, heads, hair. It all poured out. The torn trousers, a needle and thread piercing the fabric, deft hands mending a tear. Kale shaded with meticulous precision, pulling out every shape. When there was nothing left, he regarded his work: a beautiful portrait of his mother and Thomas, faceless.

Closing his eyes again, he struggled to pull their faces into focus. He could feel what it was like to have his mother smile at him, but he couldn't recreate it. All he had was blurry perception. Kale had told Jason once that it wasn't about the details, that people rarely remember them, that art was about perception and evoking feelings. All well and good, but this was his family. Every time he tried to focus the image, he was left with the unsettling realization that it wasn't quite right.

The blank faces stared at him. It was disturbing. Holding the clearest picture in his mind that he could, he filled in the eyes, nose, and mouth on each face. He remembered to sprinkle freckles on the bridge of Thomas's nose. He didn't forget the wrinkles around his mother's eyes or the scar that cut through her right eyebrow. Little details, but it was the whole he couldn't see. The result was an intricate drawing of two people who looked similar to his mother and brother.

Kale cursed himself for not drawing them earlier, for failing to capture their images when they had still been fresh in his mind. His fourteen-year-old self wouldn't have been up to the task. And even if he had been, he wouldn't have been able to keep the drawing through the years. When he had been sold, he had known he would never see them again. He'd found no point in torturing himself with their likeness.

He could draw nothing else after that. Kale gathered up his supplies and placed them back in the saddlebag, withdrawing a book. He still had a good hour before hunger would drive him back to the house, an hour he could spend lost in another world where none of his problems existed.

CHAPTER EIGHTEEN

"A rancher from up north has inquired about purchasing a bull." John lifted the letter in question. "I've never heard of him, though."

"Does he know how much our bulls go for?" Robert puffed his cigar from the brown leather armchair where he was propped up behind his imposing, walnut desk. As a boy, Jason had been afraid of that desk and, more often than not, the gruff man who sat behind it. Jason had abandoned such fear long ago and now sat across from Robert next to John. He had wanted to spend time with his father, and apparently this was what his father did. It wasn't a bad idea to start showing some interest in the family business.

"He sounds like he does, but who knows? I hate selling to someone we don't know."

"I agree. See what you can find out about him, and let me know." Robert exhaled the smoke and surrendered to a coughing fit. Jason didn't know how his father could maintain such a dreadful habit when he sounded likely to cough up a lung.

"I'm confused. If he has the money, why does it matter?" Jason couldn't understand the business logic in that. He had been in the study for hours, listening to talk of things he didn't comprehend. This was at least something he felt knowledgeable enough about to ask a question.

Robert still struggled with the cough, so he motioned for John to answer. "Our value comes in our reputation. Wadsworth bulls produce high-grade cattle. It takes work to maintain that standard. If we sold to anyone who asked, it would diminish our value."

"So you work on exclusivity?"

"It's not being exclusive we're after. It's quality. Say we sell to this fellow and it turns out his cows are sick, ugly things. They pass their bad breeding on through one of our bulls, and we've got subpar cattle roaming around sired by a Wadsworth bull. When he goes to sell his miserable offspring, he's going to brag about it being the product of a Wadsworth bull. His buyer's going to take a look at the scrawny calf and think there must be something wrong with Wadsworth cattle. Our bulls produce the best because they're only allowed to breed to the best. You understand, boy?"

Jason nodded. "I guess so. It's a different business than steel."

"Of course it is. We're dealing with living animals here." Robert had overcome his cough and settled back in his chair. "If someone wants a Wadsworth bull, they've got to show that they're committed to the same quality we are."

"Well, not quite the same. No one has the quality your daddy does." John nodded to Jason and grinned with pride. Respect shone through his eyes when he looked back at Robert.

Robert chuckled. "All right, but close. That's why we only enter Cattleman's Roundup. It's the most exclusive auction in the country. If this fellow is contacting us by letter, it probably means he doesn't meet the standards to be allowed in to the auction, or he doesn't know about it. Neither one is a good sign, but I'm not against helping another man get a start as long as he can prove himself." Robert coughed again.

"Why don't we take a break? I need to see if the boys have come back from checking the northwest fence and see if that herd got moved." Robert nodded as he continued to cough. John stood, and Jason followed him. Demetri stepped forward from the corner where he'd been silently standing and gently patted Robert on the back. In the hall, John closed the door after Jason.

"You did well in there. It means a lot to Robert that you're taking an interest, even if he doesn't show it." John nodded to him and left before Jason could even respond.

The study door opened, and Demetri emerged. "Is there anything I can get you, sir?"

"No, I'm fine, thank you. And thanks for taking care of my father so well."

"It's my pleasure, sir. It's an honor to be here for him when he needs me." Demetri lifted his eyes to Jason's, and the clear blue orbs confirmed the truth of his statement.

Jason had been a fool to think he could have taken Demetri away from his father. All he had known was that Demetri was more upper-class than any of the other slaves on the ranch. Jason had been enthralled with his tales of his previous master's household where he'd served nobility. "Why did you seem disappointed when Father didn't give you to me to take to Perdana? You clearly belong with him."

Demetri lowered his eyes in the subservient way slaves were accustomed to. "I felt slighted that he didn't think highly enough of me to give me to his only son. I was insulted that he had chosen to buy Kale instead. It was wrong of me, and I apologize."

"What? I always thought you were so smart when I was younger, but you sure got that one wrong. You're invaluable to him."

"Thank you, sir."

They stood in awkward silence. Jason wondered what Demetri could be waiting for. Then it dawned on him. Demetri had come out to see if Jason was gone so he could carry Robert to his room. Jason should have realized sooner. "I'll be in my room, should anybody need me."

Demetri lifted his eyes once again. "Thank you, sir." Jason caught the understanding in his gaze. He knew Jason had been letting him know that he wouldn't be on the path to Robert's room, and that was what he thanked him for.

Up in his room, Jason removed his vest and unbuttoned the top two buttons of his shirt. Picking up his mother's journal from the table, he positioned himself in the chair by the fireplace and lost himself in her writings. Even the most mundane entries held his attention. Each word was a comforting reminder of the woman who'd been the center of his world. He didn't stop until Kale walked up behind him.

"I thought you were supposed to be spending time with your father."

Jason tilted his head all the way back over the chair, forcing Kale to lean in for an upside down kiss. Satisfied with the greeting, he marked his place in the book and set it aside. "I was, but he's resting now. He can't get through much. What are you doing back so early?"

"Early? I thought you'd be worried about me. I got absorbed in my book."

Jason glanced at the clock on the bedside table. It was already almost three o'clock. "Me too. More time passed than I thought. You want to eat lunch?"

"That's what brought me back." Kale tossed his art supplies on the bed and headed for the door.

Darlene fixed them some sandwiches, and they ate together in the dining room. It was nice to eat with just the two of them. Jason didn't know if his father had woken up and eaten or if he'd slept through lunch. He didn't want to disturb him if he was still sleeping, but he also wanted Robert to know he wanted to spend time with him. Maybe he would see if he could find Demetri after he finished eating.

"How was it with your father this morning?"

Jason nodded. "It was good. I wouldn't say we're chums now, but I sat in on a meeting between him and John. It was quite illuminating. They have their own way of running things, and it seems to be working. He's right, I'll bungle the whole thing if I don't learn."

"No, you're smart enough to take the advice of those around you. John will stay on, I'm sure. He won't let you ruin it. I'm glad to hear things went well."

"How was your day? Did you bring me back any pictures?"

Kale shifted in his seat. He was going to try to hide something. "Nothing interesting."

"Really? So if I walked upstairs right now, there'd be nothing that would catch my eye?"

"Don't, Jason. I'll show you when I'm ready."

The curt tone clipped Jason's retort. Kale was always protective of his art, but this was more than the usual shyness. With all the upheaval of the last few days, it wasn't entirely surprising that he was drawing things he didn't want Jason to know about. It put Jason at a disadvantage. He always used Kale's drawings as a barometer of his feelings. They were a useful tool in deciphering his often silent lover.

Jason reached across the table and rested his hand on top of Kale's. "You don't have to worry. I won't go snooping. Just know that I'm always here when you're ready. There's nothing you could show me that would make me think less of you."

Kale peered at Jason, his lips pursed in thought, and nodded. Jason pulled his hand back, and they resumed eating.

When they were almost done, Demetri entered. "Excuse me, sir?"

"Yes, Demetri?"

"Your father wanted me to invite you and Kale to play cards with him in his study."

Jason bit back the question that sprang to his mind. Demetri would have, of course, seen to it that his father had eaten. "Thank you. We'll join him as soon as we're done. Shouldn't be more than a few minutes."

Once Demetri was gone, Jason turned to Kale. "I hope you don't mind."

"Not at all. I think it's great. Gives me something to do."

In the study, Robert was in the same chair as earlier. The desk in front of him had been cleared of everything except a deck of cards and rack of chips. "Have a seat, boys. I thought we'd play some draw poker before dinner." Robert tapped the ash off the end of his cigar into the ashtray on the corner of his desk.

Kale took the seat on the left, leaving Jason the one on the right.

"Do either of you know how to deal?"

"Kale's better at it than me."

"Go ahead then." Robert nodded to Kale. Kale picked up the cards and shuffled, letting Jason split the deck. While Kale dealt, Jason passed out the chips.

Poker had never been Jason's game, but he knew Kale had played it when he was a slave. They were more inclined to play billiards together. Robert had loved billiards as well, and the house even had a billiards room. That was the game they should have been playing.

Robert coughed, choking on the air he breathed. Of course they couldn't play billiards. Jason's father had just as much chance of running a foot race as standing at a table.

The hand passed in silence except for the bidding, as did the next and the next.

"Stop holding back, boy." Robert growled after Kale folded for the second time on the fourth hand.

"Sir?"

"Don't give me that. You think I'm too old and sickly for you to beat? If I wanted to win every hand, I would have just had Jason come."

Jason caught the twitch in Kale's lips. "All right. I'll see you then." Kale threw his chips in the pot. "What you got?"

"A flush." Robert laid down five clubs.

Kale nodded. "That's good."

"Not good enough, is it?"

Kale tossed his hand on the table. A full house.

"Don't be scared to beat me again."

Kale nodded as he stacked his chips. "I won't, sir."

For the next few hours, Jason watched them play. He found it fascinating watching these two men size each other up and call each other's bluffs. While Jason played each hand, he was really no more than a spectator, and he was perfectly fine with that. Seeing Kale and his father together gave him hope. Robert finally treated Kale as he would any other man. Any hope at a relationship with his father was doomed as long as Robert couldn't accept Jason's relationship with Kale, making this a promising sign.

A shrill ringing, muffled by walls, pierced the air. Jason eyes snapped to Kale. Robert rarely, if ever, used the telephone, so this was likely the call they'd been waiting for. A minute later, a slave Jason didn't know entered the room.

"Sir, there's a telephone call for Mr. Kale. A Mr. Grimlock."

Robert nodded to the slave. "Thank you, Billy."

Kale didn't even look at Jason or Robert before following Billy out the door. Jason turned to his father. "This is what we've been waiting for."

"Go on, then. It's not like there's much of a game without Kale anyway."

Jason was halfway to the door by the time his father finished speaking. When he reached Kale, he was already talking to Martin. Hearing only Kale's side of the conversation wasn't very enlightening. Jason tried to read Kale's face for any sign of what was being said, but Kale seemed as calm and composed as usual.

"Thank you, Martin. This has all been very helpful. Give my love to Sophie, and Jason's too." Kale nodded, even though Martin couldn't see him. "Goodbye." Kale leaned against the wall, deflated and seemingly exhausted.

"So?" Jason came to Kale's side.

"Martin and Mr. Smithson were able to track down court proceedings regarding some unpaid debts. Just like George said, they didn't want to give up their land—it's been in their family for generations—so they sold off their slaves to pay the debts, and then just left because they couldn't keep up the place without the slaves. They're living in a cousin's property in Shalae County on the outskirts of Rushing. The court allowed them to sell their slaves at auction in Shalae County since it's more affluent there. There's no record of which slaves were sold or even what auction house they went through. My family could be anywhere."

Kale's voice broke at the end. His calm exterior showed signs of cracking: tight lips, tense muscles around the cheeks and eyes. "Let's go upstairs." Jason wanted to get Kale to a place where he could break down if he needed to. Kale didn't resist when Jason guided him to their room with an arm around his back.

"They could be anywhere, Jason." Kale looked up at him from the bed where Jason had sat him.

"We'll find them." Jason sat next to him and grabbed his hand.

"Will you come with me? I hate to take you away from your father, but I don't know if I can do this without you."

"Of course. You don't even have to ask. We'll leave first thing in the morning." Kale's eyes looked pained. "You know we'd leave now if it made sense, but there's no way we can reach Shalae County tonight." That wasn't Jason's only concern. Kale looked as though he would fall apart if a draft blew through. He needed sleep.

"You're right—"

A knock on the door interrupted Kale.

"Yes?" Jason called.

The door opened to reveal Demetri. "Excuse me, sir, but your father was worried about you."

"Oh, yes." Jason turned back to Kale. "Why don't you get ready for dinner, and I'll be back in a moment." He had completely forgotten about his father. Jason followed Demetri downstairs to where his father still sat in his study.

"I'm sorry, Father. I didn't mean to leave you for so long."

"Was it good news or bad?"

"A little of both, I suppose. We found out Kale's family was sold off, but we have no way of knowing who to."

"Well, don't feel like you need to make an appearance at dinner on my account. You can have something brought to your room if you prefer. He probably doesn't want to see anyone."

"Thank you, Father. I think we'll do that."

"Have a good night, then."

"You as well."

When Jason got back to their room, Kale was exactly as he had left him, staring vacantly ahead. "Do you want me to have dinner brought up? There's no need to go downstairs."

"I don't know if I can eat. My stomach's in knots."

"Well, you're at least going to try."

Kale finally met Jason's eyes. "You might as well eat with your father. I'm not going to be the best company. I'm going to be taking you away, so you should spend this time with him."

"Are you sure?"

"Yes. We'll have plenty of time together."

Jason was hesitant to leave him in such a state, but he doubted there was anything he could do at the moment. They both needed to eat, and Jason thought the time with his father may actually be productive. Jason tugged on the pull cord by the bed, and a few minutes later a slave girl he didn't recognize came to the door.

"Have some dinner brought up for Kale, and let my father know I'd like to dine with him if he's feeling up to it, please."

"Yes, sir." The slave left as quietly and quickly as she'd come.

With nothing else to do, Jason reclaimed his spot next to Kale and held his hand. Silence could be just as comforting as words. Jason mentally prepared for the coming day, running over the many possibilities of how it could unfold. He'd have to ask John where they could buy some fuel. It wasn't possible to make it all the way to their destination on what they had. Jason's most important role would be as a support to Kale. Jason had no idea how he must feeling; there was nothing in his experience to compare it to.

A gentle knock on the door preceded it opening to reveal a different slave carrying a covered tray.

"You can place it on the desk."

"Dinner is served downstairs as well, sir."

"Thank you. I'll be along in a moment." Once the door softly clicked closed behind the slave, Jason squeezed Kale's hand. "Eat. I'll be back as soon as I'm finished, and we can go to bed." Jason leaned in and softly kissed Kale's lips, not terribly surprised when he received no response. "Try to eat something."

"I will. Please make my apologies to your father."

"No need, he's the one who suggested it. I'll see you soon."

In the dining room, a cream of broccoli soup was served right after Jason took his seat.

"How is Kale doing?" Robert asked between spoonfuls.

"I think he'll be fine. It's a bit of a shock, but I think he appreciates knowing—having something to go off of. We'll be leaving early tomorrow morning. I don't know when we'll be back. I'm hoping it will be a quick trip." Jason thought he saw a tinge of sadness in his father's eyes at the mention of leaving.

"Where are you off to?"

"Shalae County, around Rushing."

"That's quite a drive. Even if everything goes well, you should get a room for the night before heading back. Do you think you'll bring his family with you?"

"That's the hope, although if I'm honest, I have to admit I don't think it's likely, at least not in the next two days."

"You can't let him know that. Let him hope for the best

while you prepare for the worst."

"Thank you, Father."

"I'm not the heartless tyrant you seem to think I am."

"That's what Kale says."

Robert chortled. "Is that right?"

"He's tiresomely practical. He has a talent for explaining things to me that I think he takes too much pleasure in."

"He does seem to be pretty calm and collected. That's good. You're exactly the opposite."

Jason stamped down his initial instinct to let his father's words sting. "He's a good match for me."

"You know, that's why I bought him for you. I suppose he was just a little better of a match for you than I'd intended. I certainly never envisioned this happening."

The rest of dinner proceeded with comfortable conversation. By the time dessert came around, Jason was anxious to get back to Kale. He barely tasted the peach cobbler. Once he had devoured the last of the buttery crumbs, he wiped his mouth and then set his napkin on the table while he pushed his chair back. "Thank you for dinner, Father. I probably won't see you before we leave tomorrow."

"Have a safe journey. And call to let me know how's it going and when to expect you back."

"I will, Father."

"Give Kale my regards, and let him know I hope he finds them."

"Thank you." Jason held his father's eyes for a moment, noticing the winkles around them and the gray that dusted the hair framing his face.

Upstairs, no light peeked beneath his bedroom door. Jason's heart sank. He had really wanted Kale to still be awake. It was early for him to be in bed, but it was probably for the best. Jason quickly undressed and crawled in beside Kale. He reached out to cuddle, only to be shocked when Kale shrugged him off.

An awkward silence hung in the air as Jason contemplated

what to do. He wasn't sure letting Kale brood was a good idea, but he didn't want to push the issue. He could go a night without cuddling.

"I just can't tonight. I'm sorry." Kale's pained voice breached the silence.

Jason wondered if Kale meant cuddling or sex. Neither answer would make Jason feel better, so he didn't ask. Respecting Kale's wishes, he settled on his back with one arm across his stomach and the other across his eyes. In a few minutes, Jason heard Kale's breathing fall into the familiar pattern of sleep. Every muscle in his body was tuned to the man lying next to him. He wanted to curl around him, comfort him in sleep, stave off the nightmares. But he didn't. He wanted Kale to know he was loved, and right now the best way to do that was to hold back. Experience had taught him that loving someone meant doing what that person needed to feel loved, not indulging his own desires. He lay rigid, muscles tense against the urge to reach out.

CHAPTER NINETEEN

Finally, they were out on the open road. Clear blue skies meant the top was down, and Kale relished the breeze on his skin. They had eaten breakfast before they left and had purchased fuel at a local farming supply store, so there was nothing but hours of driving ahead of them. The next stop would be in Rushing, where Kale would finally get the answers he sought.

Kale rested his hand on the seat between him and Jason. Things had been awkward between them all morning. It probably would have been better if Kale had just let Jason cuddle him last night. His self-loathing hadn't permitted him to accept the comfort even though he logically knew it would help. Quiet drives were usually pleasant, but this was the silence of two people who didn't know what to say to each other. Even the rumble of the air as the car sliced through it couldn't drown out the silence. Kale tapped his fingers on the seat. What started out as a steady rhythm turned into frantic shaking. Instead of being an outlet for his anxieties, it keyed him up even more.

A tight, warm weight restrained his hand. Kale glanced down to see Jason's alabaster hand holding his. Jason gave a firm squeeze and then intertwined his fingers with Kale's, stalling any hope of further tapping. Jason smiled. Kale returned it. The touch—the connection—was welcome. Kale regretted not letting Jason hold him last night. Sometimes, it just felt good to brood, to retreat into himself. This was unfamiliar territory for both of them. The fact that they were both trying had to be enough. They'd work things out when all this was settled.

After a few minutes, Jason reached into the back seat and retrieved a book from his bag. "I thought I could read aloud, help pass the time."

"It depends. What book did you bring?"

"*The Grisly Tale of Hunter Humphreys*. We never finished it."

"That sounds good." As Jason read, Kale thought of Naiara and the nice little life they had carved for themselves there. Since arriving at the ranch, he'd almost forgotten that he and Jason had a whole life together back home. The last few days seemed so separate from it.

Once Jason finished that book, he pulled out another. "I borrowed this from my father's library. I don't think he'll mind." It was a nice mystery with the kind of plot that was easy to follow without much thought.

While the hours had seemed to drag by as they were driving, once Kale came into Rushing, it felt like the time had flown. Kale parked in front of the first place he found that served food. Approaching the Monroes on an empty stomach would be a mistake. He and Jason ate quickly, and Kale finished off his meal with a shot of whiskey to calm his nerves.

Jason asked the bartender for directions to the address Martin had given them, and then they were back in the car. "Go down this road about a kilometer and then turn right on Maple. Follow it for six kilometers, and there'll be a left turn onto Grove and then a quick right onto Monroe. Jedediah lives in the smaller of the two houses."

Kale nodded and started the car. This was it. Ten minutes later, they were parked again and staring at a two-story white house that was nicer than the place Monroe had left in Malar.

Kale straightened his clothes, twisting his shirt cuffs into place and tightening his tie. He had almost insisted on his regular, more comfortable dress for the long drive, but Jason had been right to suggest the nice clothing. It gave Kale a confidence that he wasn't entirely sure was warranted.

Knocking on the door, Kale wished they had called first, but it would've been more difficult to get Monroe to give him the information he needed over the phone, and they might not even have one. However, the phone had the benefit of avoiding a face-to-face confrontation. With it being around lunchtime, there was a good chance Monroe would be home.

Jason introduced them to the unfamiliar butler as Mr. Wadsworth and associate, and they were led into the parlor to wait. There was no mistaking Mr. Monroe when he entered. Time had softened the sharp angles of his face. Gray hairs had turned white, and light brown had turned gray. The long nose and bushy eyebrows were just as off-putting as they had been to Kale as a boy. The cold blue eyes and mouth that habitually twisted into a sneer soured Kale's stomach. Salty acid crept up Kale's throat. His heart raced, urging him to run or fight, to do anything other than stand where he was.

In an instant, he was no longer in a parlor in Shalae County. He was outside a slave hut, trying to catch a garter snake with his brother while his mother yelled at them to let it be. Then he was being pulled to a wagon, having just been sold, his brother clinging to his legs as Kale tried to stay strong. Thomas made leaving so difficult. Mama had stood back, crying silent tears. She hadn't wanted to make it any harder on Kale than it already was. She'd already said her goodbyes. Thomas was too young to notice or care. It took a lash of the whip for him to finally release Kale. Riding in the back of that wagon, Kale had closed his heart. He couldn't afford to feel when there was only pain. He couldn't let the pain and fear of the unknown interfere with his ability to do his work and survive. That had been the last lesson his mother had taught him.

Kale didn't know how long he was submerged in the memory. Jason must have noticed because he strode forward to shake Mr. Monroe's hand. The slight breeze of his movement felt cool on Kale's skin, and he realized it was because a film of sweat covered him. Jason's voice as he introduced himself grounded Kale, and he was able to speak.

"We're interested in some slaves you owned…" Kale's voice trailed off. He didn't know what to call the man in front of him. The only address he had used for him was master, and that was certainly out of the question. Affording him even the respect of mister disgusted Kale.

Jason picked up the conversation while Kale was still trying to figure it out. "I owned a slave who was related to them, and I liked his look and features, so I was wanting to get another of the same. Since the slave was bred at your estate, I hope to find the slave's mother or brother." Hearing Jason talk about his family like they were livestock made Kale's insides churn, and he was grateful Jason was the one doing the talking. Kale didn't have the stomach for it. "The mother's name is Adele, and the boy's is Thomas."

Kale caught the precise moment that the names registered in Monroe's head. His eyes flashed to Kale. "You. You're the slave." A weight dragged Kale's head down, but he struggled against it. Never again would he lower himself before this man. Kale's skin prickled under Monroe's glare. He felt like a slave again, scrutinized purely for his market value.

"You must be mistaken." Jason's attempt was futile. Monroe's eyes pierced Kale's. Kale steeled himself, staring back with as much venom as he could muster. The first fourteen years of his life had been spent as the property of this man, but Kale had never once stared into his blue eyes.

"No, I'm not. You were my slave, weren't you, boy?"

Kale wasn't about to lie. He couldn't. "Yes, I was, Monroe." Kale sneered, all hesitation gone. "I'm a free citizen of Naiara now."

Monroe's face twisted in contempt. "There's no way I'm

helping an uppity slave with anything. You'd better get out of my house before I show you what happens to slave filth who act like they're free."

The fear was irrational, but that didn't make it any less real. Monroe didn't have any power over him. In fact, Kale had more power than Monroe, since he was under the protection of the prime minister of Naiara.

Off to the side, Kale saw heat rise in Jason's face. This wasn't the embarrassed blush Kale so often provoked in him. Jason was on the verge of exploding, which would do nothing for their cause. Kale had risen above, not only his previous station in life, but even above his old master. Nothing riled men like Monroe more than knowing he hadn't been able to get a rise out of the person he terrorized. Kale had the upper hand. "I'm sorry for wasting your time then, Mr. Monroe. Thank you for visiting with us. Jason, it's time for us to leave." He sounded more high-class than he ever had in his life.

Jason stood there, not willing to relinquish his anger. Kale walked to the door, trusting that Jason would follow. "I'll have you know we're two of the richest men in both Arine and Naiara." Kale couldn't help the little smile that tugged at his lips. Bless Jason. As if Monroe cared who they were. When he felt Jason's presence behind him, he proceeded out the door without even a glance backward.

CHAPTER TWENTY

"Who the fuck does that man think he is?" Jason had a mind to jump out of the car, moving or not, and go punch that disgusting man in the face. "Calling you filth. That's rich. And speaking of rich, what gives a man who can't even manage his own financial affairs the nerve to stand up to us? Must be pretty embarrassing having your former slave waltz in with more money than the gods."

"We don't have quite that much, and it's not mine. I just lucked into it."

"Lucked into it? You were the one who arranged the whole damn thing. You have more claim to the Arlington Steel empire than any man alive. I'm going to telephone Martin first thing, and we're going to find out about every bit of debt that man has. We're going to buy out all of his creditors, and then we're going to call every loan he has due. No way does a man like that have his business in order. He's going to show you what happens to a slave who acts like a free man? I'll show him what happens when a piece of cheap trash insults his betters."

Out of the corner of his eye, Jason saw Kale holding back a smile. "You think this is funny? We'll see how funny it is when I buy the bank that holds his mortgage."

Kale burst out laughing. "Really? And what we would do

with a bank? Use it as our own personal tool for revenge? Besides, his family's probably owned that land for generations."

"Why not? Sounds good to me. His stupidity is likely hereditary. I bet they've had to mortgage their place just to pay the bills." Jason crossed his arms across his chest and leaned back in his seat. He wanted to hit something, release his rage on an object, preferably Monroe's funny looking head.

"You really know how to cheer me up. Here I am laughing mere minutes after finding out I'll probably never see my family again."

Jason unfolded his arms and reached for Kale's hand. "I'm sorry. I know I'm being ridiculous, but he insulted you, Kale. You, the most amazing man I've ever met, and he dares to talk down to you? You're a bigger man than I am."

"I've had more practice holding my temper. Truth is, I pity him. The man's lost everything, living with his family, and here I am living a life that most free people can't even dream of."

"You pity him?"

"Yeah, don't you? I loathe that man, but he's not going to help me find my family, and if he still owned them, he wouldn't have been able to resist telling me, so I really have no further use for him." Kale shrugged. "I really had held out hope he hadn't sold them. I knew it wasn't likely. Mama and Thomas weren't particularly useful to him personally. I know he's horrible, but he wasn't cruel, and I hoped—I needed—him to still own them."

That's the best Kale could hope for, that his family was owned by someone who wasn't cruel. Jason worried about the blow to their pride while Kale hoped his family hadn't been sold to someone crueler than Monroe. And it wasn't even probable that they'd been sold together. "We'll find them, Kale. I swear."

"I know. I trust you."

"And after we do, can I please at least fantasize about destroying that little slug?"

Kale laughed some more. "Yes. I'll even get you some salt and show you how normal boys relieve their slug-destroying urges."

It was good to see Kale laughing. Jason wished it could last, but he knew it was just a momentary respite, a release of tension that prevented Kale from falling apart. "What do you want to do? We can stay in town or go back to the ranch."

"Let's stay in town. It's likely that anything we find will just lead us right back here. Unless you want to go back. I know you need to spend time with your father."

Kale's tone was deceptively nonchalant to anyone who didn't know him as well as Jason did. Kale was a master at bottling up his own needs, especially in favor of Jason's. "There's nowhere I need to be other than here. Rushing is big enough that they should have a decent hotel."

The first hotel Kale pulled up to did not meet Jason's definition of "decent," which included having a telephone, and neither did the second. The third, however, not only had a telephone on the main floor for guests, but a restaurant as well.

After they were checked in, they took a look at their room, and Jason dropped off his bag. All it contained were two books, some snacks, their bank book, and travel documents. Another set of clothes hadn't been necessary when he'd thought they would just be driving home the next day. "We'll have to go shopping for a change of clothes."

"No need. I can wear the same thing tomorrow." Kale despised shopping.

"It's something to do, and it gives us an excuse to talk to some of the locals, to see if we can find out anything else. I'll call Martin before we leave and let him know about the new developments so he can investigate. We can't just go around town asking about Monroe"—Jason couldn't keep the venom out of his voice as he uttered that vile name—"and where he might have sold his slaves. All that's going to do is draw suspicion. We're in his territory. Two gentleman shopping and making small talk with the locals is nothing out of the ordinary. With your people skills, we should be able to find out a good bit."

"Fine. I forget how good you can be at this sort of thing."

A half hour later, they walked down the street their hotel was on, in search of a clothier the concierge had recommended. Jason had spoken to Martin and let Demetri know they would spend the night in Rushing. The day was beginning to cool, and it felt good to burn off energy stretching his legs.

A tiny bell tinkled over the door when they entered the shop. A medium-sized man with spectacles greeted them. "What can I help you fine gentlemen with today?"

"We were looking for a couple of suits, one each. The train lost our bags, and we are without clothes until the whole mess is sorted. We need something we can take tonight."

"I can certainly help you with that. My name's Edward Pillston, and I'm the proprietor here." Edward shook both their hands before focusing back on Jason. "We have some options that could work very nicely and will require minimal adjustments. Let me show you. Did you have anything specific in mind?"

"Something nice, but not too fancy. We're here on business and will be in meetings most of the day. Price is of no concern." Jason fingered a suit coat, testing the fabric.

"I see. Well, I think something like this might just do the trick for you, sir." Edward showed them a full three-piece suit with matching cravat and cufflinks.

"Yes, that appears to fit the bill."

"And for your companion, might I suggest this?" Edward assembled another suit, this one with a cut that would emphasize Kale's broad shoulders. Jason pictured Kale filling out the fabric nicely.

"What do you think, Kale?"

"It'll do, but I'd prefer a tie to the cravat. I don't need to look like a stuffed cock strutting around."

Jason smiled. It was nearly impossible to get Kale into a cravat, which was a shame because Jason loved them on him. "We'll take them."

"Excellent. In the back there, we have dressing rooms. If you'd like to try them on, I can measure the adjustments that need to be made and have them ready for you shortly."

Edward snapped his fingers, and a tall young man equipped with a measuring tape and a pincushion around his wrist appeared. It was apparent from his bowed head that he was a slave. "Luis, take these suits into the dressing rooms for these gentleman. They want to take them tonight, so you'll need to do the adjustments."

"Yes, Master." Luis picked up the suits. "If you would follow me, sirs, it's right this way."

Kale looked stunning in the suit. It accentuated his trim waist and broad shoulders without making his chest or arms appear too bulky. Luis pinned the pant legs while Edward observed.

"You have quite a capable slave here. He's a credit to you." Jason wondered if Kale's words were for the slave or for Edward. Probably a little of both.

"Thank you. He performs his work well, and not just the mundane things. He can sew anything. I merely design the patterns and hand them off to him. In fact, he's even created a few patterns that I was able to tweak into decent designs. I can only say that I'm happy I own him. My competitors would love to steal him from me."

Kale's easy smile gave no hint of the day's ordeal. "I can imagine. It's hard to come across quality slaves. Do you mind me asking where you acquired this one?"

"Not at all. He came from Lyman's."

"I'm not familiar with the name."

"Oh, I'm sorry. I forgot you're not from around here.

Lyman's is a brokerage specializing in slaves with specific skills. I wish I could take credit for Luis's ability, but I'm afraid I can't. He came to me fully trained. It was worth the extra cost to not have to spend the time teaching him."

Luis continued to work as if he weren't being spoken about. Jason remembered when Kale had been like that. Jason still had trouble acting as though slaves were less than other people when Kale was such stunning proof to the contrary. Luis would have done well on his own with his talent. Instead, he was stuck working for a man who barely acknowledged him. Another life wasted.

"Yes, time is often worth more than money. I'm in search of a valet myself. I doubt I need such a thoroughly trained slave as this Lyman's could provide. Are there any auction houses you can recommend? I always feel I get a better deal when I have several options to bid on." It was impossible to tell from the way Kale spoke—his voice sure and smooth—that he had ever been a slave, or that he spoke on a subject that revolted him.

"Certainly. You might want to give Harrison's a try. They hold weekly auctions. If you're going to be in town long enough or don't mind traveling back, you'd do well to wait for Rogers and Son's monthly auction. Either option is good."

"Thank you. I'll be sure to look into it."

Once Kale was done, it was Jason's turn. He didn't think he looked particularly good in the suit, but Kale's appraising gaze said otherwise. Gods, he was lucky to have found Kale.

"If you gentleman would like to shop elsewhere on the avenue for a while, I should have these ready for you shortly."

Yes, he would have them ready, not his slave who would do the actual work. Jason knew he really didn't have room to talk when his own business used slaves, but it irked him. Having slaves working at the mills bothered him, but he and Kale had discussed it many times. Kale was adamant that if he started using free men instead, the slaves he currently used would be headed for worse fates. Maybe it was time to at least re-evaluate working conditions.

"We'll see you soon then." Jason tipped his head to Edward and then to Luis, not caring about the odd look Edward gave him.

Outside, there were plenty of shops, and they had no problem filling the time until their clothes were ready. They were able to gather the names of two other slave dealers operating in the county. Purchases in hand, they headed back to the hotel.

CHAPTER TWENTY-ONE

Dinner had been pleasant enough. Kale found it strange to think that the last time he had eaten was before the confrontation with Monroe. The food helped to steady his fraying nerves. In all the years of bondage as a slave, he had never been under so much stress. As a slave, his worries had been for himself. Having his family depending on him to find them was an entirely different situation. The knowledge that there was practically no way for them to know he was free or even to hope that he would find them gave him no comfort. It was his responsibility, and it weighed heavy on his shoulders.

Kale watched Jason as they undressed for bed. He was fortunate to have an ally in Jason. Jason's mind constantly looked for more information. That was how he had expanded the Arlington Steel empire. Jason had always believed in the power of knowledge. It was why he'd insisted they stay for drinks in the lounge after dinner, even though Kale was tired and wanted nothing more than to collapse into bed and dull the memory of the day with sleep. It was in the lounge that they had discovered what Kale had suspected: the Monroes were an old family in the area, but one whose power had greatly diminished in recent years.

Once undressed, Kale slid between the sheets, leaving

Jason to put away their new clothes. The bed did not offer the respite Kale had hoped for. Shame plagued him, twisting in his gut until he wished the bed would devour him, remove him from sight. It wasn't the way Monroe had treated him, but the fact that he had failed that hurt so much. By this time, Kale had expected to know where his family was, when in reality he wasn't really any closer. His shame was self-imposed, but that didn't make it any easier to bear.

Jason's weight shifted the bed beside him. Just like last night, he moved to hold Kale. The touch of Jason's skin burned. The undeserved warmth and comfort acted as a white hot poker to his shame. This time when Kale pulled away, Jason held firm. It was a strange feeling from a man who practiced little dominance in bed.

"I don't need to have sex with you, Kale. We don't need to do anything, but I do need you to know that I'm here for you, that I won't let anything bad happen. I need you to know I love you. I understand you can't make love right now, not when you're feeling this way, but you are loved, and I'm going to show you. Just let me hold you."

Kale couldn't argue. Jason had given him everything. Kale wouldn't deny him this. Although it would have been easier if he'd wanted to simply take Kale. A quick, hard fuck. Fucking would even take his mind off his situation. But Jason would never consent to having sex if Kale weren't visibly aroused, and try as he might, nothing stirred within him. Kale flirted with the idea of trying to fake it, but it would be worse to act interested in sex and then have Jason stop. It would bring back all of Jason's insecurities. For too long, Kale had let Jason believe he was a rapist, and the scars from those thoughts ran deep. The remembrance of the pain he'd caused Jason added another layer to his shame. Kale could never apologize enough for it, even though he had tried on countless occasions to undo the damage.

Kale nodded his consent to the cuddling, and Jason settled into a more comfortable position for the night, holding Kale against him in a grip that seemed unbreakable.

The touch of Jason's bare skin was as comfortable as any blanket. Kale smelled the sweet scent of Jason surrounding him. He could never make out exactly what it was—only that it was uniquely Jason—and it never changed no matter what soap he used or where he was. Kale's limbs stretched within the confines of Jason's embrace. He wasn't ready to be rid of the warmth, and Jason's grip had loosened during the night, allowing for careful movement. Muscles soft as jelly, Kale settled back into his spot. There was no need to even open his eyes, much less rouse himself from bed.

"How are you this morning, love?"

Kale had never been one for using pet names—Jason liked hearing Kale use his first name anyway—but sometimes he was glad Jason didn't share his aversion. It was a warm, gentle reminder that he was, indeed, loved. Kale twisted around to kiss Jason. "Good. And you?"

"Happy you didn't have any nightmares, or at least none that woke you."

"And none that I can remember."

"That's good. Do you want to go down for breakfast?"

Kale didn't think he ever wanted to move again. Life was perfect right here, but he knew it couldn't last. "Sure."

Jason gave him another quick kiss and then rose from the bed. The blissful spell broken, Kale stood. The weight he had avoided during sleep settled back on him.

After breakfast, they climbed in the car to visit the slavers they had heard about the previous day to see if they could find any information. It was unlikely a reputable business would discuss past sales with strangers, but it was better than sitting around the hotel waiting for a message from Martin. At least Kale had the satisfaction of driving.

◆ ◆ ◆

"Let's go back and get some lunch." Jason commanded more than asked. They had started at Harrison's and spent the rest of the morning in the area asking at the other nearby slave operations and talking to anyone they could find. Each dealer insisted all transactions were considered private, and if anyone around remembered the Monroe sale, they weren't saying.

"No. Let's keep asking around. Someone is bound to remember something." If only Kale could find one person who could confirm that Monroe had even sold his slaves in the county, it would be a small victory. At the moment, he was concerned that perhaps Martin had gotten it wrong somehow and the slaves were sold elsewhere. Maybe the judge had changed his mind and insisted the slaves be sold in Malar County since that's where the debts originated.

"You're exhausted. Let's take a break and see how you feel after lunch."

"I've only been up for a few hours." Kale had laid rail for as many hours as the sun shone for part of his life. A few hours walking around talking to people was hardly tiring work.

"I know, but being around all this slavery, these people who deal in humans, asking for someone to give you hope that you'll see your family again and being subject to their whim, it's taking a toll emotionally, and it's manifesting itself physically."

When Kale stopped to listen to Jason's words, he realized they were true. Even though his body could still move, inside he felt drained, as if he was navigating an empty shell down the road on two sticks. Muscles weren't holding his bones together, packing twine was. "You're right. But I'm still driving. My nerves couldn't handle you behind the wheel right now."

Kale took momentary comfort in Jason's laughter. Going back to the hotel would also allow them to see if Martin had left a message. As much as he wanted to be actively doing something, logically, he knew it wasn't necessarily productive. He tried to let the air whipping through his hair calm him as he drove.

After lunch, they didn't even make it to their room before the concierge let them know they had a message from Martin. Jason looked at Kale. "Do you want to call him back?"

"Can you handle it? I think I need to take a nap." Truth was, Kale didn't think he could bear hoping for good news only to get nothing from Martin. Nothing short of seeing his family would placate him at the moment, and he needed to sleep off this mood.

"Sure. I'll be up as soon as I'm done."

Kale trudged up the stairs to their room and collapsed on the bed as soon as the door shut behind him. He didn't remember drifting off, but there was a line of drool on his chin when Jason entered. Kale wiped his chin and saw Jason beaming down at him.

"What?"

"He's done it." Jason joined Kale on the bed while Kale was still trying to sit up. "He found the name of the auction house that was used for Monroe's slaves. It was McAllister Labor."

Kale snatched the piece of paper Jason held with the name of the dealer on it, as if that would somehow make it more real. "How? That's not even one of the names we gave him."

"He and Smithson pulled a list of all the registered dealers in Shalae County. Copies of all the records are in Perdana. Then they went through and called—or apparently in some cases telegraphed—each one posing as an auditor confirming that the court-ordered sales had been completed."

Kale shook his head. "I didn't think Martin had it in him

to be so devious."

"The man is smarter than I think either of us knows. Finish your nap, and then we'll go by McAllister's. It's not very far from here. We'll be able to walk."

"What? Why wait? Let's go now." Kale moved to get up, still looking at the paper, the proof that his hope wasn't futile. Jason jerked Kale's hand back down to the bed.

"You're exhausted. It won't do anyone any good for you to collapse. You need all of your wits for what's coming."

"Don't be ridiculous, Jason. This is my family we're talking about. I'm not waiting another minute." Kale tried to rise again, but Jason's grip on his hand was firm.

"Kale, this is our battle, and I only want what's best for you and your family. At this precise moment, that includes a nap."

Kale saw in Jason's eyes that he wasn't going to relent. He was right. Jason had a dying father back at the ranch, but he was here with Kale. Jason had made it his battle even though he didn't have to. "Fine."

"I'll wake you in an hour. I promise."

Kale nodded and lay down. He expected to struggle with his mind, but exhaustion overwhelmed him. It seemed as if hardly a minute had passed when Jason shook him awake.

"Kale? It's time to wake up."

Kale's eyes focused on the clock by the bed. It was an hour to the minute since his head had hit the pillow.

"I think you could probably do with sleeping through 'til morning, but I promised. We can go to McAllister's now."

Kale's muscles were heavy with sleep. It felt like walking through water to get ready to leave. Once outside, it didn't take long to find themselves staring up at a large green sign with red script that spelled out "McAllister Labor." The building housing the business was well kept. The sign stated they bought, sold, and held regular auctions.

Inside, they asked the secretary to see the proprietor. They were left waiting a few minutes before the secretary returned and showed them to an office. A short, balding man sat behind a large mahogany desk. Behind him stood a slave girl dressed in a clean and revealing light blue dress. She couldn't have been more than sixteen.

"Mr. McAllister, I'm Kale Wadsworth, and this is Jason Wadsworth." Kale hoped they could pass as cousins. He had forgotten that it would seem strange for them to both have the same last name. Kale had been so accustomed to using Jason's last name that it wasn't even a thought anymore. "We were hoping for a minute of your time."

McAllister stood and shook their hands, gesturing to the two chairs opposite his desk. "Please, have a seat. What can I do for you today?"

"We're following up on a phone call you received from our associate, Mr. Grimlock. In order for us to clear up this business with the Monroe estate, we'll need to see the sales records for his slaves."

"I'm afraid you've wasted a trip, gentlemen. As I told Mr. Grimlock, those records are private. I can't do anything more than confirm that the sales took place as prescribed by law. Anything more than that will require a court order."

Jason nodded. "I understand. However, we were hoping that, in the interest of expediency, there might be a way for us to simply look at the records. We don't require a copy of them or even to take them from the premises. Just a quick glance to make sure everything is as it should be, and we can be on our way."

"That's unacceptable. Our clients depend upon our discretion. Even at our auctions, we allow anonymous bidding by proxy. I can't divulge any information other than that Mr. Monroe's slave holdings were liquidated through this establishment."

Tears pricked Kale's eyes. Why couldn't any of this be just a little easier? They weren't talking about an estate. They were talking about his family. This one man got to decide if Kale would ever see his mother and brother again. It was wrong.

Frustrating. Intolerable. "Please, sir." Kale paused, attempting to gain more control over his voice. "We only need to see two records, for the slaves known as Adele and Thomas. Please. That's all we need."

"Why only those two? I thought you were settling an audit."

Kale had nothing to lose. Desperation drove him. "They're my mother and brother. I'm a free citizen of Naiara now, but before that I was a slave. I'm just trying to find my family so I can purchase them. That's all."

"I can't help you, and I don't appreciate being lied to. This is exactly why we don't free slaves in this country. It causes nothing but trouble. Abigail, see these two men out." Mr. McAllister's gruff voice displayed the anger of a culture where the very idea of equality was offensive.

The girl stepped forward and gestured to the door. Kale couldn't control the tears that flowed down his face. He had come so far, had fought every step of the way, and this was how it ended? All he wanted was his mama. How hard was that to understand? Why did his family not matter simply because they could be bought and sold? He allowed himself to be led out of the office and to the door. His body moved without his direction as his mind fell apart. He barely heard the whisper in his ear as the slave girl opened the door.

"I go to Cardinal Steakhouse each night at six-thirty to fetch my master's dinner. Meet me there."

Hope. The words were so welcome that Kale couldn't believe she had actually said them. All he could do was stare at her in amazement. She couldn't be real.

Jason stepped forward. "We'll be there. Thank you."

If Jason was replying, it must be real. Kale found his voice. "Thank you."

Once out of the building, Kale strode quickly down the street, as if rapid movement would speed up time. It didn't. None of the shop signs came into focus. Everything seemed to race by: people, horses, cars, window displays. It was all a blur. Jason's hand on his arm finally stilled him.

"Kale, slow down. This is good, but you need to get control of yourself. Let's go into the bookshop over there and look around. It'll take your mind off the waiting."

Kale followed Jason, trusting that he knew best. All Kale could think was that six-thirty seemed an eternity away. Inside the shop, Jason released Kale's arm and started browsing. Kale tried to imitate him, but it was no use. Every title he scanned was just a jumble of letters. The words they formed refused to enter his mind, as if the words "Cardinal Steakhouse" and "six-thirty" took up every available space in his head.

Out of the corner of his eye, Kale noticed the shopkeeper glancing his way. When his path crossed Jason's, he leaned in and murmured, "I think I'm making the owner nervous."

Jason threw a glance over his shoulder. "I think you're right."

"This isn't going to work. We might as well go back to the hotel."

"All right. Let me buy something, and we'll leave." Jason selected a book and pulled some money out of his billfold, refusing the change.

The walk to the hotel was too short. Kale's legs yearned to stretch, and his hands searched for activity. In the room, Kale immediately tidied all their clothes, putting everything away in its proper place. The room was a mess he could clean and make right. Retrieving a washcloth from the washbasin, he dampened it and proceeded to dust every available surface, taking great pleasure in the gleam his hand left behind.

"Kale, what are you doing?"

He didn't even look up from his work. "Cleaning. This place is a mess."

"No, it's not. You're a mess. Put the cloth down, and come here."

"I can't sit still."

"Kale, stop." Jason's voice reached a volume Kale was not accustomed to hearing. His head snapped up at the tone, and he saw Jason had come to stand behind him. "You need to relax." Jason's hands on his shoulders made Kale realize just how tense he held them. With some effort, he forced them down, rolling his head to release the kinks.

"How do you expect me to relax when that girl knows something? How can I sit and do nothing as if I'm not going to finally find out where my family is after almost fourteen years in less than three hours?"

"Relaxing isn't nothing, Kale. It's important." Jason's hands began to gently massage. "You need a clear mind right now."

Kale let Jason drag him to the bed. Pressure on his shoulders told him Jason wanted him to sit, but Kale couldn't let his body rest.

"Sit, Kale." It was the same tone as earlier. The same tone Jason used when defending someone he loved. It caught Kale's attention and alerted him to the seriousness of the situation. If Jason felt Kale was in some sort of danger, then perhaps he was worse off than he'd thought.

Kale reluctantly sat. "I'm not taking another nap."

Jason chuckled. "I wouldn't dream of asking you to. There's no way you'd be able to manage it."

"As long as we're clear on that."

"Kale, I love you."

It seemed to come out of nowhere, but nothing made Kale happier than hearing it. He knew Jason must derive the same pleasure from the words that he did, but Kale had a much harder time expressing such intimate feelings in such simple words. "I love you too, Jason. I just want to be useful right now."

"Then read to me."

"That's not exactly useful."

"It is to me. You know how I love hearing your voice, and it will give you something to focus on that won't drive your body to exhaustion. Please, Kale. I hate to see you like this. We're so close to finding what you want. You need to be able to enjoy the experience and be present in the moment."

After all this time, the man in front of him still amazed Kale. It was so easy to fall into complacency and think he knew everything about Jason, that Jason couldn't surprise him anymore, even when he regularly proved Kale wrong. Jason always had more depths than Kale thought possible and more heights he was willing to travel to, even if he had to drag Kale along. "What do you want me to read?"

Jason grabbed the book they had started earlier. "You can start with this. If you finish, we have the book I just bought."

"I don't know if I'll be able to comprehend the words right now."

"That's fine. We have the rest of our lives for you to read it. Right now, I just want you to read it to me."

Jason curled up against Kale's chest, and Kale read. A few paragraphs in, he realized Jason was right. Reading was incredibly soothing. While his mind wasn't immersed in the story, it also couldn't muster the energy to travel to anxious thoughts. Jason's weight grounded him. Kale had done this right. He had ended up with this man, and that had to count for something. Sure, he'd messed it up royally in the beginning. He had caused so much suffering in their lives, but they had been able to come back stronger.

"That's enough, Kale. It's time for us to go." Jason took the book and set it on the bedside table. Kale had become so lost in the task of forming his mouth into the words on the page that he'd lost track of time. His throat was scratchy and his mouth dry from reading. "Come on, love. Let's go."

Hearing Jason refer to him as love was usually too sappy for Kale's taste, but at the moment, it reminded him that he was loved, and he needed it. It was a reminder that, regardless of what was about to happen, he still had Jason.

Chapter Twenty-Two

Jason clasped Kale's sweaty palm in his own. It was the only way to stop his pacing in front of Cardinal Steakhouse. They didn't need to draw any extra attention, and two men holding hands was more discreet than Kale's frantic walking. With his free hand, Jason withdrew his pocket watch. There were still a few minutes before Abigail was due. He had made sure they were early, so there was no chance they would miss her. As he put the pocket watch away, Kale's grip tightened on his hand. Jason followed Kale's gaze and saw Abigail coming down the street.

Kale's hand relaxed in an effort to pull away, but Jason held firm. If Kale confronted her, it might scare her off. It was better to let her take charge of the situation. She was the one doing them a favor.

She made no movement that indicated she recognized them. Jason wondered if she'd decided it wasn't worth the risk. That could be why she was a few minutes early. When she passed them on her way to the door, Jason despaired. He didn't know if Kale could handle another disappointment.

"Thank you." Kale's voice was soft. It wouldn't carry more than a few inches in front of him.

"Good luck." The girl's voice was equally quiet. The entire exchange took only a second. Jason had almost missed it.

Kale led them down the street until they reached an alley. He ducked between two buildings, and Jason released his hand. Kale produced a piece of paper from his pocket. The girl must have handed it to him somehow. Jason hadn't been able to see it.

"Slaves are exceptionally talented at slipping things to each other unnoticed. It would have gone smoother if I'd realized she was going to pass a note. I didn't expect her to be able to read..." Kale's voice faded as he read the message.

Jason wanted to snatch the note and read it for himself, but he contented himself with watching Kale's face for a hint of its contents. He caught the exact moment Kale's face fell. "What is it?"

"They were separated."

Kale handed over the note, and Jason looked down at four different names in awkward handwriting, one across from Thomas's and another across from Adele's. "I'm so sorry." Jason reached over and rubbed Kale's back. "We knew this was a possibility."

"I know, but I couldn't help hoping."

"This is good, Kale. You'll reunite them soon enough." Jason gathered Kale in a hug.

"I can't believe she was willing to help me." Kale spoke against Jason's hair.

Jason pulled back. "Why not? You're a symbol of hope to her. You couldn't see it back at McAllister's? I imagine she's rooting for a happy ending."

At the hotel, Jason took the piece of paper to the concierge while Kale went upstairs. "Do you know these two people?" He pointed to the names across from Thomas's and Adele's.

"Absolutely. Those are both well-known family names in this area."

"Do you know where I might find them?"

"Well, Mr. Ellington passed away a few years ago. His

widow still lives at their house just outside of town." The man wrote down an address and directions on the piece of paper. "As for Mr. Driggson, I know the name, but not that particular member of the family."

"That's fine. You've been incredibly helpful. Thank you."

"My pleasure, sir."

Before he joined Kale in their room, Jason called Martin. He gave him the names to research in case he could find anything else. The fact that Mr. Ellington was dead was not promising. Widows often found themselves in the position of selling slaves to preserve the lifestyle their husbands had provided for them.

"Martin and Sophie both send their love and best wishes." Jason tossed his suit coat on the desk and sat in the chair opposite Kale.

"Thank you. It's nice to know so many people care."

"They really do, Kale. Martin's going to see if he can find any information that could be helpful to us. I got directions to the Ellington house, so we can start there tomorrow." Jason didn't want to diminish Kale's hope, but he also wanted to prepare him for the possibilities. "You should know that Mr. Ellington died a few years ago."

"So there's a good chance my mother was sold to settle the estate." Kale appeared calm, but Jason knew there was a turmoil of emotion beneath the surface.

"Not necessarily, but there's the possibility. Try not to worry. We'll know everything soon enough, and if we have to go to every slave owner in Arine, we'll do it, and we'll find her. I'm not going to let anything stop us, Kale. You're going to see your mother again."

Kale nodded, but Jason knew there was no amount of words that could put Kale at ease. Nothing would do that except for the sight and touch of his family. He ordered dinner to be brought to their room with some chamomile tea. He could only pray to the gods that they would be able to get some sleep.

CHAPTER TWENTY-THREE

The hot tea calmed Kale's nerves. He hadn't wanted any, but found it impossible to deny Mrs. Ellington's offer. She had been in the middle of her morning tea when they'd arrived and had insisted they join her. The floral china looked picturesque on top of the lace cloth covering the small table. Mrs. Ellington herself completed the image, her willowy frame and stark white hair appearing almost angelic against a white lace dress that matched the table. The crow's feet around her dark brown eyes softened her face and led Kale to believe she had spent much of her life smiling as unabashedly as she was now.

"Thank you for your hospitality, Mrs. Ellington. You may be wondering why we're here."

"Oh, I welcome the company. Is there something I can do for you?"

Kale no longer possessed the energy to act as if he was anything other than what he was. "Yes, ma'am. You see, I used to be a slave."

"Used to?" Her face didn't change from its pleasant demeanor, and her voice held a curious lilt instead of condemnation.

"Yes, ma'am. Jason here used to own me. We moved to Naiara so I could be free. I'm a citizen there now, and I'm visiting here legally."

"Of course, dear. I wouldn't have assumed otherwise."

She made it easy to confide in her. Kale only hoped she had answers for him. He wasn't likely to find anyone else as sympathetic to his plight. "Thank you. My mother and brother are still slaves here in Arine. I've been searching for them so I can buy them and take them home with me. I've found out that you purchased my mother, and I was hoping you could tell me where she is." Kale didn't mind letting her see the plea in his eyes.

"I've owned a great many slaves. What was her name?"

"Adele, ma'am. If you have any information about her, it would be greatly appreciated."

"Oh yes, she was a wonderful woman." Mrs. Ellington's eyes peered off into the distance, into another time.

Kale's heart sank. "Was?"

Mrs. Ellington focused back on him. "I hate to be the one to tell you, dear, but she died, oh, six or seven years ago."

Kale's mind crumbled. The strength to hold up his own body fled, and he slumped in his chair. Jason dove out of his seat and knelt on the ground to support Kale's body against his. All this searching and working for nothing. It couldn't be. Kale was here to rescue her, to make everything right. How could he make this right? She had died a slave. His dear, sweet mother. He had failed her.

The world melted. Kale felt Jason's arm around him, but his body was numb and the sensation muted. The voices around him sounded far away.

"Would you mind telling us what happened, Mrs. Ellington?" Jason took control. Kale didn't know if he'd ever be able to speak again. What words were there to say?

"Not at all. Adele was wonderful, one of the best housekeepers I've had. She organized the most extraordinary parties. One day, she took ill with a fever. It spread throughout the house. We lost her and three others. I miss her dearly. I was never able to find anyone else like her. I should have known she was your mother. You have the same green eyes."

Kale shut the eyes in question, only to see his mother's staring back at him. He opened them, not knowing what to do. This was where his mother had spent her last days, in a stranger's home. "Where is she buried?"

"Here on the estate. I'll have someone show you." She rang a bell. The sharp peals pierced Kale's ears, making him wince. "Stacy, take these two gentlemen to the burial plot so they can see where Adele is buried."

Jason supported Kale's weight as they walked outside to the back of the house. Off to the left, they were led to a grassy knoll next to a family plot. "This is where all the slaves are buried." Jason dismissed the girl as Kale crashed to his knees.

Of course it was an unmarked, mass grave. No headstone, nothing to commemorate the woman who had born him, had raised him, had saved him from a life of hard labor. Somewhere beneath this ground rested the woman who had first taught him about love. Kale sunk his hands in the grass. He didn't even know where she was, which specific piece of ground held his mama the way she'd held him.

Tears poured down his face, wetting the earth beneath him. There was nowhere for him to come back to in order to pay his respects. A hand touched his shoulder, and he jerked away. "Don't touch me, Jason. This isn't something you can fix." He was all alone, just like his mama. Oh, gods. His insides twisted. Every part of him hurt with an endless ache. He wanted to puke, but he couldn't. Not here.

Eventually his body broke, finding release as crying turned to sobs. And when he broke, Jason was there to catch him. Kale leaned into the comfort. He clung to Jason the way he had clung to his mother as a child. Jason didn't say a word. He just held Kale and lightly rocked. When there were literally no more tears in his eyes, when his sobbing had turned to dry heaves, Kale lost himself in the steady rhythm of Jason's rocking body. In time, he calmed enough to say the only thing he could think of. "I need to find Thomas. I need to take him away."

"We will, Kale. We will. I promise."

Soon after, Kale composed himself enough to stand. He took one last look at his mother's final resting place and walked hand in hand with Jason back to the house. They found Mrs. Ellington sitting right where they had left her. She stood when they entered.

"Oh dear. I'm sorry I didn't have better news for you."

Kale nodded. "Thank you for your hospitality." She moved to embrace him, but he acted as if he didn't notice. He couldn't be around her much longer. She was a nice lady, but she had owned his mother and had let her die. It was a childish thought, but Kale didn't see the harm in it when he would never see her again anyway.

"Thank you, Mrs. Ellington." Jason kissed her hand and took Kale out to the car. "Do you want me to drive?"

Kale wordlessly handed over the key and climbed into the passenger seat. A few minutes down the road, he spoke. "Pull over."

Jason obeyed. Before the car was fully stopped, Kale hopped out and emptied the contents of his stomach. The bitter taste of vomit broke through the haze he'd been in since he heard his mother was dead. The reminder made him want to cry, but there was nothing left in him. His mother had taught him about love, but she had also taught him when to fortify his heart against pain. He was done crying. A slave shouldn't dwell on things he couldn't change. There was only one person left he could save. Only one word could direct his actions. Thomas.

CHAPTER TWENTY-FOUR

It hadn't taken any coaxing to get Kale to sleep. After he had thrown up, he'd drifted off in the car on the short ride to the hotel. As soon as he was in the room, he'd curled under the covers and passed out. Jason removed his clothes to make him more comfortable. The only response Kale gave was shifting as Jason needed. He didn't even open his eyes. If Jason were in his place, he didn't think he'd ever want to wake up.

Jason wasn't tired at all. It was barely lunchtime. Once he had Kale situated, he went back downstairs to use the telephone. "Martin?"

"Jason?" It had taken nearly six months after Jason had promoted Martin from secretary to president of Arlington Steel to get Martin to call him by his first name. "How did the visit to Mrs. Ellington go? By your tone, I take it not well."

Martin's voice was a welcome change. It was hard to believe he had talked to him only yesterday. "No. Kale's mother passed away some time ago."

"Dear saints. How is he?"

"Asleep, thank the gods. I thought his mind was going to snap when he found out. There's not even a grave marker for him to visit."

"There wouldn't be, would there? I'm so sorry. Is there

anything I can do? Do you need me to come? You know Sophie and I could take the next train and be there by tonight."

"That's not necessary, but thanks for the offer. The best thing any of us can do is help him find his brother. That's the only hope I have of him getting over this."

"Well, I do have some news on that front. Mr. Driggson registered Thomas as a valet."

"That's excellent news." If Thomas was a valet, then he was reasonably well taken care of.

"Yes, it is, especially since Mr. Driggson sold him. He's passed through several hands, and each owner has maintained the registration."

Registering slaves wasn't a legal requirement, but it gave more value to the slave and allowed the owner broader protections under the law should his slave be stolen or destroyed. The fee involved discouraged most owners from registering any slaves other than valuable house slaves. Even then, a lot of country folk didn't like the government in their business and preferred to simply sign over the title. The back of some slave titles were filled with signatures as one owner signed him over to the next.

"Where is he now?"

"Cooperville."

"Cooperville? That's in Millner County."

"Yes. He belongs to a Mr. William Conroy."

"How much did Mr. Conroy pay for him?" Jason scrawled the information on the back of the paper with Mrs. Ellington's address on it.

"Twenty-one thousand. It was a private sale, not an auction. In fact, all of the sales since Mr. Driggson were handled between private parties, so that's good news."

"Excellent. This should cheer Kale up."

"I do hope so. Please give him my love and Sophie's too. She'll be heartbroken when she finds out."

"Of course I will. Thank you so much, Martin. We

couldn't have done any of this without you. And even though Kale's hurting now, it's better that he knows the truth than to be left wondering." Jason didn't know how much he believed that last sentiment, but he hoped it was true. "I can't wait to give him the news."

"If there's anything else I can do, please let me know."

"I will. Thank you, Martin." Jason hung up the receiver and went upstairs with a little hope that things would soon be better.

Kale woke after an hour and a half. Jason set aside the book he had been reading at the desk and sat next to Kale on the bed. It would have been nice if he'd slept longer, but given that it was still early in the day, it was the most that could be expected. At least the puffy redness was gone from his eyes.

"How are you feeling?" The question felt stupid, but Jason didn't know what else to say. He brushed the hair from Kale's face.

"My head's pounding, but it could be worse." Kale sat up. "Jason, I don't know what to do. Before, I at least had this hope in my head that she was still out there somewhere, just waiting for me. Now I don't even have that. When I was a slave, I was resigned to the fact that I'd never see her again. You would think it wouldn't hurt this much."

"Don't say that, Kale. You have every right to hurt. You can kick and scream or sit and cry. None of it's wrong. The only thing that's wrong is that you've been deprived of your mother. Don't you dare entertain a thought to the contrary."

"So what do I do now?"

"You can start by eating. They're serving lunch downstairs. I can have something sent up."

"No. I'd like to go down. I can't stay in this room. I'm liable to fall asleep again and never get up."

"Well that wouldn't do. I'd sure miss you if you decided to stay in that bed forever." Jason gave Kale a half-hearted smile. "Throw some clothes on, and we'll go down. Don't worry about how you look."

Kale nodded and laboriously dressed. It took him twice as long as normal. He looked as nice as ever, but his face seemed to have aged. The lines crossing it from his years in the sun appeared deeper. His hair had lost its shine, and his eyes looked dead, as if there was no spark of intelligence behind them. Jason schooled his expression, not wanting to worry Kale.

"You look great. Let's go. I'm starving." Jason led Kale downstairs. His hand was limp inside Jason's, as if he didn't have the strength to grip.

After a silent meal, Kale at least had a little bit of color back in his cheeks. It had taken some urging for him to eat, but once he started, he'd devoured a hearty portion. When the plates had been cleared away, they each had a cup of coffee. "Kale, Martin had some news for us."

The listless look in Kale's eyes turned to dread. Jason could only imagine Kale suspected the worst.

"It's good. Really good actually. Your brother was registered as a valet. He doesn't belong to Mr. Driggson anymore, so he isn't here, but each of his owners has kept up his registration. He's in Cooperville with a Mr. Conroy."

Kale nodded and drank his coffee. As Jason spoke, Kale's eyes had come more alive. Now they stared at nothing, but there was an awareness in them that had been missing earlier. "Cooperville's in Millner County, on the other side of Malar County, isn't it?"

"Yes. I thought we could go back to the ranch and spend the night there. If we leave now, we can arrive in time for a late dinner."

"Let's go then." Kale placed his coffee cup on the table and headed out of the restaurant. Jason was a few steps behind him. When he followed Kale into the room, Kale already had Jason's bag on the bed. He threw their clothes and books into it.

"Are you all right, Kale?"

"Fine. There's no point staying here any longer. You have a father at home who needs you, and it'll be nice to sleep in familiar surroundings tonight. I'll drive."

Jason surrendered the keys and followed Kale back downstairs. He stopped at the front desk to check out and call his father to let him know they were on their way. When he finished, he found Kale in the car with the motor running. As soon as Jason shut his door, Kale headed out of town.

CHAPTER TWENTY-FIVE

The drive back to the ranch was as peaceful as Kale could have hoped for. It was quiet, or at least if Jason had spoken, Kale didn't hear him. He was too focused on the road ahead. In a world devoid of purpose or sense, he had been given a goal. As long as he kept driving, he would complete it. All his energy focused on getting them to the ranch, getting Jason to his father. These were simple objectives with measurable results. Each kilometer that passed was proof of his success. It was a small victory, but he needed the triumph.

All too soon, he pulled the car up the drive to Robert's house. Time to focus on another goal. He took their solitary bag upstairs and unpacked, putting everything in its place. The clothes would need ironing. No need to ask a slave to do it. Kale had ironed thousands of shirts in his life. He relished the idea of smoothing out wrinkles, seeing the pristine fabric after he had ironed it. Such a visible sign of accomplishment.

"Kale, what are you doing?"

He was opening the door of their room to go in search of an iron when Jason's voice stopped him. "I need to iron our clothes."

"We can have someone else do that."

"I can do it." Kale stayed resolutely turned away from Jason.

"I know you can, love, but you don't need to."

Kale felt Jason near. "Yes, I do." He needed to keep doing, to keep moving. If he stopped, he didn't know what would happen.

"No." Jason's hand covered Kale's where it rested on the doorknob. "I'll not have you spend the rest of your life outrunning your grief. I understand you want to stay busy, but we need to go eat with my father. He held dinner for us. Since he sleeps most of the day, time's pretty relative to him right now. After we eat, we're going to bed. If you need to focus on anything, focus on those two things: eating and then sleeping."

Kale adjusted his mind, replacing ironing with the task of eating. Sleeping seemed too tall an order. One thing at a time. Eating he could manage. When Kale nodded his understanding, Jason released his hand, and they walked down to dinner.

Robert was paler than he had been before. Or maybe it was just that everything seemed less vivid to Kale. He took his seat, placed his napkin in his lap, and eagerly awaited the soup. When it arrived, he focused on one spoonful at a time. As long as he had something to do, he could get through this. The emptiness inside would abate sometime, or maybe he would simply learn to live with it.

"I was sorry to hear about your mother, Kale."

Robert's voice interrupted Kale's steady rhythm of one spoonful after the next. He looked up at the older man's eyes and was relieved to see concern there, not pity. "Thank you, sir."

"It's a shame. Losing a parent is always difficult. I imagine it must have been even worse, given your circumstances."

Kale nodded. He didn't want to talk about it. He couldn't. Not if he wanted to make it through dinner.

The soup warmed him. He hadn't realized how cold he had felt inside. Instead of sating his hunger, the soup had only ignited his appetite. The steak and potatoes tasted heavenly. No other meat tasted as good as Robert's fresh beef. The food not only energized his body, but it cleared his mind. His thoughts went to Thomas and what he needed to do to get his brother.

"Sir?" Kale broke the peaceful silence.

Robert looked up from his plate. His steak sat untouched, but the mashed potatoes were nearly gone. "Yes?"

"We found out where my brother is, and I intend to buy him. When I do, I was wondering if he'd be welcome here or if I should make other arrangements." Kale was returning with Thomas one way or another, even if he had to steal him. It was not only polite to ask Robert's permission, but Kale also wouldn't tolerate Thomas being mistreated. If Robert was going to treat him as just another slave instead of as Kale's brother, it would be better for all involved for Kale to get a hotel room for them.

"Of course he'll be welcome here. He's your brother. He's welcome to all my hospitality for as long as he would like it."

"Thank you, sir."

"Thank you for showing me the courtesy of asking, though it was hardly necessary."

"Just the same, I appreciate your support."

The silence resumed. When the meal was finished, Kale and Jason bade Robert goodnight and retired.

"Was it just me, or did my father look worse than when we left him?" Jason undressed while Kale put away his clothes.

"No, I noticed it too."

"I know the doctors say it's terminal, but I didn't really expect him to get worse."

Kale settled into bed and opened his arms. Jason snuggled close, making everything in the world seem a little better. "I understand. There's nothing wrong with hoping that the doctors aren't right. At least you have this chance to be with him."

"What time do you want to leave tomorrow?"

"I want to call first. If Mr. Conroy paid twenty-one thousand for my brother, I'm sure he has a telephone. I want to try to negotiate a deal before I get there. I don't trust myself to do it in person. I'll give too much away. With your father in the condition he's in, I don't want to leave without a deal and then end up having to be away for days the way we were this time."

"That sounds reasonable. I can call him if you want."

Kale ran his finger up and down Jason's arm. "No, I want to do it, but you're sweet for offering."

"If you change your mind, let me know."

There was one matter left to be discussed that Jason had clearly not thought about. "I was wondering if you would be all right with me offering to pay twice what Conroy paid for Thomas." The thought of haggling over his brother was sickening. "I know it's more than we need to pay, but I don't want Thomas thinking we were only willing to buy him if it was a good deal."

Jason looked up into Kale's eyes. Their warmth did more to melt Kale's muscles than a massage could have. "Of course. You don't even need to ask. It's your money as much as mine."

"Well, I felt I needed to because I don't want your name on the title. I intend to purchase him using the same corporation that holds my title."

Jason ducked his head, but Kale saw the hurt in his eyes. "It's not that I don't trust you, Jason. You have to know nothing is further from the truth. I don't want Thomas to feel scared of you or worry about you wielding any power over him. I know you would never give him cause to fear, but he won't know that. It will just make things simpler."

"I understand. You still don't have to ask to spend the money. You know it's yours to spend however you'd like."

Kale snorted. "I barely make enough to cover our expenses."

"And you're the one who arranged the marriage to Renee

so I'd inherit Arlington Steel. We're even."

Kale marveled that Jason saw it that way. Instead of dwelling on the fact that Kale had almost destroyed their lives by insisting Jason marry Renee, Jason focused on the good that came from it.

Jason yawned and settled in closer, content to cuddle. Kale was grateful. As much as he loved Jason, his physical passion was nowhere to be found. There was only hollowness inside of him. During his years of hard labor after Jason sold him, the sheer exhaustion of his body and the hopelessness of his life had chased away his sexual desire. Jason had been the one to coax it back. Kale was frightened that he no longer responded to the call of Jason's body.

Kale's fingers traced Jason's spine in the darkness. Blindfolded with nothing but a lump of clay, Kale knew he could shape it perfectly into the form of his lover. Each curve, every plane, dip, and angle of Jason's body was permanently etched in his muscle memory. The fire that the mere thought of Jason usually lit was extinguished, leaving not so much as a warm coal in its wake.

Kale wanted the comfort of their lovemaking. He yearned for it. His body refused, as if there was no hope for happiness. His body betrayed him, and he cursed it, feeling out of place in his own skin. In his mind, he knew he didn't deserve the comfort—that he had failed in so many ways—yet he still craved it, and his body refused to give it to him. A part of him had died with the news of his mother. He could only hope that once their lives returned to normal, Jason could bring it back to life.

CHAPTER TWENTY-SIX

Jason choked on the smoke from his father's cigar. "How can you smoke those things when you're coughing every few minutes?"

"They're one of my last pleasures in life. I'm not about to give them up now."

Robert reclined on the sofa in his office. He could no longer sit all the way up. Jason sat in a chair next to him. After breakfast, Kale had called Mr. Conroy and set an appointment with his secretary to call back later. Kale had insisted Jason not worry about him and spend time with Robert. The sight of Kale collapsed at his mother's grave had shaken Jason. It seemed more important than ever to make an effort with his father. "I've never liked them."

"I know. Your mother did, though. The smell, that is. She never smoked one."

"Really? I didn't know that."

"Your grandfather smoked them, and the smell always made her feel at home. There's a lot about her you don't know. Despite what you think, you don't hold the monopoly on loving her."

"I'm not the one who stole her life away. She deserved more."

"Don't you think I know she could have done better? Do

you honestly believe there's a single person in this world who knows better than I that she could have had any man she wanted? I don't know why she chose me, but she did. Sometimes in life, you learn to just shut up, and be grateful."

"She didn't belong here. She belonged in the city, around culture, the arts."

"Yes, and she's the one who decided to leave it all and live here. I was willing to move to Perdana with her. I was prepared to sell everything and follow her wherever she wanted to take me. She decided to stay here."

Jason didn't even try to keep the shock and incredulity from his voice. "What could she possibly have seen in this place?"

"She saw that it was a part of me, which is more than you ever have. She thought it would be a good place to raise children. She saw value in building something that we could pass on to the next generation."

Jason felt his father's condemnation. "I'm sorry I wasn't the son you always wanted, the one who would carry on the family name."

"All your mother and I ever wanted was for you to be happy. We wanted the best for you. It's what we worked for. I've never loved anyone else as much as I loved your mother. I would have never allowed her to stay here if I thought it made her unhappy."

"You sure have a way of showing it. You acted as if she never existed. I'd just lost the center of my life, and you went on like nothing had happened."

Robert paused in lifting his cigar back to his lips and lowered it. "Is that really what you think?"

"What am I supposed to think? You never talked about her. You put all of her stuff in storage. I didn't even understand that she had died. Darlene explained it to me."

A violent cough racked Robert's body. Demetri stepped forward, refilled Robert's water glass, and helped him to drink. When the cough subsided, Demetri retreated back to the corner. "I handled it badly, and I'm sorry, but it's not because I didn't love her. When your mother died, I wanted nothing more than to follow her. I didn't know how I was supposed to continue without her. There were times when I even came close to doing it. One night, I remember sitting right here in this study with a revolver in my hand, just staring at it."

A chill filled Jason's chest. He had never seen this side of his father. "What kept you from doing it?"

"You. Literally." Robert chuckled and then coughed. Jason handed him his glass of water. "You came banging on my door, upset that it was locked. It was time for dinner, and Darlene had sent you to come get me."

Jason found a vague memory of the event in his mind. Mainly, he remembered being perturbed at his father for locking him out of the normally open study. "I never knew."

"Of course not. That was the point. I had to lock away all traces of your mother, or I would have gone insane, and I didn't have that luxury. I couldn't be surrounded by her. I had you to think about."

"All I ever wanted was to talk to you about her. I thought you didn't love her or me." Jason's world slowly shifted. Everything he had taken as a sign of his father's apathy had actually been a sign of his love.

"It would have torn me to pieces to talk to you about her. How was I supposed to talk to my son about the woman I had spent my entire adult life loving? I had no way to relate to you. You had lost a mother, but I had lost a lover, a confidante, a friend, a companion. You couldn't possibly comprehend at that age the void she left in my life. And I didn't want you to feel like you had to fill it, because you couldn't. I thought it was best if I just acted like things were fine. Perhaps if I acted long enough, things really would be fine." The last words rattled with phlegm, and Robert was overcome by a coughing fit.

"I suppose I can understand that."

"No, you can't. But thanks for saying it. You were always like your mother. She needed to talk about everything. I was never one to pour my heart out. I was selfish. I should have taken better care of you. I should have realized that you were a scared little boy who needed me to show my love in a way you could understand, no matter how uncomfortable it made me. Except, the person who normally would have pointed that out to me was your mother, and she was gone."

"Thank you for explaining it to me now." This was the most his father had ever said to Jason privately at one time. Jason realized that, even though Robert had raised him, Jason really had no idea who he was. Robert had always just been his father. It was difficult to picture him with a whole other life outside of him.

Robert continued as if Jason hadn't spoken. "When you got older and the pain of her passing wasn't so fresh, I thought about trying to talk to you, but by that time the rift between us was too large."

"I thought you hated me."

"No, I could never hate you." Robert's face softened as he shook his head.

"You seemed to despise me for liking the things I did."

"Never. They were all the things your mother loved. It was painful to look at you and see her. Every day was a struggle just to keep living, and there you were, a constant reminder of the wife I had lost. I didn't detest those things in you, I loved them. I just didn't know how to show it when it caused me so much hurt."

Why hadn't Jason ever been able to look back on his childhood and see his father's point of view? They had each been wrapped up so tight in their grief that they hadn't been able to help each other. Jason was too young to have realized it at the time, but as he got older, he could have given his father a chance. Instead, he'd viewed him as the enemy, the antithesis of his sweet mother. "I'm so sorry I ever doubted you."

"I didn't give you a reason not to. I thought I was showing my love for you by providing for you, paying to send you to university even though I felt I was losing the last little bit of Lena when you left. If she had been here, she would have boxed my ears and told me to love my little boy the way he needed to be loved, not the way I wanted to love him. Who's the adult anyway?" Robert chuckled again. "She liked to use that phrase on me."

"I can picture that." Jason smiled as his mind constructed the image.

"I noticed you would go into her sewing room as a child. I suppose you found her journals."

"Actually, I only just found them the other day."

"Really? I couldn't bear to read them. I didn't need to. I already knew all there was to know about her. I always assumed you read them."

"No, I'm reading them now, though, when I have the time."

"Good. You should. I know you loved her as your mother, but there was so much more to her, things you would have learned to appreciate about her as you grew older."

Jason hesitated to confess his next concern. However, Robert had overcome his fear of judgment and laid himself bare. Jason could do the same. "As I'm reading them, I try to picture her, but I can't. I don't remember what she looked like."

"Oh, Jason." Robert patted his son's hand. The light frailty of the touch astonished Jason. "That's all right. It's natural. Memories fade. Do you know, sometimes I'll be thinking about her and realize I'm remembering something that never happened? I'll have made up an entire story just because I miss her so much. It's no wonder you don't remember her. We don't have many portraits of her, but what we do have is in the attic." Robert looked to the corner. "Demetri, when I'm asleep, you should go to the attic and bring down the paintings of Lena. Jason deserves to see them."

"Yes, Master."

"How could you stand to go so long without seeing a picture of her when they're right there in the attic?"

"I cheated." Robert reached down and pulled out his pocket watch. Flipping open the cover, he revealed a miniature portrait of Jason's mother. "I see her every day."

Jason gasped. For the first time in almost twenty years, he saw his mother's face. His mind travelled back to his childhood when his father constantly checked his watch. "It wasn't punctuality you were obsessed with, was it?"

Robert grinned. "Hell no. Lena could never get me anywhere on time. It was the one thing I allowed myself. I always carried her with me. It helped me keep it together around you. Without it, you would have been in the awkward position of comforting your old man."

"I would have been happy to do it." All Jason had wanted to be was a comfort to his father, but he had never been given the chance.

"I know you would have, Son, but you shouldn't have to. I shouldn't have kept her pictures from you. Feel free to display them. It's long overdue. Besides, I wouldn't mind seeing more of her just now."

"I will, Father."

"You don't have to be afraid to talk to me about her. Ask me anything you like."

Jason had so many questions. For some reason, one memory nagged at him. It was one of the clearest from his childhood. "Did she used to cheat when we played Hide the Thimble?"

Robert laughed. "Oh, I wondered if you ever figured it out. That wasn't really her doing, but mine. She insisted we play games together as a family when you were a little boy. There was an age when you simply adored her thimble for who knows what reason. As a toddler you used to climb up on her as she was sewing and pull it off her thumb. As you got older, she introduced you to Hide the Thimble. Every day that you were a good boy and didn't steal it from her while she was working, she would hide it for you in the evening, and we would direct you saying hot or cold until you found it. She thought this was a marvelous idea."

"I can remember waiting for the six chimes of the grandfather clock when she'd let me search for it."

"That's right. It was always at six o'clock. That one we learned the hard way. If we didn't have a set time, you simply pestered her all day. Anyway, the first night of this game, you took over an hour to find it, but you wouldn't let anyone else find it for you, and you wouldn't let me give directions. Anytime I tried, you would stomp your foot and say, 'No. Mutter o'ly.' After about fifteen minutes, I stood up to go get it, and you burst into tears. I was about ready to give you something to cry about, but your mother shushed me and told me to sit. She said it was important that you learn and that you'd improve with time. You didn't. After a week of this, I was beside myself, so I convinced Lena to hide multiple thimbles. You didn't know she had more than one, and I pointed out that you wouldn't be able to tell the difference. She didn't like it, but for the sake of my sanity, she agreed. She started out by hiding three. That night, it took you a mere fifty minutes. The next she went to five. I think she was starting to get tired of the game as well. Eventually, she was hiding two dozen thimbles, and you would run to her after five minutes having found one, beaming with pride."

Jason joined Robert in a full-bellied laugh, the happiest he'd been since he'd arrived.

His father told story after story about his mother, and Jason asked every question he could think of. As the time passed, Robert's coughing fits grew increasingly frequent, and each seemed to tire him a little more. Jason would have to leave him to nap soon.

"I have one more question for you. Don't be mad." Jason felt like a child again, about to ask something that he felt was

163

taboo. "I've always wondered…the baby mother had…I never knew…was it a boy or a girl?"

Deep sorrow etched Robert's face. "It was a girl. You had a little sister. Your mother wanted to name her Lydia."

"But her grave marker says Baby Wadsworth."

"Yes. It made it easier on me. We had dreamed about little Lydia for years. Lena always wanted a sister for you. I couldn't stand the thought that we had lost her, that bringing her lifeless body into the world had killed your mother. I didn't want to picture our little Lydia under the ground. Your mother never even saw her. How could she be our Lydia if Lena never saw her?" Robert's voice cracked. It was the first time in Jason's life he had heard his father's voice falter with emotion.

Jason took Robert's hand in his. "That's enough, Father. Thank you. I always wanted to know."

Robert nodded. "I think I should sleep now. For a little while. You go check on Kale."

"All right, Father. Sleep well." Jason stood and kissed his father on the forehead before departing. His heart ached for how few days he had left with the man he was only just getting to know.

CHAPTER TWENTY-SEVEN

"Mr. Conroy, this is Kale Wadsworth from P and C Enterprises."

"Yes, Mr. Wadsworth, my secretary told me. What business do you have with me?"

"I understand you have a valet named Thomas. My company would like to purchase him from you."

"Thomas? Why would you want to do that?"

"Our company is in possession of his brother. We want the other to make a matching set." Kale swallowed the bile that rose in his throat. This was all for Thomas's good.

"I see. Well, he's quite a capable valet. I would have a hard time replacing him."

"We are prepared to compensate you adequately."

"I don't think you understand the hassle this is going to cause me. I'm going to have to wait for an acceptable slave to become available and then train him to my tastes." Kale really didn't want to consider what Mr. Conroy's tastes included. "I bought Thomas a couple of years ago. Prices have gone up for good slaves. I could be out a lot of money and time. I don't need to tell you that time is a valuable thing."

"No, you don't, Mr. Conroy, and I don't want to waste yours. I think it is you who doesn't understand. We are willing to pay forty-two thousand for your trouble. We certainly don't want P and C to get a reputation for stinginess."

"Forty-two thousand?"

"Yes."

"Why would you pay forty-two thousand? What's so special about him?"

He's my brother, you greedy prick. "Nothing other than his value to us as a match in appearance to his brother. The price is more a sign of the value we place on your time and cooperation. It should be plenty for you to find a suitable replacement and even rent one in the interim."

"All right. I hate to see him go, but if you're fool enough to offer that much for him, I won't be the fool who refuses it."

"Excellent. If you can have the paperwork ready, I'll be by tomorrow to sign it and take possession of the boy."

"Bring cash. I won't accept anything else."

"Very well, cash it will be. I will probably arrive by early afternoon."

"That's fine. I'll have the registration and title ready for you."

"Thank you, Mr. Conroy. It's been a pleasure doing business with you." The call disconnected. It was done. All Kale had to do was get the money, and he would see his brother in a day. He had one more call to make.

"Martin?"

"Kale? How are you doing? I was sorry to hear about your mother."

"I'm fine, thank you." Kale remembered he was talking to a friend. "Or at least as fine as I can expect to be. I'm doing a lot better, thanks to you. I just got off a call with Mr. Conroy. He's agreed to sell me Thomas for forty-two thousand."

"That's great news."

"Yes, it is. He wants the payment in cash. I was hoping you could speak with the bank and arrange for me to pick up the money from the branch in town today. I don't want the regular delays from withdrawing such a large amount."

"Of course. Consider it done. I'll be able to make the call before you can get there."

"Thank you."

Martin didn't balk at the amount. He knew how much had been paid for Thomas previously. Kale had half expected Martin to fight him on spending so much money. He should have thought more of Martin, especially after all this time.

After the call disconnected, Kale went in search of Jason and found him in the dining room eating a sandwich.

"Here, I had one made for you too." Jason slid a plate in Kale's direction.

"Thanks." Kale seated himself and bit into the roast beef sandwich. There was just the right amount of horseradish and cheddar cheese. The lightly toasted bread had a pleasant crunch.

"How did it go with Mr. Conroy?"

Jason's attempt at a neutral voice was amusing, and Kale was tempted to have a little fun with him. However, he couldn't help the grin that split his face. "I'm going to the bank as soon I'm done eating to get the cash. I'm picking Thomas up tomorrow." The reality began to sink in, and a happy flutter tickled his stomach.

"That's excellent." Jason threw down his sandwich and crossed to Kale, planting a sloppy kiss on his cheek. "I told you it would all work out."

Kale wiped off the breadcrumbs Jason had left on his cheek. "Yes, well, it's not a done deal. Plenty could still go wrong." Kale tried to rein in his excitement.

"Things are done going wrong." Jason took a big bite of his sandwich, storing it in his cheeks as he chewed like a little kid.

"I hope so. But even if everything goes right, there's no guarantee he's even going to like me."

"How could anyone not like you?"

"You didn't when we first met."

"Well, the likelihood of your brother being a blathering

idiot is extraordinarily slim. He is related to you."

"Especially the blathering part. Blathering isn't a desirable quality in slaves." The jovial tone outshone his fears of not connecting with his brother. What would be would be, and Kale would always love him, even if Thomas couldn't warm up to his stranger of a brother. "How were things with your father?"

"Really good. We've never talked the way we did this morning. I felt like I was meeting him for the first time."

"Good. Any particulars you want to share?"

"Do you know I always thought he didn't love my mother, but he's been carrying a miniature of her around this entire time? Every day, right there in his pocket watch, and I never knew."

"It's amazing what you can learn when you decide to listen."

"Yes, yes, I know. You're right. He told me the funniest stories from when I was a child."

"Which you will be telling me when we have more time. I can just picture little Jason toddling around." Kale smiled at the image. Jason would've been an entertaining child.

"Yes, I will regale you with tales of my childhood later, despite never hearing any of your stories."

"I'm willing to bet all the money we have that my stories aren't nearly as cute as yours."

"Fair enough." Jason finished off the last bit of sandwich and wiped his mouth on his napkin. "I did learn some interesting tidbits and got the facts straightened out regarding some issues."

"Oh?" Kale suspected there were a quite a few things Robert set Jason straight about.

"For starters, my father offered to move to Perdana for my mother. She's the one who insisted they stay here."

"Really? I wouldn't have guessed that."

"Me either, which is why I always assumed it was the other way around."

Kale shook his head. "When are you going to learn to stop assuming things?"

"Probably around the same time you learn to accept just how amazing you are."

"Hmph. What else did you discover?" Kale stuffed the last piece of sandwich into his mouth.

Jason's voice lowered. "That I had a baby sister. Lydia. She died the same day as my mother."

Kale struggled to swallow the huge bite of roast beef in his mouth. He reached across the table for Jason's hand. "I thought you knew your mother died in childbirth."

"Yes, but I didn't know the gender of the baby. Her headstone simply says Baby Wadsworth. Father didn't feel right about putting her name on it since she never lived."

"I'm sorry."

"Don't be. I'm glad I finally know."

"It can be comforting, but don't torture yourself with thoughts of what might have been." Kale could imagine Jason staying awake at night, envisioning a little sister who would never be.

"I won't. I promise. It's nice to know that at least my mother died trying to fulfill her dream of having a little girl. It gives it meaning somehow. I don't know why that matters, though. It doesn't change anything."

"It makes it easier for you. That's something."

"I suppose it is." Jason tossed his napkin on the table. "Anyway, Demetri is finding the paintings of my mother that Father stored in the attic. I have permission to display them."

"That's good." Kale withdrew his hand and leaned his elbows on the table.

"Don't you want to know why he put them there to begin with?"

"I imagine he did it for the same reason I never drew my mother or Thomas and why I never let myself think about them in those early years."

"I suppose it is the same reason when it comes down to

169

it. Who would have thought you and my father had something in common?"

Kale chuckled. "I always figured I was more like him than I am you."

"I can see that."

Kale stood. "I'd love to stay and talk, but I need to get to the bank before it closes. Do you want to come with me?"

"Sure. Father will be asleep for a while. Besides, I've never seen forty-two thousand in cash before."

"Really?"

"Really. I always deal in transfers and checks."

"Then this should be fun." Kale retrieved their documents and a valise from their room. In less than an hour, it would be heavy with the exact amount of cash required to buy a man's life.

CHAPTER TWENTY-EIGHT

"Demetri, where's my father?" Jason had just entered the dining room with Kale. He hadn't seen his father since they'd parted earlier in the day. The seat at the head of the table was conspicuously empty, and Demetri stood dutifully behind it, as if unaware that his master was missing.

"He wanted me to send his apologies, sir. He's not quite feeling up to dinner tonight."

Robert hadn't been able to sit all the way up earlier, but Jason had assumed he would be fine once he was able to rest. It dawned on him that he may never see his father sit in a chair again. The thought winded him. "Please, tell him not to worry. Kale and I are fine on our own."

"Of course, sir. Is there anything else I can do for you?"

"No, go back to my father."

"Thank you, sir." Demetri's tone was thick with gratitude.

When Demetri passed, Jason grabbed his arm. Demetri stopped, and Jason gave him a gentle shake until the slave met his eyes. "Make sure he eats something. And come get me if you think anything's wrong. Do you understand me, Demetri? If *you* think anything's wrong, whether or not he does."

"I understand, sir. Don't worry, between myself and Darlene, he doesn't get away with an empty stomach."

Jason nodded and released his grip. Robert's vacant chair at the table seemed as strong a presence as the man himself. It was strange to be eating dinner in this room without him present. Jason had begun to take their nightly meals together for granted.

"I'm sure he's fine, Jason. Probably just tired. He can take soup in his room without having to worry about entertaining us."

The smooth strength of Kale's voice lulled Jason into the lie. There was nothing fine about a man who was too weak to sit up to a table.

◆ ◆ ◆

Jason heard the footsteps creaking on the wood floor outside the bedroom door. He had been half awake all night listening for the sound. Slithering out of Kale's hold, he stepped softly to the door, opening it before the visitor had a chance to knock.

"Sir!" Demetri's startled exclamation was what Jason expected. He hurried to close the door behind him, muffling the sound of their voices. No need to wake Kale.

"I was awake and heard you approaching. It's my father, isn't it?"

"Yes, sir. He didn't hold down any of the food he's had today. His breathing is shallow, and I'm worried he'll stop breathing or choke on his own phlegm."

Demetri's impeccably distanced demeanor fell away, and Jason saw the man who had cared for his father for more than two decades. "Can't we telephone a doctor?"

"The doctor's already said there's nothing he can do. He'll send a nurse with some drugs, but the master hates being fussed over."

"Well, the master is going to have to learn to deal with things he doesn't like. Send for the nurse. If need be, I can fetch her in the car. I'll go sit with him. Come back to his room when you're done."

Demetri headed downstairs, and Jason walked down the hall to his right. He hadn't been in his father's room since he was a little boy, shortly after his mother had died. Out of habit, he stepped over a loose floorboard outside the door. As a youngster, he had spent many a night creeping into his parent's room when a bad dream had scared him from his bed.

The room was dimly lit by a gas lamp. Not enough light to disturb Robert, but enough to see if anything was amiss. A straight-backed chair was pulled close to the bed. Demetri must have been using it. Jason sat and examined his father. Each quick, shallow breath rattled the phlegm in Robert's throat. Every so often, the breaths would be swallowed in a cough. It was tempting to wake him, to tell him to clear his throat, spit out the mucus, and go back to sleep, but Jason wasn't naïve enough to believe that would fix the problem.

Demetri returned. "The nurse is on her way. It will probably take her close to an hour to get here. Is there anything I can get for you?"

"No, thank you, Demetri. Here, take your seat back." Jason's movement to rise was halted by the mortified look on Demetri's face.

"I'm find standing, sir. Thank you."

"Worried my father will wake and see you sitting here and me standing?"

"He wouldn't like it, sir."

"He doesn't seem that strict with you, not as strict as I would have thought."

"Only because I don't give him reason to be. He wouldn't tolerate me acting above my station, sir."

Jason knew that all too well. His father was incapable of viewing people in terms of human relationships instead of the roles they played. When he saw Demetri, he saw a slave, not the man who had cared for him for years when no one else was around. When he saw Kale, he saw a slave, not his son's lover and life companion. Then again, that seemed to be changing. Robert had been treating Kale as more of a person. Between dinners together, the card game, and offer of hospitality to Thomas, the last few days had shown Jason a different picture of his father. However, it was hard to let go of such ingrained views, especially when confronted with more proof of his old assumptions. Besides, he needed more than politeness from his father; he needed acceptance.

"Excuse me, sir?"

"Yes?" Jason kept looking at the father he was quickly abandoning hope of ever truly knowing.

"It's his way of protecting me. I've earned a place in this household and in the master's esteem. He respects that. But it doesn't do him or me any good to allow me to act as if I'm more than a slave. To sit when a free man stands is to say with my actions that I think myself better than him. It's not true, and if your father didn't punish for me it, I'd lose respect for him. I'd rather take punishment at his hand than get myself into the kind of trouble he can't protect me from, sir."

Demetri was right. Jason had a habit of finding himself in the presence of slaves who were wiser than him. If Robert encouraged his slaves in dangerous habits, they could get in serious trouble should they be sold or act out of turn in front of someone who would demand punishment or even legal action. Kale had held the same concerns when he was a slave.

Jason nodded his understanding to Demetri and settled into a silent vigil.

"You're not nearly as sneaky as you think you are." Jason nearly jumped out of his skin at the sound of Kale's voice. It was the last thing he'd expected to hear.

"How'd you know I was in here?"

"There's only one place you'd be this time of night besides our bed." Kale handed him a warm mug of coffee. "Drink this."

The rich aroma perked Jason up before he even tasted it, and he sipped the hot liquid. Several scoops of sugar and a generous helping of cream already sweetened the bitter drink. "Who made it?"

"I did. You don't think anyone else would make it up like that for a grown man, do you?"

Kale's familiar teasing was a welcome bit of normalcy. "I didn't know you knew your way around the kitchen here. You'd better hope Darlene doesn't find out."

"Kitchens are easy enough. She won't find out. I left everything cleaner than I found it." Kale rested his hand on Jason's shoulder as Jason drank. "How is he?"

"I don't know, but he doesn't look good. A nurse is on the way. We'll know more when she gets here."

"I'll sit with you."

"No, you should really get back to bed. You're driving. I can sleep on the way tomorrow." Jason wasn't going to let anything ruin Kale's big day. He had worked too long and too hard for it.

"You're not really still planning on coming, are you?"

"We'll see. I'll come to bed as soon as the nurse says it's all right. There's a good chance everything's fine, and we're a bunch of overreacting dolts. But no matter what happens, you have someplace to be tomorrow."

Kale didn't move.

"Please, Kale. I can't be worrying about you not making it to Conroy's. I'll be along soon."

Kale leaned down and kissed Jason's temple. "Wake me if you need me."

Jason nodded and patted the hand resting on his shoulder. When the warmth and weight of it were gone, he missed it. He wanted nothing more than to have Kale sit with him, make him feel not so alone. If it was any other night, he would have begged him to stay. As it was, Jason wasn't about to let his selfishness ruin Kale's reunion with his brother.

Jason sipped at the coffee, barely noticing when it cooled.

He didn't know how much time had passed when he heard a horse's hooves clip-clop on the driveway. Demetri left to let the nurse in before she woke up the rest of the house. When he returned, Jason stood to allow the nurse to take the place closest to Robert.

"Thank you for coming at this time of night."

"It's not a bother, Mr. Wadsworth. It's what I'm here for." The nurse listened to Robert's breath sounds and felt his pulse. "It's nothing to be worried about. This is one of those things that sounds worse than it is."

"But it sounds as if he's going to choke." It was odd for Demetri to speak out of turn. "Ma'am." His panic was poorly concealed on his face. This was more than just loyal concern. Jason wondered exactly what kind of relationship the slave shared with his father. Jason hoped Demetri had been able to provide companionship for his father, to prevent him from being so lonely.

"He won't. His heartbeat is strong. If the phlegm becomes too much, he'll cough it up. As long as we can hear it, it means breath is getting through. I can stay awake with him and monitor his progress. There's really no need for both of you to stay awake. It will all look better in the morning. You won't be any use to him tonight."

"Are you sure? If something happens, I'll never forgive myself if I'm not here." Jason was certain of it.

"I'm as sure as it's possible to be. He doesn't have much time left, but he's not going anywhere tonight."

"All right then." Jason turned to leave and came face to face with Demetri. The slave's eyes dared Jason to dismiss him. He looked as set in place as stone. Looking back at the nurse, Jason asked, "What was your name?"

"Sadie, sir."

"Sadie, this is Demetri. He's my father's personal attendant. He's to be allowed to stay for however long he wishes."

"I understand, sir."

The gratitude in Demetri's eyes was unmistakable.

◆◆◆

Jason slipped as gently as he could into bed. Kale didn't stir. Jason was tempted to curl around Kale's warmth, breathe in his familiar smell, and remind himself that the man lying next to him made the worst things in life bearable, but he didn't want to wake him. He had already robbed Kale of enough sleep tonight.

Lying on his back, Jason's mind drifted to his father's room. He wondered if Demetri was going to stand there all night. Seeing his father fading away was startling, a slow agony made more distressing by the knowledge that Jason didn't have enough time left to make up for all the lost years. It wasn't entirely his fault. His father had decided to disapprove of Jason's relationship with Kale. No matter what progress they had made, Jason couldn't entirely forgive his father for pushing him away, for disowning him, for preventing any possibility of a reconciliation.

Sleep pulled at his consciousness. Thoughts of Robert turned to thoughts of Kale. The dying man in the other room assumed Kale's face. As surely as his father was about to leave them, Kale would one day leave too. In a flash of selfishness, Jason hoped he would be the first to die. He sent a silent prayer to the gods. It would be easier for them to take him first than to grant him the strength it would take for him to weather such a blow. It was hard to feel greedy when he knew Kale had the mettle to survive without him. The thought of Kale grieving over him left a dull, bleak pain in his chest. He couldn't wish that pain on his lover. If he did die first, he hoped Kale would move on to find some happiness. He'd have the opportunity to choose a companion instead of clinging to the man who had freed him.

Jason hoped death for either of them was many years

away, after they had lived a long life together, filled with travel and art and dreams and lazy days reading under a shade tree. Dread consumed him at the thought of it all being cut short. He couldn't dictate to the gods when to take his companion. It could happen tomorrow. Any night could be their last.

Temptation turned to necessity, and Jason curled himself around his lover. Kale would have told him to stop being stupid and wake him if he needed him, but his presence was enough. Words couldn't chase away the specter of death. Kale shifted slightly, moving to accommodate him. Jason reached up and pulled Kale's arm around him. As soon as he was settled, Kale's arm gently squeezed him in an automatic gesture. Snug against Kale—where he knew he belonged—it was impossible to think that death would ever separate them. Kale would always be there to comfort him.

Chapter Twenty-Nine

Kale was not surprised to find Jason absent from bed. He knew he had returned at some point in the night because he'd had to peel Jason's arm off of him so he could pee. That was sometime after midnight, and he hadn't expected him to stay. When Jason worried, he didn't let himself rest much. Boy couldn't get out of bed before eight o'clock to save his own life, but he'd be up before dawn if he thought it would help someone he loved.

Kale quickly dressed. He was anxious to start the long drive. He dressed in a comfortable suit, not as casual as he would have been at home, but not the same level of formality Jason had insisted they wear in Shalae County. Kale had secured the deal. He didn't need to appear as if he had forty-two thousand personally, just as if he was the type of man who would be employed by a company who could spend that kind of money on a single slave.

Jason was in the same spot Kale had left him in last night. It would have been easy to believe he had never come back to bed. There was a new addition to the room. A nurse sat in a chair on the other side of the bed. Demetri was in a chair at the foot and stood when Kale entered.

"Good, you're awake. I was going to send someone to knock on the door if you weren't up soon." Jason smiled up at Kale.

"How is he?"

"He's woken up a few times. Never for very long. Sadie was able to get him to take some medicine, and we were able to feed him some broth. So far, he's managed to keep it down."

"Good."

"I came back to bed."

"I know. You should come have breakfast with me."

"I'm fine here."

"You need to eat. It won't take long, and it will give us a chance to talk."

Jason looked to the nurse, who said, "He's right, you should eat. We'll send someone for you if he wakes."

"All right, I'll go, but only if a tray is sent up for Demetri, and he promises to eat everything on it."

Kale glanced between Demetri and Jason. This was a new development.

"I promise, sir."

Jason nodded and stretched when he stood, joints popping in his back and neck. "I'll be back soon."

The dining room wasn't much brighter than Robert's room. The sun was just starting to rise. The kitchen hadn't known when to expect them for breakfast, so they waited a few minutes for the food. Jason looked like he was going to devour whatever was placed in front of him and dart back upstairs, so Kale was grateful for the time to talk.

"I'm going to leave as soon as we're done eating. If everything goes as planned, I'll be back late tonight. Don't hold dinner for me. I'll ask Darlene to leave something out for us." Us. Him and Thomas. The next time Kale sat at this table, Thomas would be with him.

"I'm sorry I can't go with you."

"Don't. There's nothing to be sorry for, Jason. Do you really think I'd let you come with me today?"

"I suppose not, but you shouldn't go by yourself."

"I can take a slave with me. It would probably make Thomas more comfortable." There was no telling how Thomas was going to react to him. He probably wouldn't even recognize him. Having a slave along could smooth the transition. Thomas would see that the slave didn't fear Kale, and he'd have someone who he would assume knew Kale's preferences to mimic. It was a great idea.

"That's not what I meant. You shouldn't be traveling alone with that much money. It's not safe. A slave can't help if someone tries to rob you."

"If someone tries to rob me, he can have the money. I won't put a slave in that position." Kale shuddered. A slave would be obligated to protect his master, but would be violating the law if he struck a free man. Kale had once found himself in that impossible situation. Just another example of how ridiculous Arine was.

"I'd feel better if John went with you. I trust him, and he always carries a gun. It would also be nice for you to have someone with you so Conroy doesn't try to change the deal."

Kale didn't know John very well, but based on the time he had spent with him, John seemed like a decent enough man. "I don't want to intrude on his time. He has things to do."

"I'll ask him." Jason gestured to a nearby slave. "Billy, go get John for me, please."

While the slave was gone, another served their breakfast. Just as Kale had predicted, Jason ate so quickly Kale was concerned he'd choke. A few minutes later, the slave returned with John on his heels. "You wanted me, sir?"

"I was wondering if you'd be available to go with Kale to Cooperville today. I was supposed to go, but I need to stay here with my father."

"I don't see why not. Billy caught me just as I was saddling up to go check on the boys who are out with the herd. Let me go get someone else to do it, and I'll be ready to go. Say, ten minutes?"

"Sounds good." Jason smiled triumphantly at Kale.

"Thank you, John. I'll meet you at the car." At least the time would pass more quickly with a passenger. Kale was reluctant to discard the idea of taking a slave, but Jason had a point. If this kept Jason from worrying about him, then he would do it. It would be too crowded for such a long drive in the car to bring a slave as well.

Jason finished his plate just before Kale did. "Be safe, Kale. If you get too tired to drive, get a room."

"I will."

"You know, you could take the train."

"Nah, I prefer the car. I don't like the thought of bringing Thomas back on a crowded train. I don't want to overwhelm him."

"You do know we have enough money for you to hire an entire train car for yourself?"

"Things are already set to take the car." Sitting on a train with nothing to do would drive him mad. Driving would occupy him and not really take too much longer when the stops were factored in, and he wouldn't have to a hire a cab at the other end.

"I'm going to miss you. I wish I could be there to see the expression on your face when you see your brother again."

"I suppose it'll be the same expression that's always on it." Kale hoped so at least. He knew his emotions were going to be overwhelming when the moment came, but he didn't want to scare Thomas or make Conroy suspicious.

"I look forward to meeting him. If I'm asleep for some reason when you get back, wake me. I'm excited for you, Kale."

"Thanks. I'll try to call if I can find a place, but don't worry if you don't hear from me. Try to sleep whenever you can. You're no good to your father if you're exhausted."

"I'll try."

Kale didn't expect Jason would try at all. He wished he could be around to make him sleep, but he'd make sure Jason got caught up tonight.

They stood, and Jason crossed over to Kale. He planted his lips on Kale's, his tongue demanding entrance. Kale complied. As the kiss deepened, Jason moved his hand from Kale's face to his back, crushing their bodies together. It was a marked change from the quick pecks and gentle caresses that had been so common lately.

"I love you."

"I love you, too, Jason. You do realize I'm just going to be gone for the day? I'm not circling the globe or even leaving the country."

Jason stepped back. "I know. I should get back upstairs."

"All right. Don't get too lost in your own head. I don't like the thought of you sitting up there with nothing to occupy your mind. Take a book with you at least."

Jason nodded. "I will. See you tonight. Good luck."

"Thanks."

After Jason left, Kale entered the kitchen, not minding the shocked faces of the slaves. "Darlene—"

"Thank goodness you stopped by. It saves me an errand. I wanted to give you this, and I just heard that John's going with you, so I packed enough for three." Darlene handed him a basket overflowing with fruit, bread, cheese, nuts, and dried meat.

"Why is everyone under the impression I'm leaving for days?"

"Hush. Now, I'd tell you to wake me when you get in so I could feed you and this brother of yours, but I doubt it'd do much good. I'll have a pot of soup and some plates in the oven for you. If it's not gone when I come into this kitchen to fix breakfast, there'll be trouble."

"Thanks, Darlene. Could you also make sure Jason eats?"

"Boy, it's a good thing you're free now, otherwise I'd whack you. Who do I look like? Do you think I let anyone in this house, slave or free, go without a meal?"

"No, ma'am."

"That's better." Darlene winked at him before going back

183

to her work.

John waited for him at the car with several canteens. "You ready to go?"

"Yeah, Darlene was just making sure we won't starve to death should we get stranded for a week."

John laughed. "I figured. That's why I got the canteens. You know she'll check that basket when we get back."

Kale put the basket in the back seat with the canteens. It was a good thing he hadn't asked one of the slaves along. With all the food and the valise, there wasn't any room for a fourth person.

"Are you sure you don't mind coming with me? Mr. Wadsworth might need you."

"You mean Mr. Wadsworth might pass. No, Robert's going soon, but not today. He'll be here when we get back. Besides, we've already said our goodbyes, and he doesn't like me seeing him this way." John settled into the passenger seat.

Kale took one last look in the valise to make sure the money was there along with his travel documents and pulled out of the driveway.

Chapter Thirty

"This is the fanciest car I've seen. If I were ever to get a car, this is the kind I'd want. None of those boxy things that look just like a carriage. This feels free, cutting through the wind, the same as a horse."

They were off Robert's property and on the open road where Kale could accelerate. The sun rose at their backs, chasing the night chill from the air caressing Kale's arms.

"That's why I got it. You get the same thrill driving it that you do running a horse on a long stretch. It won't take you as many places as a horse will, but it'll get you to the places it can take you pretty quick."

"I bet." John slid his hand across the leather upholstery on the door.

"Have you ever driven one before?"

"Nope. Never had much reason to. Like you said, a car can't take me to the places I need to go. I have driven a tractor, though."

"Really? I didn't know Robert had one."

"I know Jason thinks his father's backward, but he's not. He always keeps up with the latest tools to help his business. He just doesn't see much point in spending money on luxuries. It's the same thinking he had in the early days. He only likes to invest his money back into the business."

That sounded familiar. As much as Jason had wanted all the fanciest things when he was younger, now that he was a business owner, he watched his money. He wasn't stingy, but he didn't ever spend money on things just so other people could see them and know he had money.

"Well, if you've driven a tractor, then you know how to drive a car. I'll pull over in a couple of hours, and you can take a turn."

"Sounds good to me."

Kale blessed Jason. Bringing John had been a brilliant idea. The conversation was easy, and he didn't have to worry about fatigue or being too tired to make it home tonight.

◆ ◆ ◆

Kale was behind the wheel when they made it to Mr. Conroy's. They had alternated so that John would take a turn after they got Thomas to allow Kale to spend some time with him. A plethora of stories about Jason and Robert, told by both men, had kept Kale's nerves calm. Once they had made it into Cooperville, the conversation had gradually abated. This was the moment Kale had never thought would arrive.

When he parked the car, he reached back for the valise only to be stopped by John. "Let me get that."

"It's no trouble."

"I didn't think it would be. It'll just look better if I'm the one carrying it. You're the man in charge, not the man who handles the money."

John made sense. It was a good suggestion. "Let me just get my documents out of it. That way he can take the whole thing." Kale retrieved the papers and put them underneath the driver's seat. It was a wearing necessity to carry them with him at all times in Arine. They were little protection should anyone truly wish him harm, but if they were ever lost or stolen, especially without Jason to vouch for him, there was no way for Kale to prove his identity. The old fear of being captured and sold still lurked in the recesses of his mind. It was ridiculous. No one had cause to try to steal them, but he still liked to keep them out of plain view.

Mr. Conroy's secretary led them into his study and shut the door, remaining inside, out of the way. Kale was glad he had John with him to keep the numbers even. Behind a giant oak desk sat Mr. Conroy. He was a stout man with a ruddy complexion and about as much hair in his sideburns as he had on his entire head. There wasn't anything in his appearance to lead Kale to believe he was a pleasant man.

"Gentleman, please, take a seat."

"We're fine standing, thank you. This shouldn't take long." Kale was too on edge to sit. He wanted to hand over the money, sign the papers, get Thomas, and be gone in five minutes.

"I'm afraid there's been a change of plans. Upon further reflection, I can't let Thomas go for anything less than fifty."

Kale took a step forward before he could stop himself. "We had a deal." Kale was tired of disappointments, but his voice was pure steel without a hint of weariness. He was leaving with Thomas in the back seat of his car whether Mr. Conroy agreed to the terms or not.

"I know, but I've been thinking about it, and there must be something I don't know about this boy if you're willing to pay so much for him."

John stepped forward and placed the valise on the desk. "Well, we have forty-two thousand cash for you as promised. That's an awful lot of money. It seems to me you can take it and be happy at your good fortune, or you can decline it, in which case we'll have ourselves a bit of a problem." After John placed the valise on the desk, he brushed his coat back and put his hands in his pockets. Kale realized at the same moment Mr. Conroy did that this placed John's revolver in plain view.

Mr. Conroy eyed each man. Neither Kale nor John

moved. John was taller than Kale and pure muscle. It wouldn't be hard for him to intimidate anyone.

"All right. No need to make a fuss. A deal's a deal. Gereson, count this and make sure it's all there." The secretary opened the valise and started to pull the money out.

"I don't take kindly to being called a liar." John's voice was low.

"No offense intended. Business is business." Conroy held his palms up in a gesture of helplessness.

Gereson thumbed through all forty-two bundles of cash. "It's all here, sir."

"Good. Then if you would just sign here, Mr. Wadsworth, Thomas will be all yours." Kale scanned each copy of the bill of sale before he affixed his signature to them and did the same with Thomas's title and registration papers. As soon as Kale finished, Conroy clapped his hands together. "Excellent. It was nice doing business with you. Gereson, bring the boy in."

It was then that Kale realized Mr. Conroy had sold him Thomas sight unseen. Kale didn't mind. He hadn't wanted his brother around for the money part of it anyway, but it did make him wonder at Conroy's motivation. He was probably worried there was some mix-up, and Thomas wasn't the slave they wanted. Either that or there was something wrong with Thomas that Conroy didn't want them knowing about before he had his money. Kale didn't delve down that path. It was simpler to assume that Conroy was afraid they wouldn't want Thomas if it turned out he didn't look enough like the brother Kale had told him P and C already owned. Kale would find out soon enough.

The door opened, and Kale was awestruck. Before him stood a man where Kale had expected to find a boy. Thomas stood barely an inch shorter than Kale, or at least he would when his head was raised. His long, gangly limbs had filled out. The freckles on his nose and cheeks were faded.

"Thomas, you've been sold." A flutter of his downcast

eyelashes was the only movement that betrayed his surprise. "This is your new master, Mr. Wadsworth."

Thomas began to sink to his knees. Kale's stomach churned. He wouldn't let his brother kneel to him. Instead he grabbed Thomas's arm, perhaps a bit too gruffly, before his knees could hit the floor. "No time for all that. Let's go." Kale kept his voice low. It was the only way he could control it.

Once out of Conroy's office, Kale released Thomas's arm and strode to the car, confident that Thomas and John followed. Kale climbed into the back and John got behind the wheel, putting Thomas's papers under the seat to join Kale's. Thomas moved to get in the front, but Kale grabbed his hand and tugged him into the back. The moment Thomas's door closed, the car jerked forward.

Once John had them off of Conroy's property, Kale collapsed back in his seat and breathed easier. To his right, Thomas sat awkwardly on the edge of his seat with his head bowed and one hand limp inside Kale's. He had no idea how to even begin to talk to Thomas. It didn't feel right to just blurt out that he was his brother.

Kale could imagine what was going through Thomas's head. What he really wanted was to put him at ease. "You must have a lot of questions." Thomas perked slightly at the words. "You've noticed my hands are rougher than any man you've served in a while. You would have seen the valise full of cash on the desk. You're wondering what you did to get yourself sold. Was it something you said, a mistake you made? Or did the master just get tired of you? You're right back at the beginning, having to learn new preferences and rules. John's revolver is an unexpected variable. You haven't been manacled, so are you expected to do something? How can you please someone who you've already upset merely by trying to pay the proper respect on your knees? I'm sorry about that, by the way. I didn't mean to be rough with you. And now you're wondering how any free man can know what you're thinking so well. It's a bit scary."

Kale lifted Thomas's face. Thomas had inherited the soft curves of their mother's bone structure. "Lift your eyes to mine." The pale green eyes that met Kale's were imprinted with a lifetime of experiences Kale had no knowledge of. There was a depth that hadn't been there the last time Kale had seen them. The light behind the irises had dimmed. Slaves never really had innocence, even as children, but there was a certain spark, a hope, that had persisted in Thomas when he was young. Kale had envied it. When had it been extinguished? Had it been when Kale was sold? Or when Thomas was finally separated from his mother? It was time to bring some understanding to dispel the confusion clouding Thomas's eyes. "I know what you're thinking because it's what I would have been thinking if I were you. It was the way our mother taught us to think." There was a flicker of something on Thomas's face, not quite recognition. "It's me, Thomas. Kale. Your brother."

Thomas's eyes widened so much they reminded Kale of the time he had shown Thomas a three-foot snake he had killed near the pond. "I know it's hard to believe. It doesn't make any sense, but it's true."

"Kale?" It was the first time Thomas had spoken. He had an unfamiliar voice, deep and richer than when Kale had last heard it.

"Yes." Thomas's eyes flashed to John in the front seat. "Don't worry, John's a friend. You don't need to worry about anything. John doesn't own you, and he won't hurt you. A company I own just bought your title. It's a little complicated, and I don't expect you to make sense of it right now. All you need to know is that I've got you, and I'm going to take care of you."

"You're free?"

"Yes, Little Brother, and I'm taking you home."

CHAPTER THIRTY-ONE

A little after eleven o'clock, Robert finally woke up for more than just a few minutes. Jason set his book aside as soon as he heard the change in his father's breathing.

"What are you doing hovering over my bedside? Aren't you supposed to be with Kale?"

Jason handed his father a glass of water. "Kale's fine without me. I wanted to be here with you today."

"I'm not going to die today. You should have gone." Robert lifted his head and drank. He handed Jason back an empty glass.

Demetri piled pillows behind Robert and helped him get comfortable in a near sitting position. Once he was situated, Robert eyed the nurse. "Thank you for your help, but your services are no longer needed."

"Excuse me, sir, but I'd like to stay. I can be of use here, help make you more comfortable."

"I have Demetri for that."

"Yes, and as long as Demetri doesn't need sleep or food, I'm sure that would work out fine. As it is, you need help, Mr. Wadsworth. You're only going to get more uncomfortable as time goes on."

"I'm fine."

"No, sir, you're not. You're dying. Men in your condition

don't get better. You've held on a remarkably long time. It's time for you to make peace with what's coming. If not for yourself, then for your loved ones."

Jason braced himself for Robert's explosion. It didn't occur to him that his father didn't have the strength for one. "What's your name?"

"Sadie, sir."

"You may stay, Sadie. I don't have the energy to fight with you."

Sadie smiled. "That's why most of my patients agree to have me around, sir."

"Son." Jason leaned forward in his chair, eager to help in any way he could. "Go eat something."

"I already have."

"Then go look at the portraits Demetri pulled down from the attic."

"That can wait, Father."

"How about this: leave because your old man needs to piss, and I might be bossed into keeping nurses around, but I will retain some dignity in front of my own son."

Jason blushed, embarrassed he hadn't understood his father's meaning.

"Gods, you blush just like Lena did. Kale must have fun with that."

Jason blushed even hotter, and Robert made a gurgling sound that was supposed to be a laugh. "I'll be back soon."

Taking his father's advice, he went to the parlor where Demetri had set the paintings. There were four in all, leaned up on the sofa. Jason sat cross-legged on the floor in front of them. It felt like being a child again, sitting on the floor, looking up at his mother as she sewed or read aloud from a book.

To the far left was a picture of her as a young woman before she'd married his father. She looked barely fifteen, with round pink cheeks and bright hazel eyes. She looked so young and carefree. The painting to the right of it was a wedding portrait of her with his father. Robert's arm was possessively around Lena's waist, as if he was scared he would lose her at any moment. His smile was much more reserved than Lena's, but it was the happiest Jason had ever seen him. The next was a bust of his mother. Jason couldn't determine her age, but he assumed it was around the time he was born. The final canvas was a family portrait. Jason was around four. He could remember sitting for it. The wool trousers had been itchy, and he wasn't allowed any toys to play with, but his mother had sneaked him treats when his father wasn't looking. Robert was much more relaxed in this one. Not only was he happy, but satisfied as well, as if his wife and child were his greatest accomplishments.

Jason picked up the family portrait and carried it with him to his father's room.

"I thought you might like to have something to look at other than the bare walls." Jason perched the picture on top of the dresser opposite the bed.

"It's been a long time since I saw that. It's hard to believe I was ever so young."

"Yeah. We were one happy little family, weren't we?"

"Yes, we were. Thanks for bringing it here. That was the best time of my life."

"I had completely forgotten that it existed until I saw it today."

"Probably blocked it from your memory. You threw a fit every time we tried to put you in those trousers after that day. The only way I could get you to keep still was to bribe you with sweets."

"You? I thought Mother gave them to me."

"Where do you think she got them from?"

Jason shrugged. "Do you ever wonder what she'd say if she could see us?"

"No. I know what she'd say. She'd tell us to stop being stubborn and realize we're the only family we're going to get, and that's more valuable than pride or foolishness."

"I wonder what she would think of me and Kale."

"The same thing I do. She'd be happy that you're happy."

Jason's blood ran hot at his father's lie. "You hate the fact that I'm with Kale."

"No, I don't. You're a good match."

Jason wouldn't let his father pretend like nothing had happened. "If that were true, why didn't you accept Kale when I first brought him back here?"

"Your mother would have, once she saw how in love you were with him and that he returned it. If she'd been here, she would have talked me out of my idiocy. At the time, I didn't know he loved you. I thought he was manipulating you."

"It should have been enough that I loved him."

"Perhaps, but you love far more easily than you should. You can thank your mother for that. Don't think I didn't hear about you and Eric Vanderhoff. First, it was him, and then it was Kale. It could have been someone else the next week for all I knew."

"You threatened to beat him."

"Yes, Jason. He was a slave, no matter how much you wished he wasn't. I wanted to end it. All I saw for you going down that path was hurt. You had to go and fall for the one person with whom it would be most difficult for you to build a life. It was never anything against Kale personally. I liked him. That's why I bought him for you. I just never imagined you would end up falling in love with him."

"Kale persuaded me to come here, to try to mend our relationship. He always blamed himself for our problems."

"I'm glad he convinced you to come. I wanted to write you, but I couldn't bear the thought that you might refuse, and I had given you every reason to."

"I didn't think you'd want to see me, since you disowned me."

"I regretted that as soon as you left. I didn't mean what I said that day. I must have started two dozen letters, but I could never find the right words. I was ashamed of myself, if

I'm honest. Then you began courting Renee, and it didn't seem there was much point. After the wedding, I thought everything would be fine, but when things fell apart with Renee, I felt responsible. I knew it had to do with Kale. You never looked at Renee the way you did him, even on your wedding day."

"I loved her." Jason didn't want his father thinking he'd married Renee for her money. "In a way, I still do."

"I know. You loved her the way you love most things, but you weren't in love with her. You were too young to know the difference, to know that you can love many different people, but that doesn't mean you bind yourself to them."

"You terrified Kale that day. He thought you still held his title."

"I'm sorry about that. I was wrong to treat him the way I did. I only wanted to protect you. I reacted badly. I'm sure he was happy to get back to Perdana."

"No, actually, he was furious with me for not giving in to you. I got quite the earful on the journey back. He insisted I was a fool, that he was just a slave, and you were my father, my family."

"Kale's a good man."

"Yes, he is."

"I like him, Jason. I really do. I think he's good for you. I wish things had been different. When you both showed up here, I fell into my old habits. I didn't know if he really loved you or if he had just used you to gain freedom. It doesn't take long around the two of you to realize the truth."

"And what's that?"

"Kale loves you enough to risk enslavement again to bring you here. You support each other. It couldn't have been easy for him to come back here, and even once he was here, he didn't have to push so hard for our reconciliation, but he did. He talked to me as if he didn't have any reason to fear me."

"He doesn't. He knows that."

"Perhaps, but he didn't need to make himself vulnerable to attack the way he did. It would have been easier for him to avoid me altogether, but that wouldn't be serving you. I don't know how it could have ever worked with him as a slave, but I'm glad you found a way around it. I would have liked more time to get to know him."

"You still have time."

"Not much. I can feel it."

"But you're so much better than you were last night."

"That's only because of the drugs Sadie gave me to calm my stomach and get me to keep food down again. It won't last."

"Then we'll have to make it count."

"When Kale gets back, I'd like to meet his brother. I also need to apologize to him. I wronged him as much as I wronged you, probably more given that he didn't have any choice in the matter."

Jason grinned. "If there's one thing you need to know about Kale, it's that he's always exercised more choice than you'd expect. He did manipulate me, but only for my own good, or so he thought. I would have never sold him and married Renee if he hadn't maneuvered me into it."

"He has balls. When he kept me from striking you, I was so stunned I didn't know whether to admire him or beat him. Obviously, I made the wrong choice. It wasn't my place to threaten him. You took a dangerous path with him, but it was your prerogative, and I shouldn't have intervened."

"Thank you. There's no point in dwelling on the past anymore."

"No, there's not. Why don't you tell me about him and your life in Naiara? I'd like to know about it."

"Naiara's wonderful. We've made a nice little home for ourselves. Kale loves gardening. He keeps the entire place in bloom and grows vegetables for our kitchen. Oh, and he's an artist."

"Really?"

"Yes. He's quite famous actually. Right before we came, he had a big opening at one of the most prestigious galleries in Calea. People came from all over the country for it."

"I would have never thought."

"He's shy about it. The only reason he lets people see his work is because he feels like he has to contribute financially."

"Aren't you one of the richest men on the continent?"

"Don't get me started. That's Kale for you. He never wants to be a burden."

Jason talked and talked, sharing tidbits about his life, funny anecdotes, stories about their friends, all the things only a parent would be interested in. Robert listened, asking questions where appropriate, and paying rapt attention. After a couple of hours, Robert's eyelids began to droop, and he visibly struggled to stay awake.

"Why don't you go to sleep now? We can talk more after you've had a nap."

"That sounds good. I just want to know one thing before I go back to sleep. What's going to happen to this place? You and Kale have a home in Naiara. I don't expect you to uproot and move here, but the thought of it fading away, it's unbearable."

"I won't ever let that happen." Jason's voice was fierce as he took his father's hand in his own. "John and I, we'll work something out. I promise you. Please don't worry about it. We'll grow the ranch, make it bigger than you could ever imagine."

"Thank you, Son." Robert reached over and patted Jason's hand with his free one. "I'm just going to close my eyes now. Keep talking. I want to hear about everything."

Jason obliged, never letting go of his father's hand.

CHAPTER THIRTY-TWO

Little flutters of light escaped the thickness of the tress. They were almost to the ranch. Only their headlights—and now the lights from the cabin—broke the black of the moonless night.

"Thomas." Kale shook his brother's arm to wake him. "We're almost there."

Thomas opened his eyes, disoriented in the darkness. Kale and John had switched off driving a few times, but Kale had spent most of the drive in the back seat with Thomas. He had explained what had happened since they were separated, how he came to be free, who Jason was, and what to expect.

The drive had still been long and awkward. Thomas didn't know how to react to all of the information he was given or his new, altered reality. Kale couldn't blame him. It would take time for them to build a relationship. The two things that had made the drive more bearable were the food and sleep. They were both great excuses not to talk, and Kale was sure Thomas could use more of both.

"Remember, no one in this house has any power over you. Other than observing basic good manners, there are no expectations, but you can behave however you feel most comfortable. If it's easier for you, just keep your head down and don't speak unless spoken to. If you have any questions, you are always welcome to ask. No one will ever be mad at you for asking."

"Yes…" Thomas's voice trailed off. Kale had asked him not to call him sir, and certainly not master, so that didn't leave Thomas with many options. It would take more than a day to the break the habit of replying to everything with a "yes, sir" or "no, sir."

John parked the car and grabbed the empty basket and canteens. "I'll take care of everything, Kale. You two go on in the house."

"Thanks, John. I really appreciate you coming with me today. I don't know how I could have done it without you."

"Don't mention it. When else am I going to get a chance to drive such a fancy car? Go see what happened while we were gone."

Kale took Thomas's hand firmly in his and led the way. As soon as they were in the door, Jason leapt into his arms and greeted him with a kiss. Kale didn't even have a chance to see it coming. He wrapped Jason in his arms and pulled him tight, breathing in the scent of his hair. It had been a long day, and having his arms full of Jason made Kale aware of the amount of stress he'd been managing.

As quickly as Jason had leapt into Kale's arms, he jumped back. "So this is Thomas?"

"Yep. Thomas, this is Jason."

Thomas nodded his head, but Jason was having none of that. He stuck out his hand, and Kale nodded to Thomas. Jason would let his hand hang there in midair all night until Thomas took it. As soon as Thomas met him for the handshake, Jason pulled him into a hug. "It's so good to meet you. We've been waiting for you."

When Jason stepped back, he turned to Kale. "Father wants to meet him."

"It's late. That can wait until tomorrow." Kale wanted nothing more than to get into bed with Jason and talk through it all. His own head reeled, and he needed time to resolve all the changes in his life. Kale didn't know how Thomas was holding it together when he was having such a hard time.

"No, Kale, it can't. Please. It's important to him." It wasn't the pleading tone of Jason's voice that convinced him. It was the raw urgency in his eyes.

"All right. For you." Kale gestured for Thomas to follow them.

Jason stepped into the room first, and Kale followed with Thomas behind him. As soon as Thomas cleared the door, Jason introduced him. "Father, this is Thomas."

Kale positioned his body between Thomas and Robert, off to the side. It was instinctual, as if Robert might leap out of bed and attack. He was prepared to step in should he need to shield Thomas from Robert's words.

"Thomas, it's a pleasure to finally meet you. I wanted to personally welcome you to my home. It's important to me that you make yourself comfortable here. I consider you an honored guest as the brother of my son's companion, and I extend you all the courtesies as such. No one here expects you to act as a slave, and no one other than your brother has any authority over you."

Kale was stunned. He hadn't really expected for Robert to be rude, but he hadn't expected this either.

"Thank you, sir." Thomas, at least, had his wits about him, which was more than Kale could say.

"My pleasure. I had the room next to Kale and Jason's readied for you. If you need anything, just ask." Robert didn't wait for a reply before he settled his focus on Kale. "As for you, Kale, I owe you a long overdue apology. I was out of line all those years ago. You've never done anything other than try to protect my son, and I terrorized you for it. I'm ashamed of myself. I deeply regret my actions and the consequences of them. Losing my son was too high a price for my pride." Frequent pauses for breath and the rattle behind his voice punctuated Robert's speech.

Kale struggled to muster a response. The only reason it was even possible was because he couldn't let such a gesture go unanswered.

"Thank you, sir."

"Call me Robert. Hell, you can come give me a bear hug and call me Dad if you want."

Jason sniggered. Someone had been telling tales. Kale smiled. "Thank you, Robert. I don't know how to express my gratitude, and not just for the apology, but for your generosity as well."

"There's no need. You've done enough just making my boy happy. I'm glad you gave me the chance to reclaim my family before I die."

Robert held Kale's gaze as Kale absorbed the full meaning of what he'd said. There was a shared moment of warmth between them. A coughing fit overcame Robert, and the moment was broken. Jason was immediately at his father's side, leaning him forward and patting his back. Robert waved him off. "Don't fuss. I'm just tired."

"I think we all are. Good night, Robert. We'll see you in the morning."

"Good night. That's a fine brother you've got there."

"I know." Kale nodded and ushered Thomas from the room.

Thomas held himself well. He was the picture of a perfect slave, blending into the background, not bringing attention to himself. Kale found it hard to remember if he had ever been so inconspicuous. Even as a free man, he wasn't one to draw attention to himself, but he had a strong personality and wasn't shy about speaking his mind. What kind of man was his brother behind the bland façade? Did Thomas even know? For Kale, the transition from piece of property to valued human had been gradual, supported by Jason who loved him. If Jason hadn't been there to facilitate his emergence from objectification, Kale didn't know how he would have done it, or if he could have at all. The fear of freedom—or rather of hoping for freedom—ran too deep.

"This is mine and Jason's room." Kale pointed to their door as they passed. "If you need anything, don't hesitate to come get one of us. Just make sure you knock first. This room here," Kale opened the next door, "must be the one Robert had prepared." Kale turned on the lights to reveal a room that was similar in appearance to Jason's, complete with its own bathroom. A four poster bed dominated the space, and a royal blue comforter added color to the dark wood. The fireplace shared the same chimney as Jason's. There was a sitting area with two wing-back chairs on a carpet that matched the comforter and a desk complete with paper and a few books. It had been dusted and aired, but it still held the smell of a room that hadn't been used in years. Kale doubted Thomas would mind.

"Stay right here. I'll be back in a moment." Kale dashed to his room. It occurred to him that his brother didn't have any clothes other than what he wore. Kale's would be too large for him, but they would be a better fit than Jason's who was much more slender. It took just a minute for him to grab one of the outfits he was used to wearing back home and a robe. Kale had never understood the fascination with robes. He was always either naked or dressed and saw no need for one, but he wanted his brother to have the option.

"Here, you can wear this tomorrow, so we can have your clothes laundered." Thomas hadn't moved a muscle. He stood in the middle of the floor with his mouth slightly open. At least his head was raised. "You can have a seat. It's what they're there for." Kale placed the clothes in the wardrobe and sat in one of the chairs. Only after Kale was seated and had gestured to the chair opposite him, did Thomas sit.

"Thank you for the clothes. I can get a few more days wear out of these before they need to be washed."

"No. I want them laundered." Kale didn't want anything from Mr. Conroy's house here, but he couldn't exactly burn the only clothes his brother had. The next best thing was having the smell of that man's house washed off of them. "Mine will be a little big on you, but not much. We'll buy you some new clothes when there's time."

"I'm sure yours will work just fine."

"As you saw, Robert's not doing well. He'll probably pass in the next couple of days. When he does, I'm going to have to spend almost all my time with Jason. Things will get pretty hectic around here. I wish it could be calmer for your first few days, but I wasn't about to wait to get you."

"I won't be in the way."

"Oh, I'm not worried about that. You can do what you like. Spend your time in here where you know you won't be disturbed. Look around the house. You can even help out the slaves if you need to keep busy. I can imagine how confusing this must be for you, and I know how unnerving having to make decisions can be, but I really want you to do what's best for you. I want you to be entirely selfish."

Thomas nodded. "I don't know if I can do that."

"I understand. You know I own you on paper only. I don't expect any subservience from you, but if it will make it easier for you to have me give you orders, let me know. I don't like the thought, but I suppose most boys do boss their kid brothers around, so I'll try to think of it like that."

"Thank you. I honestly don't know what to think right now."

"Doesn't surprise me. It'll take time for your mind to adjust to the new situation. It'll be harder than your previous transitions since these are entirely different circumstances. Don't fight it. Don't worry about how long it takes. There's no right or wrong. I have all the time in the world."

"I can't imagine ever getting used to the fact that my brother's free. I've never even thought about what it would be like. Does it feel different?"

Kale grinned. "Gods yes. Even though things didn't change much for me on the outside when I was freed, since

Jason already spoiled me, there was something on the inside that changed. I can't describe it. You have to feel it for yourself."

Thomas started to speak and then stopped.

"I already told you, you can ask or say anything. Nothing you do could offend me."

"Are you planning on freeing me?"

"Yes," Kale stated as firmly as he knew how. "We don't have the details worked out yet, but Jason and I are friends with some very powerful people. It'll most likely happen the way it did for me. As long as we're in Arine, I can't free you. You have to appreciate the irony of a country that will allow me to kill you if I like, but not to free you."

"Can't be giving the slaves any hope, now can we? Then they all might waste their days dreaming of a long lost brother coming to buy them up, take them away, and free them. Couldn't have that."

Kale chuckled. "Nope." The atmosphere relaxed, the silence between them more natural than it had been in the car. "I'm glad to see you did well for yourself. A registered valet. I don't think Jason ever registered me. Never thought to ask."

"No, he just gave you your title."

"Yes, that he did." Kale nodded. "You should be proud of yourself. I worried you might not have listened to Mama."

"And get a switch to my backside? That woman beat me more than all my masters combined. Bless her for it." Thomas smiled, the first real smile Kale had seen. It suited him.

"Yes, bless her." This was as good an opening as Kale was going to get. He had avoided the subject since he'd seen Thomas, but it would only be harder the longer he waited. "Did you hear what happened to her?"

Thomas sobered. "Yeah. I was still in the area at the time, and word got to me. When did you find out?"

Kale relaxed further into his chair. At least he was spared

that unpleasant task. "Two days ago."

"I'm sorry."

"You didn't kill her. There's nothing for you to be sorry for." The silence dragged on between them until Kale stood, and Thomas followed suit. "You should go to bed. I know how hard it is to sleep in a new place. You'll be surprised how long it takes to get used to sleeping on a featherbed."

"You really didn't have to put me in such a nice room."

Kale hugged Thomas on his way to the door. "Yes, I did."

CHAPTER THIRTY-THREE

Robert fell back to sleep soon after Kale and Thomas left. Jason gave the nurse instructions to wake him if anything changed and went to his room to wait for Kale. It was difficult to pull himself away from his father's bedside, but he needed Kale. He was wearing thin. At the prompting of Demetri and Darlene, he had attempted to take a nap earlier in the day, but it had done nothing to refresh him. If anything, it had made him feel worse simply by revealing how bad off he was. It seemed natural to feel strained at his dying father's bedside, but it was disturbing that he couldn't find any rest in sleep.

Kale was the answer. He always was. Whenever Jason was overwhelmed or his mind spun away from him, Kale's strong presence brought him back to himself.

Jason was sitting in front of the fireplace when Kale finally joined him. It couldn't have been a very long wait, but Jason's time alone stretched on for longer than it was.

"How is Thomas settling in?" Jason rose from his chair to meet Kale and help him undress.

"It's hard to tell. He appears fine, but if he's anything like me, he'd appear that way even if he was terrified. He's been all alone in the world for a long time."

"Well, he's not going to be anymore." Jason removed

Kale's shirt and then his own, throwing them across the chair he had vacated. "I'm exhausted, and I'm sure you are too. I was worried that you might not make it back tonight."

"I should have called, but we never stopped anywhere with a telephone. I didn't want to spend time searching for one when we could be on the road."

"Don't worry about it. You're here now. I feel like I could shatter at the slightest touch, and I need you to hold me together." Jason slid naked into bed alongside Kale.

"I think I can manage that." Kale lifted his arm and gestured for Jason to assume his usual spot, nestled in the crook of Kale's shoulder against the flat of his chest. When Jason was settled into the warmth of Kale's side, he shivered. "What was that?"

"Nothing. It's just a relief having you here. I don't know how I could get through this without you."

"You don't have to, so don't waste any energy thinking about it." Kale lightly caressed Jason's arm, sending chills through his body.

It felt so nice. Jason hadn't realized how tense he was until his muscles slowly relaxed, giving up the struggle to stay strong. As his body released the determination to remain together, tears flowed. Everything he'd held at bay all day so he could be there for his father crashed down on him. The pain, the regret, the hurt, the sadness, added up to a tidal wave of emotion. He buried his face in Kale's chest, not wanting his lover to see him fall apart. Jason's hand crossed Kale's abdomen to grip his side, nails digging into the skin as he tried to pull him closer than he could ever be.

Kale's only response was to turn on his side and gather Jason into his arms. Jason let himself accept the comfort, grateful that Kale wasn't pushing for words or an explanation. Inside his head, voices of regret—the should haves and could haves—drowned out any attempts to silence them. "Why, Kale? Why is it only now that I'm getting to know him? Why when it's too late? I wish I had never come. It would be so much easier if I could just keep hating him."

"Yes, it would be, but I never took you for a man who avoided something merely because it's difficult."

"I'm such a wretched man. You didn't even have the chance to know your father, and you were taken from your mother. You didn't have a chance to see her before she died. Not only did I choose to not have a relationship with my father, but I also had the opportunity to make it better, and all I can do is complain about it. How can you stand me?"

"My situation has no bearing on yours. You're allowed your feelings. There's nothing wrong with them."

"But how can you love me?"

"You make it incredibly easy. Your actions are what matter. You came, even though you didn't want to. You put in the effort to get to know your father, even though you knew it would make what's coming more difficult. If you want me to stop loving you, you'll have to come at me with more than that."

"No, please don't ever stop loving me, Kale."

"I couldn't."

Jason clung to Kale even harder. Somehow, with all the challenges that had been put in their way by themselves and fate, Jason had ended up with a man who both knew him and loved him, a man who was strong when Jason was weak, proud when Jason was shamed, and steadfast when Jason faltered. Jason wanted him, needed him. With the realities of life swirling around him, he yearned to retreat into the heady space he and Kale could create in their passion for one another.

Jason hardened, craving the comfort of sex, the intimate exploration of familiar places, the renewed connection with a man Jason could scarcely believe was his, the spent bonelessness that came after the physical exertion, the drowsy fog that would lull him into contented sleep surrounded by the proof that he was loved. He wanted it all.

But it wasn't his to take. It was only Kale's to give, and

Jason knew Kale was not able. Guilt stabbed Jason's heart. It had scarcely been two days since Kale had discovered his mother was dead, and his lost brother had been found only hours ago. Jason knew it all weighed on Kale. He had his own guilt and pain to sort through, and for some reason, sex didn't play a role in it. Jason couldn't be so selfish as to demand what Kale was not prepared to give him.

Kale rose from the bed, the sheet falling away to reveal what Jason already knew: Kale wasn't interested in sex. Jason couldn't blame him for leaving. It no doubt made him uncomfortable to feel Jason's erection against his leg when he didn't reciprocate the feeling. "Where are you going?"

"To get some oil from our luggage." Kale proceeded to the wardrobe and rummaged around for the bottle.

"No, Kale."

"Why not? You're aching for it."

"You know my reasons. I won't, not if you're not enjoying yourself."

"Your reasons are stupid. I choose to ignore them. One of the benefits of being free. I want to do this for you." Kale returned to the bed with the oil in hand.

"I appreciate it, Kale, but you don't have to."

"Yes, I do, Jason. What kind of man am I if I can't comfort my lover when he needs it? I wouldn't do it if I didn't want to."

"I won't enter you." Jason was adamant. Never again would he breech Kale without knowing for certain Kale consented and enjoyed it.

"I don't need to be hard."

"I don't care. I won't do it."

"Fine. There are other ways I can make love to you. Just because I can't get sexual release right now doesn't mean you shouldn't, and I'd rather take part than have you take care of it yourself. I still desire you. I can still take pleasure in your body and in giving you pleasure. Please don't take that away from me. It's bad enough that I feel betrayed by my own body's failure. Don't make it worse by denying me."

Jason pushed aside his own desires in order to observe Kale with clear eyes. Nothing in his demeanor belied his words other than the lack of arousal in his prick. Nothing scared Jason more than the thought of taking Kale against his will, but Kale was eager, and Jason knew that if he were in Kale's position, he would be the same. He knew he could make love to Kale without being aroused himself and even take pleasure without a climax to finish the experience. "All right. But don't feel obligated to finish what you start if you don't want to. I won't demand anything from you."

"I know. Trust me." Kale rolled Jason onto his stomach. It was unexpected, and Jason had to adjust himself to get comfortable. Kale's hands descended on Jason's shoulder muscles, slick with oil. Jason groaned with the pressure as knots loosened. "You need to relax." Kale's voice tickled his ear, as did the lick Kale applied before he pulled away.

Kale's hands slid all over the back of Jason's body. Nothing was left untouched. Arms, legs, neck, buttocks, all luxuriated under the steady pressure and growing warmth. After only a few minutes, Kale rolled him onto his back. It was over all too soon, but upon the sight of Kale naked above him, all longing for the massage fled in favor of more expedient matters.

"It's been too long since I've touched all of you. I need to get reacquainted." Kale repeated the exercise on Jason's front, using slightly less pressure. Jason couldn't agree more and reveled in Kale's touch. He expected Kale to skip his protruding cock and return to it later, so Kale's hands encircling his cock and balls with the same touch he'd used everywhere else was a shock. The oddly asexual caress elicited a shudder from Jason. He yearned for more attention to his straining erection, but Kale acted oblivious.

After every part of Jason's body had felt Kale's touch, Kale slid his hands down Jason's sides and rested his weight on top of him. Jason reached up and stroked the delectable curve between Kale's shoulder and neck, craning his head to kiss it. Kale obliged, moving his shoulder to within kissing distance, taking the opportunity to bestow some kisses himself on Jason's neck. The inside of Kale's lips was soft against Jason's skin, a thrill after his earlier firm touch. When Kale was done kissing, he moved lower, seeming not to care that Jason wanted to taste more of Kale's skin, wanted to suck that delectable bit of flesh into his mouth and then lick the mark he'd left behind.

Kale devoured Jason's chest, lips and fingers roaming across his torso. Jason arched to meet Kale, wanting each kiss —each touch—to last longer. His cock ached with need. He wanted Kale. He wanted release. He wanted love, and he wanted the pain to go away. Once again, tears erupted.

"Let it all out." Kale continued his ministrations while Jason quietly sobbed. He yearned, he wanted, he needed, he craved. So many things. When the tears were spent, Jason was left with nothing but the unbearable tension. Kale's touch was all over him, but it wasn't enough. If only the tension would snap, Jason felt sure peace was on the other side of it.

Kale's mouth enveloped Jason's weeping erection. The hot, slick pressure was a thousand times more acute than it had been on Jason's muscles. All thought ceased. Only touch remained. Jason didn't care anymore whether or not Kale was hard. This was too incredible for him to stop. A voice of self-hatred sounded in his head, and Jason pushed it away. He trusted Kale. Kale would never do anything to harm him, including letting Jason coerce him into sex. If Kale had a problem, he would let Jason know. In the meantime, Jason relished the sensation, the freedom of falling, knowing that his lover waited to catch him.

It didn't take much. The recent celibacy and stress diminished Jason's capacity to last much longer than a few tongue strokes against his shaft. He tugged on Kale's hair to let him know he was about to come, but Kale had already strengthened his grip on the outside of Jason's thighs. Of course, Kale would be able to tell when Jason was nearing the end. He knew Jason's body better than Jason did. A few seconds later the tension snapped, and Jason orgasmed. The pain and grief of earlier didn't come rushing back from their retreat. They remained muted in the distant background of Jason's mind. Peace filled the void. It pooled inside of him, warm and thick. Kale bundled him in his arms, and Jason drifted away.

CHAPTER THIRTY-FOUR

Jason snored softly against Kale's chest. Miraculously, he had slept through the night. It was still early. The sun wasn't even all the way up yet, but Kale was anxious about his brother. He doubted Thomas had slept much, and it would take time for his internal clock to adjust to not having to be up at dawn.

Kale was loath to leave Jason to wake to an empty bed, but he needed to make sure his brother was fed and sorted. Moving carefully, he squirmed out from under Jason's weight and covered him with the sheet. He tiptoed to the wardrobe and withdrew some clothes.

"You're not nearly as sneaky as you think you are." Jason's drowsy voice turned Kale around.

"I'm sorry. You were supposed to stay asleep. I just need to make sure Thomas gets some breakfast."

"Breakfast sounds good." Jason stretched, the sheet falling away from his chest, revealing a few love bites.

"Are you sure?"

"Yes. I need to check on Father."

"He must be fine, otherwise someone would have come for you."

"I asked them to get me if he woke."

"Isn't it good that he slept through the night?"

"Yes and no. Sadie said he's going to get more tired and

weak until he just falls asleep and never wakes up." Jason's voice caught on the last word, making it come out more as a squeak.

"Jason—"

"It's fine. I have to make my peace with it. I'm grateful we at least came to understand each other."

Kale nodded. He didn't want Jason to tumble down a pit of emotion, but he didn't want him acting as though nothing was happening either. "Get some clothes on. I'll go fetch Thomas, and you go check on your father. We'll meet in the dining room."

"Thanks." Jason rose from the bed naked and took languid steps toward Kale. "For everything." He kissed him on the mouth and ran a hand across his chest.

"Thanks for letting me. It was nice." Kale didn't think Jason could comprehend how wonderful it had been for him. Pleasuring Jason gave Kale immense satisfaction. The matter of his current impotence was a source of pain. The only other time it had happened was when he was owned by a labor firm that had seemed bent on working him to death. He could only hope that once their lives settled back to some form of normalcy, his body would stop betraying him. "I'll see you in a few minutes."

Kale knocked lightly on Thomas's door. He didn't want to wake him if, by some chance, he was still sleeping. There was no need. Thomas answered the door seconds after Kale lowered his hand.

"Good morning. The clothes fit you better than I thought they would. How'd you sleep?"

"Very well, thank you."

"Thomas, I'm your brother. You can tell me the truth. I won't think you're ungrateful."

Thomas smirked. "You were right. It takes a while to get used to a bed like that. It's so soft and fluffy. I kept jerking awake, as if I was falling. Each time I wondered where I was."

Kale patted him on the back. "I'd like to tell you that

completely goes away, but there are still mornings I wake up wondering if it was all a dream."

"Then you understand how I've felt since Mr. Gereson showed me into the office yesterday. My only reassurance is that my mind could never come up with a dream like this."

Kale was grateful for Thomas's eloquence. Their mother's training and his work as a valet had refined his speech. The lack of disparity in their language helped bridge the gap between them. It would also make his transition easier once he was free.

Jason exited his and Kale's room and smiled at them before going down the hall to his father's.

"It's time I show you where the kitchen is and introduce you. We'll order breakfast." Kale led Thomas into the kitchen and was immediately confronted by a grim Darlene. "Shit." There were places for coarse language, even in the life of a free man.

"Shit is right. Why was there a full pot of soup and plates piled high with food in my oven this morning?"

"Darlene, I—"

"Did I not make myself clear? Was there some part of my instructions you did not understand?"

"No, Darlene. I'm sorry. We were tired, and it was late, and I completely forgot. After all the food you packed us, we weren't hungry at all."

"He's right, ma'am. That basket of food was delicious, the perfect accompaniment for a day's drive. After an afternoon savoring it, there simply wasn't room for more."

Darlene eyed Thomas and then glanced at Kale. "I can see charm runs in the family."

"I suppose so." Kale smiled at his brother. It was good to know that he at least felt comfortable around the slaves. Or maybe it was just Darlene. Any decent slave knew the necessity of charming the cook. "Darlene, this is Thomas. Thomas, Darlene. She keeps us all fed. A few days with her and your clothes won't fit."

"It's nice to meet you, Thomas."

"You too, ma'am."

"Call me Darlene. Ma'am makes me feel old and leads me to believe you've done something to get yourself in trouble like your brother here."

Thomas put his large smile to use. "He was always the troublemaker."

"Usually lured by your big puppy eyes asking me to do something for you."

"Don't listen to such lies, Darlene. I've always been a model of propriety."

Kale snorted. It was the first time they had teased each other as adults, and it wasn't much different than when they were kids.

"I'm sure you are, child. Now, did you boys want breakfast?"

"Yes, please. Jason's up too."

"Then I'll have it served in the dining room. Let me get you some coffee to take with you."

"Half coffee and half cream and sugar for Jason."

"Boy, don't act like I'm not the one who taught you how Master Jason takes his coffee. Try and tell me how that boy drinks it," Darlene muttered as she poured the coffee. She handed two cups to Kale and one to Thomas. "If you all will get out of my way now, I'll have breakfast for you in no time."

"Thanks, Darlene." Kale headed to the door.

"Thank you, Darlene. If there's anything I can do to help, you make sure to let me know. I can't cook worth a damn, but I can chop and peel with the best of them."

"I bet you can, sweetheart. Tell me, what are you used to having for breakfast?"

"The usual. Oatmeal. Every now and then, some hard-boiled eggs if they cracked in the pot."

"Then I'm sure you'll like what I make just fine."

"Oh, there's no doubt about that." Thomas followed Kale

218

out to the dining room. It was amazing that he acted so much like Kale when they'd spent most of their lives apart. Kale raised his eyebrows at him as soon as Thomas looked his way. "What?"

"Laying it on a little thick, weren't you?"

"Everyone knows to make nice with the cook."

"Uh-huh."

"Like you wouldn't do the same."

"Oh, I did. It's just a surprise to see my little brother following so closely in my footsteps." Kale sat down in his usual spot and gestured for Thomas to sit next to him. Jason hadn't arrived, but Kale placed his coffee in front of his place. "I told you my story yesterday. What about you? I know you were sold quite a few times."

"There's really not much to tell. After you were sold, Mama was harder on me than ever. It was as if all her attention was split in two my whole life and then it was all focused on me. She was also less affectionate. I suppose she always knew she'd lose her children, but I don't think she knew how hard it was going to be until you were gone. It changed something in her."

"I wish I could have saved her."

"Me too. She'd be so proud of you. Who would have guessed our mama raised a free man?"

"Where'd they put you to work? When I left, you were working in the kitchens."

"Yeah, but I had no talent for food. Mama was scared I'd be doing scullery work my whole life or else get myself in a world of hurt when anyone tasted my cooking. She got me put in your old job in the laundry. Mending clothes and keeping them in order didn't take much talent, just patience. When we were put up for auction, I got sold as a house slave to a family by the name of Driggson. They were decent to me, lived only a few kilometers from the Ellingtons. Old Mrs. Ellington adored Mama, Kale. She had a good life."

It was nice to know she hadn't died someplace horrible.

Mrs. Ellington had seemed nice enough when Kale met her, but it was always hard to tell. "I'm glad. It could have been a lot worse."

"Yeah, it could've. The Driggsons even let me attend the little service the slaves held for her."

"What happened? Why didn't they keep you?"

"After Mama was gone, there was no reason for me to want to stay with them. I was never going to move up in that house, so I made myself invaluable to their cousin whenever he came to visit. I was always assigned to him, and when he made his way in the world, he made an offer for me. That was Mr. Roche. It was a nice situation I'd gotten for myself. I thought I had it all. Then the fool lost me in a game of cards. That one hurt."

Kale grimaced. What kind of man used a valet as good as his brother as stakes?

"The man he lost me to was a bastard. Nickardian was his name. What kind of name is that? Man was mean as fuck. I never did figure him out. There had to have been something wrong in his head. The things he made us do…"

"You don't have to talk about them if you don't want to. I don't mind if you ever want to talk, but you don't need to."

Thomas nodded. "Suffice it to say, I was grateful when he got tired of me and sold me to Conroy. Conroy was slimy, but he wasn't cruel."

"Good morning." Jason strolled in, and Kale's eyes were drawn to the worry lines creasing his face.

Thomas stood as soon as Jason entered, and Kale grabbed his arm and tugged him back down. "How's your father this morning?"

Jason sat and took a sip of his coffee. "He hasn't woken up. Sadie says his heartbeat is losing strength. She'll send for me when he wakes, but it's not likely to happen before this afternoon. What were you two talking about?"

"Comparing masters." Kale wanted to lend Jason encouragement, but decided it was best to honor his request for a change of subject.

"Kale really lucked out getting sold to you, sir."

"I wouldn't say that. I wasn't a good master. The only good thing I did for him was free him, and to be honest, I had selfish reasons for doing it."

"That's not true. You taught me to read, encouraged my art, and didn't beat the daylights out of me the way I deserved."

"No, but if it weren't for me, you would have never been sold—"

"Let's not talk about it. I think we can all agree that I was lucky, and now it's Thomas's turn to be lucky." Kale held Jason's eyes. He felt Thomas's curious stare, but he didn't break eye contact with Jason until he was sure Jason wasn't going to bring up anything he didn't want Thomas knowing.

There was a nearly imperceptible nod of Jason's head before he looked at Thomas. "Of course it is. How are you settling in, Thomas? Must be quite a change to get used to."

"It is, but as far as transitions go, this one's worth the difficulty. Thank you for asking, sir."

"Thomas, I'm your brother's idiot lover. You don't need to call me sir. Please, call me Jason."

Three plates were brought in and set before them. Kale couldn't help the laugh he released as soon as he saw what was on them. "It looks like Darlene has a new pet."

"I should say so." Jason suppressed his laugh and began eating.

Thomas's eyes were both wide with wonder and furrowed with confusion. Each plate was stacked high with pancakes topped with blueberries, strawberries, and whipped cream. A mushroom, bell pepper, onion, and cheese omelet took up one third of the plate, and bacon and sausage took up the remaining third. A bottle of maple syrup was placed on the table.

"I'm glad you're eating with us, Little Brother. If Darlene could have gotten away with just serving you this feast, she would have."

Thomas's eyebrows shot up. "This is for me?"

Kale loved Darlene at that moment. "Yeah. She doesn't cook like this for us."

"Scrambled eggs, toast, some meat, and tomatoes is the most we ever get." Jason poured a liberal helping of maple syrup over his pancakes.

Thomas waited until Kale and Jason had both started to eat before he took a bite. Kale tried to remember the first time he had eaten a real breakfast. His had been poached eggs. That morning had also been the first time Jason had tried oatmeal. The memory prompted him to look at Jason.

"What?" Jason swallowed a bite of pancake.

"Nothing. Just remembering some of the breakfasts we've had."

Jason shook his head and went back to eating. "What are you two going to do today?"

"There's nothing we have to do. Is there anything you need? Anything we can do to make the day easier?"

"No. I'm going to spend all day sitting with my father, so I can be there when he wakes. I don't know how many more chances I'm going to get. There's no need for you to be bored all day just for me."

"You know I don't mind."

"I know. I'm not saying I'm not going to need you—I will —just not for most of the day."

"I was thinking about taking Thomas out and showing him the ranch."

"That'll be good. I'll send someone for you if I need you."

"All right. I also need to call Martin."

"He'll be dying to know how it all worked out. I'm surprised he didn't call here yesterday asking."

"He probably didn't want to bother you. I also wanted to see what he thought about something." Kale left it up to Jason to decide if he wanted to ask what was on his mind. He didn't want to force conversation on him at the moment.

"What?" Jason's eyes showed he was genuinely curious.

"I've been thinking about what we talked about at the Lady Lion before we left. It struck me last night how absurd it is that a man can kill a slave in this country, but not free him. I think that would be a good place to start with the laws."

"A bill that would allow slave owners to emancipate their slaves?"

"Yes. It would have to be approached from the perspective of the owners. A kind of, 'This is my slave, and I can damn well do whatever I want with him, including free him.'"

"That's perfect, Kale."

"What do you think, Thomas?"

Thomas looked up from his plate, clearly having difficulty hiding his surprise at being asked his opinion. "I think it makes sense, but it'll be hard to convince people of it. Free men—especially out in farm country where there are so many slaves—are terrified of slaves conspiring. They don't want us having any hope. Better if we just accept our slavery as an unchangeable fact. You know what Mama said: hoping for freedom is death for a slave."

"You're right. It'll take a lot of work, but I think that it might be possible with the trade agreement coming up for renewal. We can convince the Naiarans that it's an adequate concession, and I think we can sell it as hardly a concession at all to Arinians. We need to see how politicians and the upper class would react to it. That's why I thought I'd ask Martin to toss the idea around. See if he can gauge reaction for us."

"He'll be able to do that. He can even play it off as idle chatter." Jason slipped into a mimic of Martin's proper, exasperated voice. "'So much to do. If only Mr. Wadsworth had been able to stay in the country. Pity he had to move all the way to Naiara just to free his slave. Left me with all his work. A man should be able to free his slave if he wants to without having to move to another country.' That sort of thing."

"I'll call him on our way out." Kale finished his breakfast and pushed his chair back. His stomach hadn't been so full in ages. "You don't have to finish it all, Thomas. No one will be offended. Don't make yourself sick."

"There's no way I'm not sending an empty plate back. I don't want Darlene to think I didn't like it. Maybe she'll do it again tomorrow."

"Even if she doesn't do it again tomorrow, there will still be plenty. You'll have an abundance of food for the rest of your life, and you can eat any time you want."

Thomas reached over and took one of the remaining bites of Kale's pancake and used it to mop up his last bit of syrup. "Done."

"Have a good time. Are you going to be coming back for lunch?"

"Yes, if this one ever gets hungry again. If nothing else, I want to check in."

They all stood and walked together to the stairs. Jason brushed his lips against Kale's and squeezed his hand. "Don't worry about me. I promise I'll let you know when I need you."

"All right. Focus on the good. And don't hesitate to get me. Have someone shoot up a flare, and I'll be back in minutes." Kale watched Jason ascend the stairs. It tore at him, knowing the pain Jason faced. All Kale could offer was his love, and he hoped it would be enough when the time came.

Chapter Thirty-Five

Jason had tried reading, but ended up staring at the pages of his book. Eventually, the weight in his hand grew cumbersome, so he abandoned the pretense. Sadie sewed in the corner. Demetri sat in his chair at the foot of the bed, watching Robert as intently as Jason did. The steady rhythm of Robert's chest rising and falling entranced Jason.

"Is there anything I can do for you, sir?" Demetri asked periodically, clearing the oppressive atmosphere.

Jason shook his head. Robert's labored breathing was the only sound in the room. Over time, it became almost unbearable in its monotonous drone, like the ticking of a clock.

"You love him, don't you?" It was a question Jason had pondered for some time. There was no harm in asking Demetri now.

"Yes, sir."

"Like a father?"

"No, sir."

"More than that?"

Demetri hesitated.

"I'm not asking if you love him more than I do. Do you love him the way I love Kale?"

"Not as intensely, sir, but it's closer to that. More

companionship than passion."

Jason was glad. His father needed someone. "Were you lovers?"

"For a time, but he put a stop to it, sir."

"Why?"

"I was becoming too attached."

"Then why did he keep you?"

"It wasn't a problem of him returning the feeling. He didn't want to hurt me by making me believe I could be anything other than his slave."

"Typical."

"His way of caring for me, sir."

Loyal to the end. Jason had never heard a critical word about his father from Demetri. He doubted anyone had. "Thank you for taking such good care of him. I won't forget it."

"It's been a pleasure, sir."

Silence resumed. Jason's eyes remained riveted on his father's face. It was so different than the face he associated with the man. Hollow shadows took the place of cheeks. Bruise-like circles darkened his eyes. Wrinkles crossed his face, and skin sagged. As a boy, Jason had never thought of his father getting old. As a man, he hadn't cared. As a grieving son, he ached to see his father so frail and weak and mourned the vigor that would never again fill his father's face.

Jason noticed a slight hitch in the rhythm of Robert's breath. Just a cough. They were becoming more frequent, but this one persisted. Robert's eyes fluttered open, and Demetri joined Jason in helping him drink and clear his throat. Demetri wiped the spittle from Robert's chin with a handkerchief.

"Jason?"

"Yes, Father? I'm here." Jason clasped his hand.

"I love you, Son."

"I know. I love you too. I should have said it more."

"Shh. I knew. A father always knows his son." There was

a pause. Jason wondered if he would say anything else. "Demetri?"

"Master?"

"Come here." Jason made room, never loosening his grip on his father's hand. Demetri came to Robert's side, leaned over, and grasped Robert's other hand.

"What can I do for you, sir?"

"Nothing more. You've done enough. I couldn't have asked for a more loyal slave."

"It's been an honor, Master."

"Help Jason and John. They'll need you."

"Of course, sir."

"Jason?"

Demetri knelt at the bedside, still holding Robert's hand, giving Jason space to see Robert's face.

"Yes?"

"Be happy. It's all I ever wanted for you. You've made me so proud. You grew into such a fine man. I couldn't be prouder."

Jason's heart burst. They were the words he had always wanted from his father, but he'd never thought to hear them under such circumstances. Jason would give them back a thousand times if it meant keeping his father. If he tried to speak, he wouldn't be able to control the tears, and he didn't want Robert to see him that way. Instead, he leaned forward and kissed his father's forehead.

"My watch."

Jason didn't know if he heard him correctly, but before he could ask, Demetri was moving. "Here, Master." He placed Robert's open pocket watch in his hand and positioned it where he could see.

"Lena." Robert gazed at the miniature of his wife. A peaceful calm entered his eyes, and they slid shut.

"I love you." It emerged as barely more than a whisper even though Jason wanted to shout it.

Sadie leaned over the bed and felt for his pulse. "He's

gone. I'm sorry."

Jason felt the tears pooling in his eyes and slowly spilling down his cheeks. He took a deep breath, needing to control his voice. "Get Kale."

CHAPTER THIRTY-SIX

"How do you like Jason?" Kale rode slowly alongside Thomas. Kale didn't particularly want to go anywhere. The goal was to be outdoors with Thomas where no one could bother them.

"I don't believe he's as rich as you say he is."

Kale smiled. "I know. No one would ever guess. The money doesn't mean much to him, except that it facilitates us being able to live together without financial stress."

"So what is it you do all day when you're at home? I haven't the least idea what I would spend my time doing if I were free."

"We keep busy. Jason still runs Arlington Steel, though it doesn't take up nearly as much time as it used to. We're both politically active. Jason does a lot of charity work. I manage our household. There's a flower garden and vegetable garden that I tend. I also do art commissions to help out financially."

Thomas's eyebrows shot up. "He makes you earn your own money?"

"No. It's a point of frequent disagreement between us, actually. I don't like him having to take care of me. I didn't become free just to live off another man's money."

"I see they didn't beat the pride out of you."

"They did. It grew back." Kale chuckled.

"Is that what Jason was talking about? When you cut him off earlier?"

Kale realized his mistake. "That was nothing."

"Don't lie to me. I'd expect that from a master, not from my brother."

Kale sighed. It was a part of his life he wasn't proud of. He didn't want Thomas knowing, but honesty was an important part of building trust, and Kale needed Thomas to trust him. "I left out a few years when I was telling you what happened to me."

"I figured that."

"For a few years, I was owned by a labor firm. It's not a big deal."

"Not a big deal? Sure, after being trained and raised to be a valet, I'm sure it wasn't traumatizing as hell to be sold to a place where the average life expectancy for a slave is five to ten years."

"It wasn't that bad."

"I'd bet your back has a different story to tell. Just because you survived doesn't mean it wasn't that bad. What did you do, just shut down your mind?"

"Pretty much."

"When in your story does this fit in? I didn't notice any missing time yesterday."

"It was in the middle of my time with Jason. It didn't quite work out the way I told you."

Thomas grit his teeth, and a red flush crept up his neck. "He sold you to a labor firm? And now you're with him? What kind of twisted relationship are you in?"

"It's not like that."

Thomas didn't let him explain. "I'm going to beat him bloody."

Kale grabbed his horse's reins. "No, you're not. It's in the past. Trust me, the physical pain I underwent is nothing compared to what he did to himself. You're not going to mention a word of it to him. The last thing he needs is old guilt right now. I'm serious, Thomas. If you can't hold your tongue around him, then you turn and walk away when you see him."

"Is that an order?"

Things had turned ugly fast. Kale considered his options. Concern for Jason outweighed his brother's feelings. "Yes. If you need it to be an order for you to follow it, yes."

"So that's how it is?"

"Thomas, he is the best thing that's ever happened to me. He didn't just free me; he saved me. Maybe someday I'll tell you the story, but you won't understand until you fall in love with someone. The past is the past. We both made mistakes, and we paid for them. I won't have you digging up long buried trouble." Kale held eye contact with his brother until he gradually saw the fight leave him.

"I'm sorry. It's just that after everything Mama did for us, everything she taught us, for you to end up as a labor slave tears at my insides. That wasn't supposed to happen."

"It all worked out for the best. I wasn't supposed to end up free either. You take the bad with the good."

Thomas smiled. "Do you remember the time Mama caught you eating blueberries from Monroe's blueberry bushes?"

"Yeah, she took a switch to my backside for it."

"And then you went right back the next day and did it again."

Kale chuckled. "Yeah. What made you think of that?"

"You don't remember what you said to me when I asked you why you did it after you got switched again?"

Kale searched his recollection. The only thing he could remember was the pain of the switching and the taste of those blueberries. "No. What'd I say?"

"You shrugged and said it was worth it, that you take the bad with the good. You figured Mama was going to switch you for something, you might as well get something good out of it."

Kale laughed. "That sounds like me."

"Whatever got you to stop stealing those blueberries?"

"I'd rather not say." That particular incident was vivid in his memory.

"Come on, Kale. I'll tell you one of my secrets."

Kale considered it. It would be worth it to know something more about his brother. "All right. I started hiding them away to eat them all at once. I figured it'd be harder for Mama to catch me if I was careful one time rather than count on her not noticing every day, and I would get the same number of blueberries either way. One day, I ate my whole stash. My stomach got upset, and I crapped purple. Scared me witless. I ran to Mama and told her everything. I thought I was dying. She looked at me real solemn and said the master had found out about it and poisoned them to punish me. She told me the only way to get better was to take castor oil. That stuff was awful. I swore up and down that I would never steal from the master again. I couldn't so much as look at a blueberry for ages after that."

Thomas guffawed. "You really thought the master had poisoned you?"

"You would have too. When I figured it out, I was so mad at her, until I saw what Monroe really did to thieves."

"Yeah, castor oil didn't seem so bad after that."

"No, it did not. Now what secret do you have to share with me? It'd better be good."

Back and forth they reminisced. It surprised Kale the things Thomas remembered that he didn't and the things he could picture so clearly in his mind but Thomas had no recollection of. The easy banter was what Kale had envisioned when he'd dreamt of finding his brother.

Thomas was recounting the time he had fallen in the pond trying to catch a fish when Kale caught a flash of color in the corner of his eye. He whipped his head to the side, startling Thomas into silence. A red flare.

"Jason." Kale took off at a gallop. When he reached the

yard, John and Billy were running toward him. Kale leapt off the horse and threw the reins to Billy. "What's happened?"

John matched him pace for pace as he hurried to the house. "It's Robert. He passed a few minutes ago."

Kale barged in the house and took the stairs two and three at a time. When he burst into Robert's room, he found Jason sitting by the bed holding his father's hand, tears streaming down his cheeks and looking like the faintest touch would shatter him.

Jason made no indication that he heard Kale enter. Only knowing that Jason needed him, Kale knelt beside him, hesitant to touch. Jason appeared to be in shock. "Jason?"

"He's dead, Kale." Jason's face crumbled, and he fell forward out of his chair, his hand slipping from Robert's. Kale caught him and pulled him to his chest, wrapping his arms around him as tight as he could.

"It's all right. Everything's going to be all right."

"No, it's not. I'm never going to see him again."

"You're right. I'm sorry." Jason hadn't been able to fix it when Kale had discovered his mother's death, and Kale couldn't fix this for Jason. "I'm so sorry, Jason."

Tears soaked Kale's shirt. He had never felt so helpless in his life. All he could do was hold Jason as he cried, so that was what he did. He lost all sense of time.

When Jason's sobs quieted to simple tears, John whispered in Kale's ear, "The undertaker's here."

Kale nodded. The last thing Jason needed was to see his father's body taken away. Kale stood, lifting Jason. Immediately, Jason's weight sagged against him. Kale put an arm under his knees and one behind his back, hoisting him up. He wasn't an easy load to carry, but Kale could manage the short distance to their room.

Outside Robert's door, Thomas waited uncertainly. "Is there anything I can do?"

"Ask John what he needs help with. We'll be in our room."

Thomas followed Kale to their room and opened the door for him. "I'm so sorry."

"Thank you, Thomas. He'll be all right. He just needs some time." Kale took Jason to the bed and set him down, not letting him go as he climbed in next to him. The door clicked shut behind them.

Kale didn't know what to say. He simply held Jason and let him cry until he fell asleep.

CHAPTER THIRTY-SEVEN

Jason's breath came in shudders, the same as a baby's after a crying fit. He would only sleep for a few minutes at a time and then wake up, eyes wide with fear, as if a nightmare chased him, and then burst into tears that turned into violent sobs until his body succumbed to sleep again.

Kale reached behind him and tugged on the bell pull. Less than a minute later, a slave knocked and entered. Kale put a finger to his lips to indicate silence and waved the slave over. When he was close enough to hear a whisper, Kale said, "Get me John, please."

The slave left. Kale didn't know what John would be able to do, but he knew he needed help. Too many hours had passed without any improvement. Jason's face looked as distressed in sleep as it did awake. The usual childlike countenance of his slumbering form was gone. Before him was a man who appeared as if Death was chasing him into Hell. Kale worried Jason wouldn't recover.

"You wanted me?" John entered the room.

"Yes. I don't know what to do. He doesn't stay asleep any length of time, and when he is asleep, he's like this." Kale gestured to Jason's twitching body.

"The nurse left a couple of doses of sedative in case we needed it. Said it would knock someone out for several hours.

Let me go get it."

"Thank you."

"It has to be dissolved in a drink. Do you want me to put in a cup of tea?"

"That'll be fine." Kale nodded. He hated to sedate Jason, but he needed to break the cycle.

When John returned with the tea, Jason was still sleeping. Kale hoped, as he did every time, that it would last. "I brought you a cup of tea as well."

"Thanks." Kale made no move for the tea.

"Don't forget that you need to take care of yourself as well."

"I can't do anything until he's sleeping more peacefully. When he wakes, he's in a terror. I can't leave him until he's really resting."

"Do you want me to stay and help you get him to drink it?"

Jason wouldn't want anyone to see him in his current state, but Kale could use the help. He didn't know how easily Jason would drink what was offered him. "Thanks. I don't know how he'll react."

"No need to tell him there's a sedative in it." John pulled the desk chair near the bed and sat.

Kale nodded. Jason's health outweighed honesty.

A few minutes passed before Jason's grip tightened on Kale's shirt. Kale braced himself.

Jason's eyes flew open, pupils dilated, irises darting from left to right too fast for him to be able to see anything. "Kale?"

"I'm here. Shh." He ran his hand through Jason's hair.

Just as before, Jason's face twisted, and his body convulsed with sobs.

"Jason, please calm down."

There was no response.

"Jason, I have some tea here for you. Will you drink it for me? Please?"

Still nothing.

John leaned forward and placed a hand on Jason's arm. Jason whipped his head around, startled by the unexpected touch. "Jason, it's John. Kale and I need you to drink this tea. It'll help you feel better." John held the teacup to Jason's lips.

"Kale?" Jason looked wildly at his companion.

"Yes, Jason. Drink it. Please."

Jason nodded, his eyes still wide with fear. Kale doubted whether any sedative could calm him. Slowly he drank, never loosening his grip on Kale, letting John control the cup.

"You need to drink it all, Jason." John encouraged him when he paused.

Jason sputtered on the last bit and then fell on Kale. The sobbing resumed, but it was less volatile. A few minutes later, he slept.

John rose from his seat and moved to leave. "John, can you check on Thomas for me?"

"No need to. Some of the cows are separated from the herd. He rode out with some of the boys to go search. Is there anything else I can get you?"

"No, thanks. You've been plenty of help. Now we just have to see if it worked." Kale focused all of his attention on Jason. The muscles of his face were relaxing. The shuddering subsided. Ten minutes later, a soft snore escaped Jason's mouth. Kale had never been so grateful to hear the nasally sound. He reached behind him and grabbed the cup of tea John had left for him. Its tepid sweetness tasted better than Kale would have thought possible.

Thirty minutes later, Kale was confident Jason would sleep for at least a couple of hours. He slid out of bed and grabbed the teacups to take with him down to the kitchen. It was still early evening, but the air in the house was dark and still, as if it was far later. Or maybe it was just Kale.

"How's the master doing?" Darlene took the teacups from Kale and steered him into a chair.

"I don't know. He's sleeping now, but I don't know how

237

long it will last. I've never seen him like this."

"It'll pass. Just give it time."

"I hope so, Darlene."

"Let me fix you something to eat. I can have it taken to your room."

"I'd rather eat down here, if you don't mind. I need a break."

"Of course you do. It'll take just a few minutes."

Kale nodded and stood. It took more effort than it should have. He'd hardly been on his feet all day. There was no reason for the difficulty. "I need to make a phone call. When I'm done, I'll come back. I don't want to bother with the dining room tonight."

Kale needed Martin. He didn't know how Jason would feel about him coming, but Kale didn't care. They needed all the help they could get.

"Martin?"

"Kale, what's wrong?"

"Robert passed today."

"Oh, dear saints. How is Jason handling it?"

"Not well."

"How are you?"

"Drowning. All my time is spent taking care of Jason. I'm sure there's plenty that I should be doing, but I can't even think clearly enough to know what needs done."

"You're doing exactly what you need to. Don't worry about anything. I will be on the next train, and I'll take care of everything. You just focus on taking care of Jason and yourself."

"Thanks, Martin. I knew he'd take it hard—you know how Jason is—but this is beyond anything I'd anticipated."

"You can never tell how people will react to this sort of thing. I'd love to chat, but I've got to go if I'm going to get the train tonight. I'll get a cabbie from the station to bring me. It'll probably be early morning when I get there."

Kale was halfway up the stairs before his growling

stomach reminded him he had a date with Darlene. It almost wasn't worth the effort to turn around. When he reached the kitchen, the smell of fresh cornbread permeated the air, and he was glad he had decided to come back. When he sat at the plain kitchen table, Darlene served him a bowl of thick beef stew, a plate of cornbread with slabs of butter, and a tall glass of milk. It was the perfect meal that Kale hadn't even known he wanted.

"Thanks, Darlene. This smells wonderful."

"It tastes even better. You're not leaving this kitchen until it's all gone. I know how Master Jason gets. He hasn't changed that much since he was a boy. When he's distraught, he'll tire out those who care about him. You've got to tread a careful line between helping him and wearing yourself out."

"I can handle it."

"Not looking like the living dead, you can't."

Kale answered by shoving a heaping spoonful of stew into his mouth. It was thick and warm and filled his insides with a comfort only food could provide. It wasn't a struggle to finish every bite.

"You want more?"

"No, thanks."

Darlene cleared away his bowl and plate. Kale needed to get back upstairs to check on Jason, but he had no idea what he should do when he got there. "He survived his mama dying. He'll survive this." Darlene patted his shoulder and sat next to him.

"How did he get through it last time?"

"Well, it's tricky. When you're young, your mama's your whole world, but at the same time, you're so full of life that eventually the urge to live just overwhelms everything else. Young'uns snap back. On the other hand, I'd wager he's feeling his pa's death deeper than he felt his ma's. He knows what it means this time, but he's a man. He'll deal with it."

Kale wasn't so sure. No one felt things as deeply as Jason. His heart didn't know the meaning of half-hearted. Jason's grief could permanently change him. His grief when he'd lost Kale almost had. The only thing that had saved him was Kale's return. There was no such hope in this situation.

"Thanks, Darlene."

"Now you'd better go get yourself some sleep."

"It's still early."

"I don't care what the sun says. I say you need sleep."

"Yes, ma'am." Kale tried to smile but couldn't quite manage it.

Jason was exactly as Kale had left him. The sight of the bed turned Kale's muscles to mush. Darlene was right. He needed to sleep. Better to do it now while Jason was. Kale threw his clothes on the floor and climbed next to Jason. His bedfellow didn't even stir. Whatever had been in his tea had done its job. Kale entwined his legs with Jason's so he would be awakened as soon as Jason moved. Hopefully, Jason would be calm when he woke, but there was no guarantee. Once the sedative wore off, he could go right back to his hysterical sobbing. Medicine may have gotten him to sleep, but it couldn't cure his grief.

CHAPTER THIRTY-EIGHT

A dull throbbing was the only sensation that pierced the fog in Jason's head. The fog obscured something, a different sensation he should be feeling. What had happened?

Kale was with him. He had been with him a lot. There were tears and a hollow feeling in his chest. His father. The nurse's voice floated in the back of his mind. Robert was dead. Jason's father was gone.

Jason's limbs seemed heavy. He opened his eyes and saw the familiar expanse of Kale's chest. Following the line of his body downward, he saw Kale's legs wrapped around his own. That was part of the heaviness. He didn't want to move. He didn't want to think. All he wanted was to close his eyes and go back to sleep. The darkness of his unconscious mind was comforting, welcoming. The protective cocoon of Kale's body didn't allow for movement. Jason relished the restriction, the safety of it. There was nothing to worry about except the painful fullness of his bladder.

His arm moved first, breaking the comfortable stillness that had consumed him. He started to pull his legs from between Kale's, expecting Kale to move and allow him to free himself. Instead, the legs only tightened on his own. He looked up to see Kale staring at him.

"How are you?"

"I didn't mean to wake you."

"You didn't have a choice. How are you?"

Jason paused, considering the question. With anyone else, he would have said fine, but this was Kale. He needed Kale, which meant he had to be honest. It would only cause problems if he wasn't. "I feel better, but I'm also waiting for it to wear off."

Kale pursed his lips. "And what happens when it wears off?"

"I don't know. I'm scared I'm going to fall apart."

Kale pulled Jason's torso to him, holding Jason tight. "Don't be scared. You can be sad, angry, devastated, anything but scared. Every emotion makes sense except that one. You know why?"

Jason shook his head. Fear was so wrapped up inside him that he didn't know how to separate it from all the other emotions.

"Because if you fall apart, I'm going to be here. And you can bet I'm too selfish to let you stay that way. I'll piece you back together. I'm not going to let anything happen to you. Do you believe me?"

There wasn't a good answer. Jason wanted to lie, but if he did, Kale might not be able to help him, and Jason needed someone he could trust. "I don't think you're lying."

"That's not the same thing."

"No, it's not. I want to believe you. I just don't know if I can be helped."

"And every time you've ever thought that before, you were wrong, weren't you?"

Jason thought back through all the times in his life he had almost lost himself. "Yes. You've always made me better before."

"Damn right, and I'll do it again because you're worth it, Jason. You're worth everything I have to give and more. So don't be scared. The only reason to be scared is if you don't trust me. Do you trust me?"

"You know I do."

"Then everything's going to be all right. You do whatever you need to. I'll be here to clean it all up. I won't let you hurt yourself."

Jason noted the omission. "Don't let me hurt you either."

"I can handle it. Whatever you can dish out, I can take."

"No. No deal. You don't let me hurt you, if for no other reason than I could never forgive myself afterward." Jason knew from experience that Kale would tolerate any abuse Jason hurled at him if he thought it would help. It was a part of Jason's past he was unwilling to relive.

"Fine. I promise I won't let you hurt me either."

"Good." Jason moved to get up, but Kale restrained him.

"Where are you going?"

"I need to pee, if that's all right with you." If he waited much longer, he'd have to walk to the toilet with his legs crossed.

Kale released Jason's legs. "Yes, you have my permission."

Jason smiled, but it went no further than his lips. It felt like a lie. Nothing inside of him—no emotion—supported the smile, but he wanted to at least pretend he could be normal again. In the bathroom, he didn't have to feign his relief at relieving his bladder. It was the most positive thing he had felt since his father died.

"I called Martin. He's on his way."

Jason rummaged around the wardrobe for a change of clothes. The ones he had on were wrinkled beyond recognition. "You didn't have to bother him."

"He wasn't bothered, Jason. We need him here, and he's happy to help. He would have been offended if we hadn't called him."

"I suppose you're right." Martin would be invaluable. This was precisely the type of situation in which he shone. Jason's only objection was that he didn't want to make his problems someone else's. Martin had shouldered enough of Jason's problems over the years.

"What are you doing?"

Jason unbuttoned his shirt. "Are you monitoring my every movement now?"

"Yes. Get used to it."

"I'm getting dressed so I can go downstairs."

"And then?"

"Then I will eat, if it pleases you."

"I can have a tray brought up. You don't have to go anywhere."

"I know." Jason was about to say he wanted to, but it wasn't true. "It seems like the prudent thing to do."

"I don't want you thinking you need to do anything for anybody. If you want to go downstairs, that's great, but don't do it because you think you owe it to anyone to make an appearance."

Jason shrugged into his new shirt and began buttoning. "I just want a little normalcy before I break down again." It was coming. Jason could sense it on the edges of his mind. Once the fog rolled away, there would be nothing numbing his grief, and it would assault him again. The only uncertainty was whether it would be as powerful as before.

Kale joined Jason in dressing. "Good. There's a beef stew in the kitchen that'll make you want to take Darlene home with us."

Darlene. What would happen to her now that his father was dead? Jason supposed she belonged to him. He could take her home if he wanted, cart her off like a memento. It was impossible to imagine the ranch without her. She was as much a part of it in his mind as the house itself. There couldn't be one without the other. "That sounds good."

Jason went through the motions. He finished dressing, went downstairs, navigated to the dining room without thinking, and ate what was put before him. He wanted to taste it, but he couldn't. The stew seeped warmth into his body, but little else. The meat and potatoes sat heavy in his stomach. The cornbread was sawdust in his mouth. Dutifully, he ate until there was nothing left. Stand, walk, climb stairs, open door. His body seemed to move without any input from him.

"What do you want to do now?" Kale was behind him with both hands on Jason's shoulders.

The fog was almost gone. Grief and pain rushed in. Jason longed for a drink, for the respite of losing himself in the alcohol, for a bottle to carry him away from himself. Those were dangerous thoughts. A drink was out of the question while he was in this state. He wouldn't put Kale through that again. But there was an alternative. "Sleep. I want whatever it is you gave me earlier."

"I'll have to see if there's anymore. Get undressed and into bed. I'll be back." Kale started for the door, stopped, and came back to Jason, giving him a brief kiss. Without another word, he turned and left.

It was always the little gestures that reminded Jason how lucky he was to have Kale. Jason disposed of his clothes in an orderly fashion and took his spot on the bed. The emptiness of the room crowded in. Without Kale to talk to or hold, he was left with only his mind, and it was a place that scared him. He tried to concentrate on the clock on his bedside table. The steady movement of the second hand tormented him with how effortlessly it passed time while he struggled just to stay inside his own head.

He changed his mind. He didn't want the sedative. He wanted Kale. If only he would come back. The pressure built. He didn't want to break, not now, not without Kale. If he let enough of a crack form to let the tears flow, he would burrow inside the misery, wrap it around himself like a blanket, and get lost in it.

The door opened. Jason's head whipped toward the sound, his eyes searching out Kale's face. They frantically darted around, not able to focus on any one thing. Two hands on the sides of his face, forcing him still. Two pale green eyes locking on his, not letting him see anything else.

"Jason, it's all right. I'm here."

Shivers coursed through his body. Their source was a mystery. "Did you get the sedative?"

"Yes. It's the last dose. Darlene's going to send it up in a cup of tea like last time." Kale toed off his shoes and lay with Jason, crushing their bodies together so close that Jason's shivering ceased. "Try to relax. If you need to cry, do it. You'll feel better afterward."

Jason shook his head. "I won't be able to stop."

"I doubt that. Go ahead and try."

Tears already fell from his eyes. Jason held his breath, attempting to constrain them. When the air finally forced its way from his lungs, he couldn't hold back his cries any longer. He buried his face in Kale's chest and let it all out.

His father was dead. His father, who had always loved him, who had given him Kale, who he had only just begun to know. He was gone. There would be no more opportunities, no more chances to talk. A lifetime of memories of Jason and his mother had died. There was so much still to learn from his father, so much to share with him.

Kale's hand rubbed soothing circles on his back, but it felt so far away. "You're all right, Jason. I'm here."

Those simple words were more comforting than Jason would have thought possible. The mere notion that he wasn't alone was enough to give him some measure of hope, however small. Kale pulled away, and Jason followed, tightening his grip.

"Jason, the tea is here." He hadn't heard anyone enter the room—or exit for that matter. "Do you want it now, or do you want to cry some more?"

"Now." Jason's abdomen ached. Physically, he was exhausted, but he wouldn't be able to quiet his mind long enough to sleep without help.

The tea was warm and sweet. The act of drinking it calmed him. Once it was gone, he settled against Kale, allowing the drug to do its work. There was no reason to cry.

Soon he would be in a dreamless sleep. When he woke, he would be able to face the day. He had to be.

CHAPTER THIRTY-NINE

Something niggled at Kale's mind. It was too dark to see the clock, but he guessed, given the stillness of the house and how much sleep he felt he'd had, that it was three or four o'clock in the morning. He hadn't wakened naturally. Something had pulled him from sleep. Jason appeared fine, snoring in Kale's arms. His grip had relaxed around Kale, his posture no longer revealing deep desperation.

Not able to shake the feeling that something was amiss, Kale went downstairs. Everything appeared normal. In the kitchen, he found what he hadn't even known he was looking for. Sitting at the table was Martin, eating biscuits and drinking a glass of milk with Darlene across from him.

"I found this one wandering around outside. Will you believe he tried to go to bed without eating anything first? I set him straight on how things work around here. City folk always underestimate the value of a full stomach before bed."

"Martin! When did you get in?" Kale strode to the table, hand outstretched.

Martin stood to shake his hand, but as soon as Martin's hand was in his, Kale pulled the man into a hug. After a pat on the back, he pulled away and sat, gesturing for Martin to do the same.

"Just a few minutes ago. I called and spoke to a man

249

named John before I boarded the train to let him know when I would arrive. He said someone would be waiting for me."

"I was going to be up soon to start cooking anyway, so I told John I'd get him settled."

"Thanks, Darlene. Are you normally up this early?"

"No, but with the viewing, there's going to need to be a lot of food on hand. It's not too early to start preparing."

"The viewing. I hadn't even thought about that."

"Nor should you." Martin wiped his mouth with a napkin and took a drink of milk. "That's what I'm here for. There's absolutely nothing you need to concern yourself with other than Jason and taking care of yourself. How is he doing?"

"He's sedated again. I don't know how he'll react to seeing his father's body. He's so lost in his grief I can assure you he hasn't thought about the viewing or funeral. When is it all going to happen?"

"I confirmed with this John fellow that the viewing will be tomorrow and the funeral the day after. It's customary for there to be a private viewing the night before, so Robert's body will be brought here tonight. It'll give Jason a chance to pay his respects without the stress of having everyone else around."

"Just how many people are we planning on having at the viewing?"

"I suppose a couple hundred. They'll be coming in throughout the day from all over the county." Darlene pulled bowls down from the cupboards.

"A couple hundred?"

"The master was a well-known and influential man. He didn't have close friends outside of this ranch, but there'll be plenty of people who'll be stopping by."

Strangers parading through the house and Jason having to stand and greet them all, accept their meaningless condolences. The whole thing was dreadful. "If you're ready, I can take you up to your room, Martin."

"I suppose I should get a few hours of sleep before I

start. Thank you for the warm welcome, Darlene."

"My pleasure, sir. Kale, we've prepared the room on the other side of Thomas's for him."

"Did Thomas come back today?"

"He rode in with the others in time for a late dinner. Looked like he had a good time from the way they all were talking. They found every one of the cows."

Kale nodded. It was a relief not to have to worry about his brother. "Do you have any luggage, Martin?"

"Just this." Martin held up a small valise. "I didn't have time to pack properly. Sophie's coming later with the rest of my things."

"Good. Jason'll be happy to see her." Kale led the way. Martin's room was almost identical to Thomas's except with yellow accents instead of blue. "Thanks again for coming."

"There's nowhere else I'd rather be. Go get some sleep. Don't worry about entertaining me. I've got plenty to do and no trouble getting it done myself."

Jason was still asleep when Kale returned. The sheets were smooth, no signs of distress or fitful sleeping. Encouraged, Kale allowed himself to hope that Jason just might make it through the next few days. With Martin's help, Jason would only need to show up. Soon, Kale could take Jason home and begin the process of helping him mend.

CHAPTER FORTY

The kitchen bustled with slaves. Jason hadn't spent much time in there since he'd tried to sneak treats past Darlene as a child. He would tiptoe in, as quiet as a little boy knew how to be, and reach into the cookie jar or sneak a pastry right off the cooling rack. Before the kitchen door even closed behind him, he would run as fast as his little legs would carry him, fist held high, flaunting his victory. Watching Darlene run her kitchen, Jason had no doubt he had never truly gotten away with anything.

This morning had been better. The grief was muted, as if dulled by the profuse crying the previous day. Better was the wrong word. It was more manageable. At least he could function without breaking into tears.

When Kale asked him what he wanted to do, Jason had immediately known he wanted to be in the kitchen. He supposed it was because the kitchen was the one place in the house that held no memories of his mother or father. It was also busy, providing him with plenty to observe in his effort to not retreat into himself. He sat at the kitchen table, an untouched book in front of him, watching Kale knead dough. It was pleasant watching Kale do just about anything. The effort he put into his task, the flex of his muscles, the lines his body formed, it was all the best distraction Jason could ask for. He finally understood why Kale had liked the kitchen all these years.

Kale continually slipped glances in Jason's direction. Each time, Jason mustered as much of a smile as he could: a little lift of his lips so Kale would know that he was present and aware. There was nothing Kale could do, no action he could take that would chase away the pain. Jason had no doubt in his mind that if there was, Kale would do it, no matter what it entailed. This way, Kale had something he could do, a physical task that yielded a tangible result. Jason could give him that.

The day passed in a blur. Jason only moved to eat or use the bathroom. Kale kept busy in the kitchen, and Jason assured him there was nothing else he'd rather be doing. Martin entered several times to talk to Darlene or Kale. Jason was glad to see Martin. Or at least, he thought he was. He didn't really feel any different, but he knew logically that having Martin present was a good thing. If the circumstances had been different, he might have pondered why it was that he could feel such intense pain but not the simple pleased feeling he knew must accompany Martin's arrival. However, it involved too much thinking, and thinking was something best avoided at the moment.

At some point, Sophie had arrived. He'd managed a smile for her as he did for Kale. The slight blonde woman was a welcome sight. She worked well with Darlene, submitting to the slave's authority in her domain. Kale spoke frequently with Sophie, teasing her about her beau and catching up on lost time. A part of Jason wished he could join in, but what would he say? "How's your life going, Sophie? I just lost my father and have no idea if I'll ever be normal again?" His presence in the conversation would only make it awkward.

Jason couldn't stay in the kitchen forever. All too soon, he had to leave. He didn't want to. He knew what awaited him. Martin appeared and murmured to Kale, both of them casting worried looks at him. It was time, then. His father's body had arrived.

Kale approached Jason once Martin had left. Jason stood and spared him having to find the words. "I know."

"You don't have to do anything you don't want to."

"Nonsense. It's my duty. I owe him the respect. You know I'd hate myself if I didn't have this closure. Besides, I won't be able to avoid it tomorrow, and if I'm going to make a scene, I'd rather it not be with strangers in the house."

Kale nodded. "Whenever you're ready."

Jason had been dreading this all day, steering his thoughts away from it with the distraction of the activity around him. Jason didn't have the least idea how he'd react to seeing his father. There was slight solace in believing it couldn't possibly be worse than what had already happened.

Jason reached out for Kale's hand. Once their fingers were intertwined, Jason took a deep breath and left the kitchen.

The open casket was visible from the parlor doorway. Yellow flowers surrounded it, and Demetri stood behind, his eyes lowered. Custom dictated that the body never be left alone. The body. When Jason reached the casket, he was surprised at how peaceful his father appeared. He was dressed in one of his finest suits. The expression on his face was relaxed and smooth. To see his father before him, so still and serene, was eerie. Without life animating his body, Jason didn't know what to make of it. How was he supposed to feel? He didn't know whether seeing his father should console him or upset him. Mostly, it made him long for the last few days, the days when he and his father had been able to talk, to even play cards with Kale, to joke and laugh and reminisce. He longed for the father he had never known as a child. He longed for the man his mother had loved. He longed to reach a place where his father was a happy memory in his heart that he could carry everywhere.

Jason let go of Kale's hand and placed both of his on the casket. Fine craftsmanship. Whoever had arranged for it had spared no expense. Jason appreciated that. His father deserved the best, even though he would have hated it. "Why spend so much money on a box you're going to bury?" he'd say. "What use is it to a dead man?" he'd reason. Jason smiled. He could still hear his father's voice clearly in his mind. He knew from experience that someday it would fade until he could no longer remember it, until all he had was the memory of a memory. He wanted to hold onto it forever, to preserve his father's image. But it was all destined to fade away.

Jason reached into the casket to hold his father's hand and touch his forehead. The absence of life beneath his hands was noticeable. He leaned down and placed a kiss on his father's cheek, the same way he had as a boy when his mother was still alive and his father would come home after a day's work outside. "I love you. Say hello to Mother for me." The words were so soft, Jason barely heard them himself. He straightened and looked at Demetri. "Thank you for all you've done. I know I've been no help."

"No need, sir. It's my duty, and Mr. Grimlock has shouldered most of the work."

"You've been a credit to your master."

"Thank you, sir."

"You should go get some rest. We have a long day tomorrow."

"Excuse me, sir, but I'd like the honor of being the one to keep vigil tonight. It should be someone close to him, and you need your rest to greet everyone at the viewing."

Demetri was right. The thought of someone else taking the responsibility was irksome. A strong sense of kinship with his father's valet washed over him. Demetri must be at a loss. Like Jason, he had nothing to do. The master he had served no longer had need of him, except in this last act of devotion. "Of course you may. If John would like to relieve you, let him. He's the only other person who can lay claim to the responsibility. You need your sleep like the rest of us."

"Thank you, sir."

Jason rejoined his hand with Kale's and walked to their room. On the way, it struck him that Demetri had called him sir when the proper address was master. The will hadn't been read yet, but it was natural to assume that Jason now had ownership over him. There was something honorable in Demetri, who always followed protocol, refusing to transfer the title of master to another man before Robert was buried. It was a loyalty Jason admired and that he once again gave thanks for. It was a comfort to know that while his father had surrounded himself with few men, the ones he had chosen were worthy of him.

"What can I do for you, Jason?" Kale's voice reminded him that he had somehow lucked out the same way his father had. The Wadsworth men eschewed quantity in favor of quality when it came to the people in their lives.

Jason looked at Kale and saw in his eyes an unadulterated love for him. For the first time since his father had died, he knew he was going to be all right.

"Read to me, please. Let me lie with my eyes closed and just listen to you."

Jason allowed Kale's voice, the voice of a man whose fidelity was absolute, to chase out the dreary thoughts that threatened to creep into his mind. Peace followed the gentle realization that the way to mourn his father was not to lament the past, but to honor him by accepting the love of those around him.

Chapter Forty-One

The people started arriving around ten o'clock. Kale was wary of this idea from the beginning. He didn't understand why Jason was obligated to accommodate these strangers. Inevitably, Jason ended up reassuring and comforting the people who offered condolences. It was ridiculous.

"You need to sit." Kale had stood by Jason all morning.

"I need to greet everyone. I'm fine."

"No, you're not. I'm going to get you a chair." Kale pulled one of the simpler chairs in the room over to where Jason stood by the open casket. "Sit, or I carry you out of here right now."

"You wouldn't."

"Really? What in our history leads you to believe I won't do what's best for you regardless of what others may think?" Kale stared into Jason's worn eyes. The man's face was drawn. If Jason could see what Kale did, he wouldn't put up such a fight. As much as Kale wished Jason would decide to follow Kale's advice for his own good, he knew Jason relenting had more to do with the group of people accumulating behind Kale as he stalled the proceedings. As soon as Jason was seated, Kale pulled another chair next to him and joined him.

Refreshments were served in the sitting room. The mourners lingered about, chatting. Kale had no idea what they could be talking about. Probably gossiping. He doubted any of these people had spent enough time with Robert to be reminiscing.

The only break Jason took was to eat and only then because Kale had Darlene's support. Despite how foolish Kale thought this all was, he was proud of Jason and understood his desire to keep going until all the mourners were gone. It was like when Kale had worked laying rail. His muscles would burn, and everything in him would ache for a break, but he knew if he were granted one or let up for a bit, it would be nearly impossible to start again. Better to steel himself and forge ahead until the work was done.

Voices raised in anger floated into the parlor, muffled by the walls. Jason looked up from the woman he was greeting. Kale placed his hand on Jason's leg, giving a light squeeze to indicate he'd take care of it, and stood. The commotion was coming from outside.

In the driveway, John stared down a red-faced James Cartwright and his son Carter, as well as Mrs. Cartwright and Carter's three younger sisters. "Mr. Cartwright, I won't be telling you again. You're not welcome here." John's voice was strong and steady. He stood calmly with his arms crossed in front of him and his feet planted shoulder-width apart. Kale didn't think a bull would dare try to get past him.

There was no hesitation in Kale's gait as he approached. Jason had decreed that he didn't want the Cartwrights to attend. The gesture touched Kale even though he knew it wasn't just for his benefit. Jason wanted to avoid an altercation, and he didn't trust himself around Kale's previous owner. As far as Kale was concerned, anything that kept more people out and kept the day as short as possible was fine by him.

Mr. Cartwright seemed to search for a reply. From his flushed face, it appeared he had already gone several rounds with John, who didn't look at all ruffled. Kale took his place at John's shoulder, crossing his arms over his chest. John didn't even spare him a glance. Mr. Cartwright, on the other hand, sneered at Kale. "And what do you think you're doing, slave?"

Maybe it was fatigue, maybe it was the instinct to protect Jason from people he didn't want to see, and maybe he was just fed up with being scared of people who could do him no harm. Whatever the reason, Kale raised his chin and stared Mr. Cartwright straight on. "You heard him. I wouldn't test him if I were you."

Mrs. Cartwright shrieked from where she stood, her small frame dwarfed by her husband. "So it is true. The Wadsworths are letting their slaves behave like free people now."

Kale met her wide, ice-blue eyes. "Ma'am, you may gawk at me all you like, but you will have to do it off of Wadsworth property. Jason does not want you here."

Mrs. Cartwright's hand connected with Kale's cheek. It wasn't as painful as it was humiliating. Kale tried to cool the heat flooding his face and gave thanks that it was Mrs. Cartwright who had struck him. If it had been either of the men in her family, he didn't think he'd be able to prevent himself from striking back. The last thing he needed was to cause a scene. Or more of one, at least.

"How dare you!" Mrs. Cartwright's voice was indignant as only a country biddy's could be.

"I'm sorry you're offended, Mrs. Cartwright, but this is a private affair, and your family will have to leave."

"Don't talk to my wife like that, boy."

Kale could only assume he meant that Kale shouldn't be talking to his wife at all, and certainly not with his head raised, looking her in the eye.

Mr. Cartwright leaned in close enough that Kale could smell his foul breath. Before either of them could say a word, John appeared between them. Kale momentarily resented the man for interfering, but it only made sense. If it came to blows, there would be unneeded complications if Kale was

261

involved.

"Any problems here, John? It looks like we've got some hot tempers."

Kale was surprised by the unfamiliar voice. He looked behind Cartwright and saw a middle-aged man he didn't recognize with a woman on his arm.

"We were just helping Mr. Cartwright and his family find their buggy, Sheriff."

"I have the right to pay my respects to one of my oldest friends."

"Not if Jason says you don't." Kale kept his voice as cool as possible.

"And who is this?" The sheriff nodded to Kale.

"The slave Robert bought off me for his son."

"I'm not a slave. I'm Jason Wadsworth's partner." Kale kept his eyes trained on James Cartwright.

"You lying—"

"John?" The sheriff's voice overrode Mr. Cartwright, silencing him.

"It's like he said. Kale's family, Sheriff. We're just trying to follow Mr. Wadsworth's orders."

"Well, then, it looks pretty simple to me. James, why don't you take your family home? If you need an escort, I'd be happy to oblige." The sheriff's tone gave the distinct impression that he'd "escorted" certain members of the Cartwright family numerous times throughout the years.

James turned away, muttering under his breath and gestured for his family to follow. None of them had any problem sneering at Kale before they walked away, even the youngest who couldn't possibly remember the time when her family had owned Kale. He had never seen so much ugly in one place.

"Thanks for the help, Rich." John shook the sheriff's hand.

Kale didn't move until the Cartwright's buggy was on its way down the drive. It was the first time he'd ever felt superior for being able to afford a car. Such sentiments were usually beneath him, but maybe just this once it was all right.

When he was satisfied, he turned to Rich and held out his hand. "Thank you for your help, Sheriff."

"Not a problem. I learned early on that I would never truly be off-duty." Rich didn't hesitate before shaking Kale's hand, despite what he had just learned about his past.

"If you'll excuse me, I've got to get back to Jason. I trust John can see you inside." Kale nodded to John and then headed back to the parlor. When he sat next to Jason, Kale gave him a smile and rested his hand on Jason's knee. That seemed to be all the information Jason needed on the subject.

At six o'clock, the insanity ended. Kale didn't know whether the people had ceased coming or if someone was stopping them. Or maybe it was general knowledge that viewings ended at six just as it appeared to be general knowledge that social rules dictated one went to a viewing even if one did not know the deceased by any more than reputation. At least the funeral would be a private affair.

"Where is everyone?" Jason seemed bewildered.

"There's no one left. It's all over. You did well."

"Thank the gods." Jason slumped against Kale. "I thought they would never stop."

"I know. I'm so proud of you. If the urge to throw everyone out was even half as strong in you as it was in me, I'm impressed by your restraint. The only thing holding me back was knowing you'd never forgive me."

"Thanks for being here for me."

"Of course. Where else would I be?"

Martin entered. "Shall I allow the slaves in now to pay their respects?"

"Yes." Jason stood.

"You can keep your seat. No one expects anything of you. It's been a long day." Jason had done so well, Kale didn't want him to push himself too hard.

"No, Kale, let me show them respect. At least these

people knew him."

The slaves filed past Robert's coffin. Kale noted that there was hardly a dry eye among them. Each offered heartfelt condolences to Jason, honoring him as the son of their esteemed master. It was the only sensible thing that had happened all day. Kale felt for these men and women. Their grief was real, and they had no comfort, only uncertainty for the future.

After the last of the slaves left, only Kale, Jason, Demetri, John, and Martin remained. "It's time to seal the casket. Everyone should pay their last respects."

Kale approached first, since he was the least close to Robert. "Thank you for giving him the best parts of yourself." Kale struggled against the unexpected lump in his throat as he prepared to say the words he had wanted to say to Robert in life. "Thank you for giving me to him." It washed over Kale in that moment how much he owed the man in the casket. He turned his mind away from the dark trail his life could have taken had Robert not intervened. There was only one way to thank him. "I'll take care of him for you." Promise made, he stood back, giving the others a bit of privacy. John went next and then Demetri. Jason was last. He spent a few minutes whispering to his father then stepped backward.

"Demetri? Do you have his pocket watch?"

"Yes, sir. I brought it in case you wanted it." Demetri stepped forward and handed it to Jason.

Jason opened it and looked at the picture of his mother. Kale stepped to him, placing a hand on his back as a tear fell down Jason's cheek. Jason kissed the picture and closed the watch. Tenderly, he placed it on Robert's chest and wrapped both of his hands around it. "You finally have your Lena back." Jason stepped away and nodded to Martin.

Kale wrapped his arm firmly around Jason's shoulders as Martin closed the casket. He wished they could have the funeral now and let it all be over with, but this was the way it was done. The casket would sit sealed in the house for the night and be buried in the morning.

Sophie joined them as they all ate together in the dining room. Kale took great comfort in her presence. She had helped him and Jason through many a tough time. While Martin provided practical support, Sophie provided the emotional. Talking to her in the kitchen the previous day had been such a welcome respite. Somehow, she made everything seem so simple. Her encouragement made Kale believe they would get through this.

Jason insisted Demetri eat with them. Kale knew it had to be uncomfortable for him. Demetri would never disobey an order, but it was plain to see that this went against everything he knew. Eventually, he relaxed when it was apparent that no one expected him to join in the conversation.

There wasn't much conversation anyway. A drowsy air hung in the room. Each other's presence was enough. It communicated all that needed to be said. They sat in a silent bond of love and support. Kale caught Jason stealing occasional looks at his father's vacant chair, his eyes more wistful than pained. Thomas sat to Kale's right. Kale had barely seen him all day. It must be uncomfortable for him, not really having a place in the household. Kale patted his brother on the back, getting him to look up from his plate. Once he had Thomas's eye, he smiled and was glad to see him readily return it. Knowing he had a brother's support was an unfamiliar source of comfort.

It was a motley crew that sat around the table. John and Martin had readily earned each other's respect. They seemed so different, but they both possessed a strong work ethic and keen sense of loyalty. Martin and Sophie had both fit right in as soon as they arrived. Darlene had been invited to join them, but she had huffed about it not being right and needing to supervise the kitchen. Even so, it had been easy to see the gesture meant something to her.

After it was clear no one would be eating anything else,

Jason stood. "Thank you all. Somehow the grief is made lighter by knowing I do not carry it alone. I wish you all a good night and invite you to breakfast with me tomorrow morning before the service." Jason's gaze rested on Demetri before he stepped around the table to leave. Kale followed.

"You were exceptional today. I don't think I've ever been so proud." Kale helped Jason undress in their room.

"I'm just glad it's over."

"I know. Do you think you'll be able to sleep tonight?"

"Yes. I'm more tired than I've ever been. I don't know how my father managed it when my mother died, and he had me running around. The thought of caring for a child during something like this makes my head spin."

Kale kissed Jason's neck and took him to bed. "Then it's a good thing we don't have kids."

"That wasn't my point."

"I know. People rise to what's expected of them. In this case, you rose to your own expectations. If it was up to me, you would have spent the day wrapped in my arms, the rest of the world be damned."

"Hmm. I didn't know that was an option." Jason yawned. His eyes were already closed, and he snuggled in close to Kale.

"It always is." Kale's words were drowned out by Jason's snore. Kale smiled into Jason's hair and relaxed. They were going to be just fine.

CHAPTER FORTY-TWO

The funeral was small. Intimate. Even with the casket and chairs, they all fit nicely into the parlor. Mr. Garrity, Robert's attorney, was there both as a mourner and to ensure Robert's wishes were honored. Robert's requests for the funeral had been simple. Mr. Garrity read a letter Robert had written for the occasion. John said a few words; a prayer was uttered. Robert could never be accused of being a religious man. However, it was tradition and certainly couldn't do any harm.

Jason knew he should listen, but he only lent half an ear to the proceedings. He was focused on the feel of Kale's hand in his, the presence of the people in the room, all of whom depended on him in some form or another. His eyes never strayed far from the casket. The man who had built all this, who had brought these people together, lay at peace within it. Now, Robert had passed the mantle to Jason. It was a heavy weight, but one Jason wanted to take pride in carrying. He was a Wadsworth. Never had that name meant more to him than it did this day. He wondered how it must have felt for Kale the day Jason had given the name to him. Kale always seemed proud of it. Jason had taken it for granted his entire life. It was only a name, but it was a piece of his father that had been passed down to him. It was a standard of principles, of ethics, of character that was Jason's to live up to.

Kale stood. Looking around, Jason saw that John, Demetri, Mr. Garrity, and Martin were all approaching the casket. It was time then.

Jason hefted the weight onto his shoulder. The double doors leading to the backyard were opened, and together they carried his father out into the sunlight. The morning dew lent a fresh scent to the air. Jason squinted against the pale blue light until his eyes adjusted. Around him was everything his father loved. Thick green grass cushioned their steps. The men his father had trusted walked beside him, shouldering the same burden as Jason. They walked in step together, solemn and reflective. At that moment, carrying his father to his final resting place, Jason's heart swelled. Robert had been a great man, who left Jason an amazing legacy. The grief of the last few days receded. His father was being laid to rest with his wife and baby girl. If he hadn't fallen ill, then Jason would have never been able to reconcile with him. It could have been so much worse. Jason had made peace with Robert. He could ask for nothing more.

Slowly, they lowered the casket into the ground. Again a prayer was said, and the ground was blessed. It had been consecrated by his father's sweat, tamed by his hand to provide for a family. This was his father's land, and it would welcome him in death. Jason shoveled dirt onto the casket and watched as the others followed him. After they had each taken a turn, a slave continued to fill in the grave. Jason watched each shovelful of dirt land. He let his desperation, his fear, and his worries be buried with his father. He wanted to bury his grief as well, but it wouldn't do any good. The goal wasn't to hide his grief away; it was to work through it and diminish it by continuing what his father had started.

"How are you doing?" Kale's soft voice was a contrast to the steady thump of the dirt landing in the grave, the birds chirping in the trees, and the cows mooing in the distance that had lulled Jason into an almost trancelike state.

"Good. Better than I thought." Jason looked up from the grave to show Kale his face, that he meant it. He was surprised to see that everyone else had returned indoors. "I'm glad he's here with my mother and Lydia, that he'll always be here on this land he loved so much." Jason admired the memorials at the other two gravesites. Baby Wadsworth was marked with a cherub carved out of granite, little wings much too small to be of any use to the chubby baby. A tall, gorgeous angel peering down with such a look of tenderness and concern that it seemed completely lifelike stood at the head of his mother's grave. Soon, Jason would choose a memorial to place at his father's site.

"I heard you thinking inside. Did it help?"

"Yes. I feel like I've received some closure today. I can move forward."

"I'm glad. I honestly didn't know for a while how you would do."

"Me either. This is such a peaceful place. The weather is perfect. It's a beautiful day. I don't know how this could have gone better. I was worried that I'd be so distraught that it would be difficult to visit his grave in the future. Instead, I'll be able to remember this peaceful feeling I have right now any time I see it."

"That's wonderful, Jason. I couldn't wish anything better for you." Kale raised their joined hands to his lips for a gentle kiss.

"If only you had the same." Kale didn't have any place to visit to remember his mother, much less a place as nice as this. He deserved better. "When I order the memorial for my father, I want you to order one for your mother. We'll place it here in the family plot. That way, you have a place to come to in order to reflect on her life and honor her memory."

Kale took a deep breath, prompting Jason to look away from his family's graves and focus on Kale. His eyes were misty. "I'm honored, Jason, and incredibly grateful for the offer and the gesture, but are you sure? This is your family's plot."

"And you're my family. She brought you into the world, and I'm in her debt for it. This is the least I can do. She deserves it. She was your mother and a human being who should be respected and afforded dignity in death, even if she wasn't in life."

"Thank you." Kale's voice was husky. Jason squeezed his hand and looked into his eyes, trying to communicate as much love as he could through his gaze.

After a silent moment, Jason tugged on Kale's hand. "Let's go inside. Sophie and Darlene have prepared a luncheon, and I don't want to appear ungrateful, especially when I have so much to be grateful for at the moment." Side by side, they walked to the house. Inside his chest was a hollowness Jason knew would never go away. He would simply learn to live with it. As time marched onward, he would build new memories, share new experiences, build up his love with Kale, until the hole seemed tiny due to the sheer magnitude of what surrounded it.

CHAPTER FORTY-THREE

The smell of coffee was enough to perk Kale up after the luncheon. There had been too much food and not enough self-control on his part. His stomach was beyond full. The notion that he would need to make room for the coffee was almost unthinkable, but he needed the drink to keep him alert and free from the clutches of after-meal fatigue.

They were all together in the dining room. Kale had taken the seat on Jason's left because he was unwilling to let go of his hand when they had come in from the gravesite. Jason's offer to memorialize his mother had overwhelmed Kale. In all his years, he had never been more humbled. It was more than he had ever known to hope for.

"Do you have the will with you, Mr. Garrity?" Jason broke the comfortable silence that had settled over the room as everyone drank their coffee.

"Yes, sir, but we certainly don't need to dispense with it now if you're not up for it."

"Thank you, but I'd like to go ahead and get it over with, if you don't mind. There's no sense dragging you out here again."

Mr. Garrity rose to fetch the will from his briefcase. Demetri took the opportunity to stand as well.

"Where are you going, Demetri? I want you to stay here."

Reluctantly, Demetri sat, trying valiantly to hide his discomfort. Poor fellow. Kale could only imagine how awkward he must feel. Thomas, who sat in Kale's normal spot across from Jason, appeared to have accepted that his presence was desired, but that nothing was expected of him. The twinge of discomfort on his face was due to overeating. Kale wondered how long it would take him to realize he would never go without a meal again.

The will was short and straightforward. Robert had no family other than Jason. He left twenty percent of the business to John and everything else to Jason with an entreaty to care for the people who depended on the ranch. There were no surprises, though John seemed a little surprised that he had been left such a large ownership stake. Kale was amazed he hadn't been left more, especially given the very little faith Robert placed in his son to manage the business.

"It will take some time for the will to make its way through the courts, but seeing as there are no creditors and no one who could pose any serious claim to the estate, I don't anticipate any problems."

"Thank you, Mr. Garrity. If I may intrude upon your time for a while longer, there's something I wanted to discuss with all of you." Mr. Garrity nodded, and Jason continued. "As most of you know, Kale and I are somewhat politically active in Naiara. We've made some good friends there, and seeing as we live right outside the capital, a good many of those friends are quite influential. The treaty regulating trade between Arine and Naiara is up for renewal soon. There is a strong movement in Naiara pushing the government to discontinue trade with Arine as long as the institution of slavery is still practiced here."

"I didn't think that movement was being taken very seriously." Mr. Garrity was likely the only one besides Martin who kept up with politics.

"I wouldn't doubt the strength of Naiaran feelings on the matter. I was raised there, and the hatred for slavery runs deep. It goes against everything the Naiarans take pride in." Sophie turned to Jason. "Do you think anything will come of it? Are you planning on doing something?"

"Yes. They're pushing hard for abolition, but Kale and I have been trying to persuade our friends to take a more practical approach. We know Arine won't accept abolition right now, and we don't want to waste this opportunity. That's what I wanted everyone's input on. We would like the Arinian government to adopt a law allowing a master to free his slaves, should he want to."

"Freedom has never been a possibility for slaves. It undermines the entire institution. Owning slaves is an Arinian birthright, even for those who will never be able to afford one. It's part of our national identity. Our forefathers went forth and conquered, bringing back slaves to build our country to greatness." Mr. Garrity's voice was firm with pride but not harsh.

"I'd remind you, Mr. Garrity, that there are two slaves sitting at this table and a former slave sitting at my side as my partner."

"How slaves are treated under your roof is your business, Mr. Wadsworth. I'm simply telling you the hard truth. This is no little thing you're proposing."

"Couldn't it be argued that a master has the right to do whatever he likes with his slaves? If he wants to kill a slave, he can. Why can't he free a slave if he likes?" Kale knew from his years as a slave that perception was everything. The only way a slave could ever get what he wanted was to convince the master that it was really what the master wanted.

Mr. Garrity stayed silent a moment. "If such a bill has a chance of passing, it'd be by employing that argument."

"John?" Jason turned to his new business partner.

"I've worked side by side with slaves my whole life. Never did understand what made us different. The working class out here, though, they dream of the day they can own a slave. They won't want to give up on it."

"The working class in the city won't feel the same way. They know they're never going to be rich. Most of my friends feel the way I do about slavery. I think the key is knowing slaves. My friends and I have worked with slaves our whole lives, just like John. It makes it harder to look down on them." Sophie spoke her mind with confidence, even though she sat at a table full of men. As a working-class woman, she wasn't esteemed much higher than a slave in the eyes of the government. Perhaps it would be a wise tactic to court the support of women. As two marginalized groups, they might be able to help each other.

"What are your thoughts on the matter, Demetri?"

"Sir?"

"Come now, you must have some opinion. I'd like to hear it."

"I think there are men who would like the opportunity to free their slaves, sir. It would solve some problems if there's affection between a master and slave."

"Or it would cause some," Thomas interjected. When it was clear that was all Demetri intended to say, Kale nodded for his brother to continue. "It might not be a good thing if masters started thinking their slaves were behaving a certain way in the hopes of gaining freedom. Could cause a lot of distrust. A paranoid, jealous master is a problem for a slave."

"From what I know of the men in Perdana, there are plenty who would like the option, who will feel it should have been their right from the beginning." Martin offered his view. "There's an awful lot of noble blood flowing through bastard slave children. It's always been a problem for the aristocracy. There are quite a few nobles who don't like the idea that their child is a slave. They'd like to be able to recognize them the same as they can their free, illegitimate children. Not to mention quite a few people found it ridiculous that you had to leave the country just so you could live with your freed slave, Jason. It caused quite a stir."

"Really?" Kale found it hard to believe that anyone even

gave it a thought.

"Oh, yes. There was talk at the time among some of the men in Perdana that Jason should have been allowed to do what he wanted with you. When I put feelers out at your request, the sentiment was still the same. It's not unusual for men to form an attachment to a valet or other slave. That's why there's a law against slaves impersonating free people. It wouldn't be necessary if there weren't masters who wanted their slaves to behave as if they were free."

"I never thought of it that way. I always just assumed it was to prevent slaves from thinking about revolting." It worked. It was hard for a slave to desire freedom when even acting free meant death.

"It is, but it wouldn't need to be put into law if men weren't tempted to allow it."

"Mr. Garrity, my question is: would you support such a law?" Jason turned the conversation back to the attorney.

"I suppose so. From a property law viewpoint, it makes sense for the reason that's been discussed here. You can't claim a slave is property if you don't have the right to do whatever you like with it, including letting it go."

"Thank you. We'll count on your help when the time comes."

"If that's all, Mr. Wadsworth, I have a few appointments I must attend to."

"Of course. Let me see you out." Jason stood. Kale loosened his hand to allow him to leave, but Jason kept his grip firm. Once Kale stood, Jason let go of his hand, and they walked Mr. Garrity to the door together.

"Thank you for all your help, Mr. Garrity." Jason shook the attorney's hand.

"My pleasure. Your father was a good man. He'll be missed."

After the door shut, Kale took the opportunity to speak with Jason before they rejoined the others. "You don't have to do this right now."

"Yes, I do. For one thing, it's time sensitive. We won't get another opportunity for quite a while once the treaty is ratified."

"We have friends who can handle this. I'm just saying that you don't need to shoulder the responsibility. I know you, and I don't think you should be taking on an all-consuming project right now."

"I have to, Kale. Not just because it's the right thing to do, but because I need it. I need the purpose. I wish I could find that purpose here, but I don't know the first thing about running a ranch. I plan on giving John free rein. I can't continue my father's legacy here, but I can live up to his name by doing what I know is right."

Kale grasped Jason's arm. "I won't let you follow your father into an early grave by working yourself to death." If Kale let him, Jason would run so hard and so fast that his grief couldn't possibly keep up. He'd seen firsthand how destructive Jason could become to himself. It wasn't going to happen again, not on Kale's watch, not now when they had everything they had fought so hard for in their hands.

"I know. I'm counting on you for that. I promise I'm not doing this to avoid anything. It's quite the opposite, actually. I appreciate your concern, Kale, but this is the best thing I can do for myself right now."

Kale searched Jason's eyes. The shadow that had clouded them for days was still there, but a bright earnestness shone through. It worried Kale, but he was beginning to think he may always be worried, that it was his new normal. All he could do was trust Jason and be prepared to catch him if he should fall.

CHAPTER FORTY-FOUR

"I'm sorry I haven't had much time to spend with you." Kale was out riding with Thomas. Despite his fears to the contrary, Jason appeared to be doing fine. Kale had hovered for the last two days until Jason had demanded he stop and go spend some one-on-one time with his brother. Kale had been feeling guilty for neglecting him, even though Thomas joined them for meals and occasional conversations in the sitting room.

"Don't worry about it, Kale. You worry enough as it is. Always have."

Kale crinkled his brow. "Have not."

Thomas snorted. "Sure. Between you and Mama, I was more smothered than a free boy with a nanny."

Kale chuckled. Thomas was right. Kale did have a tendency to take those he loved on as his responsibility. "There are worse things in the world."

"Yes, there are. I love you for it. It's nice having a big brother worry over me, but I'm not a kid anymore. I know you care. You don't have to spend time with me for me to know that."

"I don't want you to ever forget how much you mean to me."

"You left your cushy life in Naiara and risked re-enslavement by coming back here. All to save me. Yeah, it's not likely that's going to slip my mind any time soon."

Kale smiled. "You never know. Anyway, any time you want to talk, you have my ear."

"Thanks."

Thomas didn't appear inclined to say more. Kale wasn't used to being the one who had to prompt conversation. "So, what do you want to do?"

"I was thinking we could head out to the western grove. You should see it. Some of the most beautiful—"

"No, I mean what do you want to do?" Kale slowed his horse and waited for Thomas to follow suit. "You have options now, Thomas. I told you I plan to free you, but I won't force anything on you."

Thomas's face fell into contemplation. Kale didn't push. It was a heavy question. "I don't know. I like it here."

"Well, that's good."

"Sure, but shouldn't I want to be free?"

"After the scare-tales our mama told us?" Free children got fairy tales and stories of endless possibilities. Slave children got scare-tales of what happened when slaves tried to be free. Kale had told Lisa about them once, and she was horrified at the cruelty of it. She didn't understand that stories like those kept skin on his back. Slave children were much like free children. They didn't have an innate desire to obey. Scare-tales were a concerned mother's way of trying to ensure her children didn't end up beneath the whip or worse.

"It's not that. I'm not afraid of wanting freedom. I suppose it's the unknown that worries me."

"That's reasonable."

"Really?"

"Sure. Thomas, when I was freed, I already knew I'd be spending the rest of my life with Jason. There were a lot of unknowns, but I was already sure about the fundamentals. I was grounded. You're not in that same situation. Even with all my advantages, it still took a long time for me to adjust.

Even now, there are days when I feel like an impostor."

"I think that's how I'd feel. What do I know about being free? It would only be an act. Let's say I decide to go to Naiara. What then? How's it all going to work? I just cross the border, and suddenly I'm free?"

"Don't worry yourself with the details. Jason and I will take care of those. Our home is yours, and I don't need to tell you that money's not an issue. There's not a single thing you have to worry about other than knowing your own mind."

"Thanks. I feel at home here. I like the work I'm doing. It gives me meaning."

"Good. That's the most important thing. Take some time to figure out who you are as a man outside of those who have owned you. Learn about yourself and what you want. When you know what that is, grab onto it. Maybe you'll decide you want to start your own ranch or expand Wadsworth beef into Naiara. Maybe you'll realize this is all just a nice safe place for you to heal and that there's something else you want. Whatever it is, take your time."

"But aren't you and Jason going to be leaving for Naiara soon?"

"I suppose so. When Jason is ready. It doesn't matter though. Whenever you decide you want to come to Naiara, or any other free country for that matter, all you have to do is call." Kale pulled his horse in front of Thomas's, blocking his path and forcing eye contact. "I mean it. If you wake up in the middle of the night wanting out of Arine, you pick up the telephone."

"So I don't have to decide today?"

"Nope. If you want to come with us, we'd be happy to have you. Roll the idea around in your head some. If you don't leave with us this time, you're not closing any doors."

"I'll do that."

They rode on in comfortable silence. Rain the previous day had left the scenery alive with vivid color. Overnight, the ground had dried, making it perfect for a leisurely ride. The air still held the pleasant scent of a refreshing shower.

"When am I going to see some of this art Jason goes on about? I would have never guessed my brother would turn out to be a famous artist."

Kale shook his head and sidestepped the question. "Have your feelings toward Jason changed at all?"

"Some. When I think about what he did to you, I see red, but it appears as if he's done a fine job of making up for it. Besides, it's clear as day you're besotted with him, so until that wears off, my hands are tied."

"Besotted?" Kale laughed. "You make me sound like a boy with calf love."

"It's what you look like."

"Well, I hate to disappoint you, but it's not wearing off."

"I figured as much. In all seriousness, Kale, I'm happy for you. What you and Jason have is special. I wouldn't want anything to spoil it. I suppose I have to love a man who makes my brother so damn happy."

"I'm glad. It'd be a little uncomfortable if you two didn't like each other."

"Nah, you'd choose him any day."

The words stabbed Kale's heart. "It wasn't like that. I didn't choose him over coming back to get you. I know I shouldn't have waited as long as I did, but I hadn't forgotten about you—"

"Whoa, Big Brother. I didn't mean it like that. I know you did your best. No one could have done better or expected different. I only meant that he's your family now. I'm thrilled. It's nice to know that you had someone."

Kale tried to let his brother's words soothe his guilt. "I want the same for you." After a moment of silence, Kale sought a little levity. He didn't want his guilty conscience to ruin this time with Thomas. "Speaking of which, who's that girl I've seen you eyeing in the kitchen?"

Thomas's face cleared to the innocent, bland expression so common in slaves. "Who?"

"Don't give me that. What's her name?"

Thomas's face broke into a sheepish smile. "Ellen."

"Ah. So is she the real reason you're reluctant to leave?"

"No."

"There's no shame if she is."

"Do you think there's really a chance your idea will become law?" Thomas's voice strained with yearning.

"Yes, but even if it doesn't, we wouldn't make you choose between the woman you love and freedom, should things with Ellen advance that far. Whoever you choose to love will always have a place in our family."

Thomas nodded, and Kale saw the relief pour onto his face. "It's admirable what you and Jason are doing. It's a little hard to believe that my big brother can have an idea here, and then it could be made into law."

"Thanks, but you're giving me too much credit. I just happen to know people in positions of influence."

"Tell me you're not that daft. You're the partner of one of the wealthiest men in Naiara. Like it or not, you are one of those influential people."

Kale had never really thought of it. He supposed Thomas was right. As soon as his mind considered it though, he felt a weight on his chest. No, influence had never been something he'd sought.

"Back to my original question, which you so neatly evaded. When do I get to see some of your art?"

Kale's horse had slowed, and he nudged him into a trot. "I can show you some sketches when we get back to the house. Would you like some drawing materials?"

"Me? No. Never did have your talent and never much saw the appeal."

"Would you like to learn how to read?"

Thomas looked over at Kale, his jaw lax in surprise. "I'd love to. I don't think I'll need that skill here, but it will give me more options in the future."

"If you come to Naiara with us, I'll teach you. If not, I'll see if John can. Robert had plenty of books you can choose from. I think he favored mysteries."

"I'd really appreciate that. Mysteries sound good."

"It's settled then. So where's this grove you wanted to show me?" Kale challenged his brother with his eyes. A grin spread across Thomas's face, and he took off at a gallop. Kale surrendered himself to an all-consuming laugh as he followed, the wind rushing against him as if he was flying. It was wonderful to finally have a brother again.

CHAPTER FORTY-FIVE

It had been a week since the funeral, and Jason was anxious to be home. There was nothing more to be done. Martin and Sophie had returned to Perdana a few days ago, and life had resumed on the ranch. "I want to book us on tomorrow's train." He and Kale were dressing for the day.

"Are you sure you're ready to leave?"

"Yes. Past ready. There's nothing more for me here, not right now."

"We should visit Renee in Timar on our way home."

There was nothing Kale could have said that would have shocked Jason more. "What?"

"If you want this idea of yours to succeed, it needs to be proposed by an Arinian. If it's proposed by the Naiarans first, it'll be dismissed immediately. If it's proposed in the Arinian government, even by a fringe politician, it has a greater chance. Then the Naiarans come to the table with their demands, and the Arinians can pass it off as something they were planning to do anyway."

"That's brilliant, Kale. But we don't have to see Renee." Jason recovered from his shock and resumed buttoning his shirt.

"Her support would be invaluable. She's already proven that she can make things happen. She's done excellent work with the women's movement."

"I agree. However, I can get her support by writing or calling her. We don't have to visit."

"I know we don't have to, but I think we should. She's your wife. It wouldn't be so horrible to see her once in a while, and it's on our way."

Jason's feelings toward Renee were muddled. He did genuinely love her, albeit in a different manner than he loved Kale. He felt a strong feeling of friendship toward her. There was only a problem when Kale was added to the mix. Renee had caused them such pain. Her offense to himself he could forgive; it was the pain she'd caused Kale that Jason had a hard time reconciling. The only reason he had been able to maintain any sort of relationship with her was because he blamed himself more than he blamed her. However, he was not eager to place Kale in a house with her.

"I'll be honest. I don't like the thought of you two together."

"Why not?"

"Why? How can you even ask that after what she did?"

"It was a long time ago, and she's apologized."

"And I accepted her apology, but I don't want to put you in that position."

"What position? I have no reason to feel uncomfortable around her. If you're worried about how she feels, that's a different matter."

"Trust me, I am not concerned about her feelings in this situation."

"Then we should do it. It's the last bit of our past that we haven't fully resolved. She's your wife, and I'm your companion and life partner. Those are the facts. There's no reason we can't all be together in a room."

Jason slipped his hands under Kale's untucked shirt and held him around the waist. Under his fingertips, he felt the scar tissue that remained from Kale's time at the labor firm. How a man could live through that and then forgive those who had put him there would forever be a mystery to Jason. It took a deep inner strength that Jason didn't think anyone other than Kale possessed. "You're right. If you don't have a problem with it, there's no reason for me to. I'll get us three tickets to Timar."

"Three?"

"Isn't Thomas joining us?"

"That's for him to decide."

"I assumed he'd want to come to Naiara so he could be free."

"That's quite an assumption. He's in a different situation than I was. Freedom isn't something you can just thrust on a man. Do you remember how difficult the transition was for me? And I had an incredibly supportive lover and absolutely no financial worries."

Jason recalled those early days after Kale had been freed. It had been an adjustment. "I have no problem with us supporting him indefinitely."

"I know that, but he doesn't, and simply telling him won't convince him. I had a problem with living off of you, and I'm your partner. It's not freedom if you're reliant on someone else. He needs to have his own plan. If that plan includes living with us, then great, but if not, we can't force it on him. He may need some time to adjust. He fits in well here, and he's safe. Not to mention there's a girl here who's caught his fancy."

"I just supposed he'd want to be free."

"He does, and I want him to be free more than anything, but he's been taught since birth to fear freedom. He'll be free someday. I'm just not sure it's today. I love you for assuming he'd live with us, though. You didn't have to."

"He's your brother, Kale, and the only family I have besides you."

"Thanks for saying so." Kale kissed him, and they went down to breakfast.

◆ ◆ ◆

"So, Thomas, Jason and I have been talking, and we want to know what your plans are. We're leaving tomorrow for home, and you're welcome to join us. If you want to come to Naiara, you'll be a free man. You can live with us for as long as you like. We have plenty of room, but it's entirely up to you."

Breakfast was done, and Jason sat across from Kale and Thomas. He found it interesting how Thomas pursed his lips the same way Kale did when considering his words.

"It's not just Kale who wants you to join us, Thomas. I do too."

"We both just want you to do what's best for you."

Thomas nodded. "I appreciate the offer. I've thought about it a lot since we talked, but I'd like to stay here if that's still possible."

"Of course it is."

"It's just that I feel like I belong here. I love the work, being outside, helping to build something. It's more satisfying than anything I've ever done. I wouldn't have the first idea of what to do if I were free with you in Naiara. I don't know what my purpose would be. I'm treated better here than I ever have been, and I don't want to leave it just yet."

"I understand. You don't have to justify it to me as long as you know your reasons. If you ever change your mind, just call, and we'll be on the next train to get you."

"Thanks, but you two have something really great. I wouldn't want to get in the way."

"Trust me, Little Brother, you couldn't if you tried."

"Maybe not, but that's not a good life for any of us. You don't need your little brother around, and I don't need to worry about intruding. I'm useful here, and I think the others like me."

"Good. If you've found your place, then you should stake

it."

"Besides, you'll be back here soon enough to free me. I have faith that you'll get this law passed. And if you don't, we can talk about it then."

"Fair enough."

"I've got to go. I promised I'd ride out with Billy to check on the herd."

"Then we won't keep you. You'll be back in time for dinner?"

"Should be. I'll see you then." Thomas smiled at Jason before leaving.

"You were right." Jason didn't know why he was still amazed at Kale's ability to read people.

Kale shrugged. "I can understand how he feels. It means a lot to him that you're willing to take him with us. It means a lot to me too."

"Well, I'm glad he feels at home here. It'll be nice to have a family member still living in the house. I don't think there's any question as to how he'll be treated, but I'll make sure to make it clear to John before we leave."

"Which reminds me, I told Thomas I'd ask John to teach him how to read."

"I'll take care of it."

◆ ◆ ◆

The next afternoon, Jason placed the last of his mother's journals back in the window seat. He'd read most of them and skimmed through the rest. He had learned a lot about his mother from her writings, mainly that she was so much more than the woman he'd idealized in his memory. He was taking the painting of her from around the time he was born back home with him, but the journals belonged at the ranch along with the family portraits.

Kale had spent the morning with Thomas and was

waiting for him at the car. They would need to leave soon to catch their train. Jason had wanted just a few more minutes alone in his childhood home. On his way to the front door, he stopped inside his father's study. He closed his eyes and took a deep breath. The smell of cigar smoke still hung in the air. His mother had been right. It smelled like home.

Jason's eyes were damp. This was silly. He and Kale would be back to see the memorials installed in the family plot when they were ready. Jason closed his father's door and went outside.

Kale was leaning up against the car, talking to Thomas. As soon as he saw Jason, he straightened. He and Thomas said a few words, hugged, and then Thomas came toward Jason.

"Bye, Jason." Thomas didn't even bother with a handshake. He threw his arms around Jason and patted him on the back.

"Bye, Thomas. Take care of yourself. If you need anything—"

"You're just a phone call away. I know. Kale's been more than a little insistent on that point."

Jason smiled. "Good. We'll see you in a few months' time."

"I look forward to it."

They nodded to each other, and Thomas ran off in the direction of the stables. Jason watched him for a moment before turning to Kale.

"You ready?" Kale stood with his hand on the door handle.

Jason walked to the passenger side and opened the door. "Yeah, I'm ready." He took one last look at the ranch, at the home that now held happy memories from more than just his childhood, and got in the car. As soon as he shut the door, Kale started down the drive. Once they were on the highway, Kale placed his hand palm up between them in invitation. Jason took it and relaxed in his seat. He would miss his father,

John, the ranch, but he was ready to get back to his home. Kale had been right. It had been worth the trip.

CHAPTER FORTY-SIX

Kale had never seen the Timar estate before. Manicured gardens welcomed guests to the expansive grounds. An elaborate stone staircase led to the intricately detailed entrance. Kale counted twelve windows—six on each side of the front door—on the first of three floors. It was a stark reminder of the wealth Jason controlled. It was easy to forget, given the simple lifestyle Kale enjoyed with him.

A butler led them into the sitting room where Renee waited for them. Kale hadn't seen her since the awful day he'd been sold. Despite what he'd said to Jason, he had been worried about how he would react to seeing her. Surprisingly, he didn't feel much of anything. She'd hardly changed. Her face had gently aged but was still as enchanting as it had been. Her dark red hair was swept up in a loose bun, and her dark blue eyes were just as fiery as before, with a few faint laugh lines around the edges.

"Jason, Kale, how good to see you!" Renee stood and gave Jason a kiss on each cheek. When she came to Kale, she hesitated. Kale brought her hand to his lips, and as soon as he did, she leaned in to kiss him on the cheek. "Please, come in and sit."

Renee had little sandwiches and tea waiting for them. Kale and Jason sat side by side on the sofa while Renee occupied a chair across from them. "Thank you for having us on such short notice." Jason stayed on the edge of his seat.

"It's no trouble. It is your house, after all."

"Maybe on paper, but it's your domain, and I never want to intrude."

"I know, Jason. You're the only one who could think you're intruding. Now, what is this matter you wanted to discuss with me?"

Kale didn't listen as Jason explained the situation. For a while, he'd harbored an irrational jealousy of Renee. She was legally tied to Jason on paper. There was no such bond between himself and the man he loved. The only paper that had ever legally joined them was Kale's title, and Jason had given that back to him. As they had built their life together as equals, Kale realized Jason had given up that paper tie to forge an even deeper bond between them. Once he had made that realization, the jealousy faded.

"I'd love to help. I know exactly the politician we can use to introduce the bill. This is a marvelous idea. I'm so happy you came to me with it. I'd hate to be left out." Renee's face was alight with the promise of a new challenge. It reminded Kale of the girl she had been when he'd first met her.

"Good. We'll need to manage this from both the Arinian and Naiaran sides for it to work."

Renee waved the hand that wasn't holding her tea cup. "Absolutely. We'll coordinate everything."

Kale could see Jason moving to rise. This was his last chance. "I'd like to take a look at the gardens before we go, if you don't mind." It was the first thing Kale had said since they'd arrived. Kale looked at Jason. He knew he was anxious to leave.

"Not at all. Renee, Kale's quite the gardener at home."

"Really?"

"No, it's just impressive to Jason because he couldn't keep a weed alive if he needed to."

Renee laughed. It was the same laugh Kale remembered

from the night he had arranged for her and Jason to meet.

"I was hoping you might give me a tour."

"Certainly. Jason?" Renee turned to Jason in a gesture of invitation.

"Jason actually has some phone calls he needs to make before we leave." Kale hoped Jason would give him this time alone with Renee. After a brief moment of eye contact, Jason nodded.

"Yes, that's right. You two go on ahead."

Kale gestured for Renee to lead the way. The gardens really were amazing. Kale thought it must take a staff of half a dozen to keep them so well maintained. Renee was quiet. She had always been an intelligent woman. She no doubt knew that Kale's interest in the gardens was secondary to his primary purpose.

He waited until they were well away from the house and on an enchanting path that led through a maze of rose bushes. "Do you get lonely?"

Renee smiled. "Heavens, no. I use the manor here to house women who have fallen on unfortunate times and help them get back on their feet. I have friends here and some who visit. I still spend much of my time in Perdana and, as you know, there's never a dull moment there."

"You don't crave companionship?"

"Not as much as you might think. There are nights when it's lonely, but then the day comes, and I realize there are more important parts of my life."

"You know he wouldn't begrudge you a lover."

"I couldn't do that to him." Kale eyed her incredulously. "It's different with you and him. You had claim to him long before I did. No, I made my bed, and I'll lie in it. If I took a lover, it would cause scandal, and my mother would push for a divorce. I like the arrangement we have. I don't wish to alter it."

"I don't wish you to live your life alone."

"Don't worry about me, Kale." Renee stopped him with a

hand on his arm and deliberately met his eyes. "I'm very close with my girlfriends."

Kale was caught off guard. He supposed it made sense, but it was the last thing he'd expected. "I didn't realize."

They resumed walking. "It's sweet of you to care after everything I've done. I know you got my apology in writing, but I want you to know how truly sorry I am for the pain I caused you and Jason. I'm amazed you don't harbor any ill will toward me."

"I can't. If he hadn't married you, he wouldn't have had the money and resources to free me or move to Naiara and have me accepted as a citizen. Besides, it was my fault as much as yours. I could have stopped Jason from selling me any time I wanted, but I didn't. That was my choice, not yours. You did what you thought was best for yourself."

"And you did what you thought was best for Jason. It's why you won in the end."

"Yes, it is." It wasn't a competition, but there was no denying that Kale had won. "Thank you for your support. It'll go a long way in getting reforms passed."

"Of course. I'm glad you asked. This is going to become a reality, Kale, and it's going to be a very good thing. It's just a first step, and the first is always the hardest. Improving the lives of slaves will improve all our lives. Someday, this country is going to realize that by helping the least fortunate, we help everyone."

"And you're the one who's going to show them." Kale smiled at her. "We should go back inside. Jason's eager to get home."

"I can imagine. Take good care of him. Don't let him lose himself."

"I won't. He's safe with me."

"I know. You're better for him than I ever could have been. You understand him in a way I never did."

"He still loves you, and I know you love him. You offered him something special, just different. If this bill passes, there's a chance we'll be spending more time in Arine. There's the ranch to check on, as well as my brother, and the business in Perdana. It might be nice for us all to visit occasionally."

"I would enjoy that."

They reached the house to find Jason waiting at the door. "Thanks for your help, Renee, but we've got to be going now if we're going to catch the train. I don't want to spend any more nights away from home than I have to."

"I understand. Thank you for coming. I hope to see you again with good news."

"We look forward to it." Kale kissed her on the cheek and then stepped aside for Jason to do the same. A few minutes later, they were in the car on the way to the station.

"How was your talk with Renee?"

Kale took Jason's hand. "We made peace with each other."

"Oh?"

"Yes. It was time." Kale smiled at the love and concern emanating from the man next to him. Life may not be a competition, but he had indeed won.

CHAPTER FORTY-SEVEN

They arrived home early in the morning. The sky was still pink from the sun stretching across the horizon like a child rising from bed. Kale didn't think home had ever looked more beautiful. The back garden would be a mess from his neglect, but he relished having the project to tackle. They had let Neissa know when to expect them, so Kale was confident they would find something waiting for them in the kitchen.

Jason unlocked the front door, and Kale followed him inside. He couldn't help taking a deep breath, inhaling the familiar scent of home. They plod up the stairs in silence. Kale had left everything in the trunk of the car except the valise that had ridden in the back seat. As soon as they entered their bedroom, he tossed it on a chair, relieved he no longer had to worry about its contents.

"I don't want to wake up until tomorrow." The bed muffled Jason's voice, and Kale turned to see him face down on top of the comforter, fully clothed.

Kale smirked and suddenly desired a little mischief. He fell on top of Jason and tickled his ribs. Jason started laughing uncontrollably, squirming underneath Kale until he had rolled over onto his back. Jason's merry face brought a smile to Kale's lips. To his surprise, he felt something begin to stir in his groin. He almost sighed with relief. It wasn't an erection, but it was a hopeful start. Maybe after they had some sleep he could try to coax his desire out from its hibernation.

"You don't need to get up. Just wiggle out of your clothes." Kale undressed Jason, his lover scooting around until his trousers came free. The sight of Jason's body made Kale feel even more at home. It was wonderful to be back in their own bed, without the worries and stresses of being around other people in a foreign house.

Kale tossed Jason's clothes on the ground, rid himself of his own, and folded down the comforter, climbing in next to Jason. As soon as his back hit the sheet, Jason cuddled against him, not even bothering to open his eyes to find Kale. The stubble on Jason's chin from the journey scratched at his chest. For the first time since Kale had discovered the letter Jason was hiding, he was able to relax. Tension poured out of him. The curtains were drawn, keeping all but a sliver of sunlight out. Kale's eyes scanned their room, pleased to see it unchanged. He and Jason had both been through such emotional turmoil and upheaval away from home. There was a certain amount of comfort in the knowledge that through it all their home remained a steady place for them to return to.

It was the first time in his life he had a place to call home, to give him the comfort and security that a home did. The entire time in Arine, he had been tense. Every moment, he'd been on edge, even when he wasn't consciously aware of it. Arine wasn't his country. He had been born there, but his freedom had come from Naiara. There had to be a way for him to reconcile the memories of his life in Arine with the life he currently lived. With time, he felt he'd be able to look upon his memories with an appropriate amount of fondness for the good times and distance from the painful recollections.

Kale ran his hands through Jason's hair. A few stray silver strands had appeared over the last couple of weeks. Some of Jason's color had faded. The luster was absent from his hair and skin. The brown of his eyes appeared as vivid as before, except a shadow had appeared behind them. Kale didn't know if it would ever completely go away. In the space of a few weeks, Jason had aged a couple of years. Kale didn't mind, other than to worry about the emotional implications. Jason was still the most stunning man he had ever seen. The changes to his appearance only spoke of a man who had given his whole heart over to experiencing life. Kale couldn't be more proud to be lying next to him.

Their troubles were far from over. They had merely moved to a new stage of healing. Kale had confidence in their ability to persevere. After all, they had each other's support. The love that swelled in his chest started to swell another part of his anatomy. Of course his lust would resurface when Jason was sleeping. If it had been any other time, Kale would have woken him, but Jason was in need of sleep. Kale could only hope that when his erection withered, it wouldn't be permanent.

He tried to think of mundane matters: the work he would need to do in the garden, making a trip to the gallery in the next few days to see what had sold, the magnitude of the mission they had undertaken in campaigning for slavery reform. Nothing worked. If anything, his erection was straining even more.

Kale tried to move from underneath Jason so he could go to the bathroom and relieve himself. The moment he shifted his weight, Jason cuddled in closer, moving his knee up so it barely grazed Kale's cock before settling lower down. Gods, Kale almost wished for the return of his impotence. Almost. If Jason was moving around, he couldn't be as deep in sleep as Kale thought. Kale lowered his lips to Jason's ear and barely whispered, "How tired are you?"

"Hmm?" Jason moved around on top of Kale more, but his eyes didn't open.

"Nothing." If they weren't going to have sex, then he really wanted Jason to stop moving. Once he was settled down, maybe Kale could take care of it without bothering him.

"All right." Jason wiggled against Kale, snuggling in for a closer fit. Kale's erection leapt as Jason's knee once again brushed against it, and Kale had to suppress a groan. Jason continued to move until his leg settled against Kale's cock. As soon as the hard heat registered against Jason's skin, his eyes flew open and he lifted his head, all traces of sleep banished.

A smile curled Jason's lips. "Why didn't you say something?"

"You're tired."

"No, I'm not." Jason moved on top of him and rubbed his own growing erection against Kale's.

Kale chuckled. "I'm glad your cock hasn't realized that you're not a teenager anymore."

Jason blushed, reminding Kale of the young man he had been when they'd first met. "Can you blame me when I have you lying here?" Jason didn't wait for a reply. He dove for the canister of grease they kept by the bed. With one hand he liberally applied the lubricant to Kale's cock. With the other he grasped Kale's bicep and then littered his chest with kisses.

Kale didn't try to suppress his groans any longer. Jason's hand was firm on his erection, doing more than simply preparing him. His lover's mouth was devouring his chest as if he had been waiting weeks for this moment. In a way, Kale supposed he had, though he wished he hadn't denied himself simply because of Kale's problem.

"Stop." Kale wrenched Jason's hand off his cock. "Unless you want this to end in your hand?" Perhaps Jason did want to simply get the job done and get back to sleeping.

"Gods, no." Jason knelt up on his knees and prepared himself. It took little more than a greased finger, and he was putting the canister away.

"Are you sure you're good?" Kale didn't want Jason to let himself get hurt in his rush.

"Yes. I want to feel you. I don't care if it hurts a little."

And with that, Jason lowered himself onto Kale's cock in one slow, smooth motion.

The tight warmth that enveloped him was intoxicating. Kale's back arched, and his hands immediately grabbed Jason's hips, holding him still. "Don't move." He needed a moment to adjust. Otherwise, this wasn't going to last very long.

Jason nodded and leaned down to suck Kale's bottom lip into his mouth. The closeness gave Kale a heady sensation. He arched into the contact until his rib cage touched Jason's. At the touch, he wrapped an arm around Jason and pulled him flush against him. Using his other arm for leverage, he flipped them over so he was on top of Jason. A little smile played at Jason's lips. He clearly liked this turn of events.

"I don't know how long I can last." Kale's husky voice communicated his desire more than his words did.

"That's all right. It's not like it's the last time we're going to do this. We have an entire night to fill later."

Kale smiled. Of course, they had all the time in the world. A dark voice in the back of his head said that wasn't true, that eventually it would be their last time, but Kale pushed it away. If he had learned anything during recent events, it was to treasure life's moments as they happened.

Slowly, he began to thrust into Jason and released a shuddered breath. The sensation was overwhelming after so much time. Slow was suddenly no longer an option. All he wanted was more of this feeling. He latched his mouth onto Jason's shoulder and raked his nails along his back, pulling Jason to him, rough with desperation. Somewhere in his mind, he registered that Jason was taking care of his own cock in time with Kale's movements.

The tension curled and built in his groin until he didn't think he'd be able to take it anymore. In a burst of sensation, the tension broke. Kale released Jason's shoulder and arched up in ecstasy. His orgasm kept going longer than he would have thought possible. Once his climax had washed over him, he fell forward onto his hands. He gathered himself in time to see Jason reach his finish, come spurting out in long ribbons over his chest. Too late, he realized the implications as Jason's ass tightened around Kale's sensitized cock.

"Ooh. Aah." Kale pulled out at the first loosening of Jason's muscles and lay next to him. Jason laughed and rolled over to give Kale a passionate kiss. When Jason pulled away, Kale marveled at the man looking down at him. "Gods, you get more beautiful every day." Jason's blush warmed Kale's heart. "I'd better go get a washcloth before we fall asleep. We don't want to wake up stuck to each other."

Jason grinned. "I wouldn't mind."

"Yeah, that's because you don't have as much chest hair as I do." Kale moved out from under Jason and retrieved a damp cloth. After he cleaned both of them, he tossed it on the floor. Tidying up could wait. Everything could wait until they had gotten some sleep.

Jason pulled Kale down and wrapped an arm around his chest. The pleasant afterglow settled around them, and Kale felt a rush of closeness to his partner that was more intense than the physical contact they shared. As wonderful as the sex was, Kale thought he might have missed the afterglow even more. The intense physical sensation enhanced the emotional bond they shared. Kale tightened his grip around Jason, seeking an outlet for the fierceness of his love.

"Hmm." Jason drifted off to sleep, his snores ruffling Kale's chest hair.

It was good to finally be home.

CHAPTER FORTY-EIGHT

"Kale, can you hand me my blue shirt? You know, the one I like to wear around the house?" Jason had just gotten out of the shower and was drying off while he looked at a list of calls he wanted to make. He'd spent every day of the last three weeks in Calea. This was the first day he was staying home and making calls instead of attending meetings in town, and he wanted to be comfortable.

"No, I can't. It's packed." Kale pulled clothes out of the closet.

"Packed? Whatever for?" There hadn't been a trip on his schedule.

"For our vacation."

"What are you talking about, Kale? I don't have time to go anywhere. There's too much to do." Jason didn't have the energy to mask his irritation.

"There is exactly nothing for you to do. You've done all you can. Renee and the others will manage anything that's left. You've worked day and night on this legislation for five months, and it's time to realize that it's done. The Arinians are either going to accept the proposal or not. There is nothing more you can do. You've let this consume your life in an unhealthy way."

"I know, but I'm doing this for you, Kale. For Thomas

and Demetri and Darlene and all the others. For the men in my mills."

Kale rubbed Jason's arms in what Jason was sure was meant to be a comforting fashion while he made eye contact. "Which is why I've allowed it for so long, but it stops today. Now, in fact. We're leaving for the train station in twenty minutes."

Jason broke free of Kale's grasp. "Kale, I can't be ready in twenty minutes."

"You already are." Damn Kale's collected calm.

"Why are you doing this?"

"I already told you. Besides, you promised me once that you'd show me the world. I'm calling that promise due."

Kale had him.

◆ ◆ ◆

Kale had been right. They had both needed a vacation. Jason hadn't worked alone to get the bill passed. Kale had taken Lisa's suggestion and done a series of pieces from his experiences as a slave. They were haunting, more so because Jason knew the truth behind them. Kale had also allowed him to see the ones that were too personal to display publicly. It had been a cathartic experience for both of them. Newspapers credited Kale with turning the abolitionist movement into a nationwide cause. It had worked perfectly. Anything short of abolition was looking good to the Arinians.

Watching Kale see new places was an endless source of delight for Jason. They hiked the Hiashin foothills, explored the ruins of the abandoned city at Parubala, and frolicked on the white sandy beaches of the Bluffington coast. Jason couldn't remember ever being more relaxed. He and Kale reconnected, reminding each other why they had chosen to spend the rest of their lives together. Each new experience was sweeter because he shared it with Kale, each new discovery more amazing because he saw it through Kale's eyes as well as his own.

They'd spent the day on cliffs overlooking the beach. There was a place where the ocean jutted inward, forming a lagoon. The water was deep, and Kale had urged Jason to jump. It had to have been at least fifteen meters above the water. After much cajoling, Jason had held Kale's hand, and they'd jumped together. It was exhilarating. Now, Kale was downstairs finding them a place to eat, and Jason was in their hotel room fiddling with the new camera they had purchased. He had just about figured out how to load the film when Kale returned.

"Where's it going to be tonight? Did you find a place with fresh shellfish?"

"Jason." Kale's somber voice brought Jason's head up from the camera. "I have some news."

Jason's heart sank. Kale stood in the doorway, appearing dazed. Jason didn't think he could bear any more bad news, not when they had survived so much recently. Surely their respite would last a little longer. "What is it?"

"The Arinian king has signed the bill into law. Slaves can now be freed by their masters." Kale continued to stand blankly, as if he didn't believe the words he had uttered.

Jason whooped and leapt into the air on his way to Kale. "That's great news!" He kissed an unresponsive Kale. "Why aren't you happy?"

Kale's head jerked to Jason as he finally focused his gaze. "Happy? I'm overwhelmed with joy." Tears pooled in Kale's eyes. "This means my brother's going to be free."

"Yes, it does. Come on." Jason dragged Kale to the closet. "We'll eat on the train. We're going back to the ranch."

CHAPTER FORTY-NINE

It took more than a week to reach Malar County. They traveled from the balmy coast back to Calea to pack appropriately for the inland chill and make a few preparations before heading into Arine. There was a nervous excitement in the air the entire way there. Kale could hardly believe that he was traveling to free his brother on the tracks he had once laid as a slave. Not only his brother, but himself. He would no longer have to worry about the precarious arrangement Jason had concocted in order to free him. There would be no question. In the eyes of the law, Kale would be a free man in the country of his birth.

When Kale and Jason pulled up to the house, it was just after midnight, and the darkness had a cold bite. The top was up on the car, and as soon as they stepped out, their warm breath fogged in the air. Kale grabbed his valise, leaving everything else until morning, and they jogged up to the front door, not even bothering to knock.

"Kale, Jason." Thomas reached the front door as Jason closed it. He knocked Kale over with a giant hug and then treated Jason to the same. "Darlene left some dinner for you. Come on in. Let me take your coats." Thomas hung their coats in the hall closet and led them to the kitchen.

At the kitchen table, a young woman set out food. She

turned as they entered, and Kale remembered seeing her there before, but never talking to her. He thought she was the same girl Thomas had been making eyes at.

"This is Ellen." Thomas strode to her side and put a proprietary arm around her waist.

Kale quirked an eyebrow. "It's nice to meet you, Ellen. I see a lot has happened since we were last here."

"Yeah, it has. I thought we might keep you two company while you ate."

Jason and Kale sat at the table. Steak and potatoes were laid out for each of them along with a glass of milk each. The familiarity was as comforting as the warmth. "So, Ellen, what lies has my brother told you to trick you into fancying him?"

Ellen smiled—a big, beaming grin, not the shy, bashful smile some women were prone to. "He can't lie to me. I can spot it a kilometer away. It's a little charming how flustered he can get. It took me a while to realize that he didn't have a stutter; he was trying to court me."

Thomas shifted in his seat, grimacing at the attention.

Jason laughed. "Good to see he got his tongue back."

"That he did."

Kale made quick work of his food. He had a good idea that Thomas and Ellen weren't awake just to greet them. "I had planned to wait until tomorrow, but there's no sense in you going to bed a slave tonight. I have your title and registration here." Kale pulled them out of his valise along with one of the dozens of writ of manumission forms they had printed when they stopped in Calea. "And this is a writ of manumission." Kale laid the papers out on the table. "All we have to do is fill it out. We'll have to file it with the county for there to be a legal record, but as soon as it's signed, you're free. I already filled out everything I knew."

"What else do you need?" Thomas vibrated with either excitement or nervousness. Probably both.

"What last name do you want to go by?"

"I'd like to go by the same last name you do, since you're

my brother. If that's all right. If you don't—"

"No, we were hoping you'd want to. I want my father's name passed on." Jason patted his hand.

"Thank you."

Kale filled out the last name then signed and dated it. "All right. Now you just have to sign it here." Kale pushed the paper and pen toward his brother, pointing to the signature line.

Thomas took the pen in his hand and inhaled deeply. With a quick flourish, he signed his name.

"Congratulations, Thomas. You're free. How does it feel?"

"Amazing. I'm really free?" Thomas looked bewildered.

"Yes, you're really free." Kale squeezed his brother's shoulder, remembering his own journey to freedom.

Jason pulled another writ of manumission from the case and began filling it out. "Ellen, what last name would you like me to put on yours?"

Thomas spoke before Ellen could. "Wadsworth."

Ellen looked to Thomas.

"You'll be taking the name Wadsworth anyway, if you'll have me."

Ellen narrowed her eyes "Are you proposing to me, Thomas Wadsworth?"

Thomas nodded. "I believe I am."

Ellen's broad smile returned even brighter than before. "Then you'd better put Wadsworth on the form, sir."

Thomas took Ellen's face in his hands and kissed her. Kale observed the scene in silence. His first instinct was to caution his brother against making such a serious decision when he had just been freed. However, the sheer joy in Thomas's face was breathtaking. What sealed Kale's happiness, though, was the fact that Ellen's apparent joy mirrored his brother's. There was no use counseling his brother to take his time to experience the world when what he wanted was already right in front of him. Kale would have scoffed at anyone who told him to explore freedom before making the choice to spend his life with Jason.

Jason grinned and signed the writ. The only slave Kale had owned was his brother. It was up to Jason to free the others. "You'll just need to put your mark there." Jason indicated the spot.

"Thank you, sir."

"You'd better make it Jason now that you're going to be part of the family."

Ellen nodded. "Thank you, Jason." She carefully wrote her name, her tongue peeking out in concentration. From the way Thomas leaned over her, it was clear they had been practicing so Ellen would have the dignity of signing her name instead of an X. When she finished, she placed the pen down, and Thomas pulled her into a hug.

"Well, we should get to bed and leave you two to celebrate. We'll see you in the morning." Kale rose with a yawn. It had been a long day.

"Thank you, Kale. Sleep in. We'll have a late breakfast." Thomas had pulled away enough to address his brother, but he still had both arms wrapped around Ellen.

Kale chuckled. "I'm sure we will."

Despite his earlier drowsiness, Kale sat in bed looking at his own writ of manumission. To avoid the strange appearance of having Kale sign his own writ in both places, they'd had Jason sign it as a designated representative of P and C Enterprises. Kale was really and truly free. His brother was free. His brother's fiancée was free. He'd be able to return for their wedding as a free man without any fear of it being taken away from him. Never again would he have to endure the stress of guarding his title as he traveled. He could live in Perdana or in Calea or anywhere he wanted. A chuckle escaped his lips.

"What is it?" Jason craned his neck to look at the paper.

"Nothing. I just realized why it's named P and C. It's for Perdana and Calea, isn't it?"

"Yes, it is. You didn't know that?"

"Don't give me that look. I never thought about it before. When a man gives you a company and then tells you that company holds his title, you don't stop to analyze the name."

Jason shook his head and kissed Kale's lips. "We need to get some sleep. We have a big day ahead of us."

Kale placed the writ on the bedside table and turned off the lamp. Many more would join his by the end of the day.

Excitement had made breakfast difficult to swallow. Kale hadn't expected his stomach to be in knots over their day's plans. Jason must have felt the same, because he ate just as little and finished just as fast as Kale. As soon as the plates were cleared away, John joined them at the table to discuss how the day would unfold.

"We're going to bring the slaves in one by one and talk to them. Any slave who wants it will be granted freedom. Any freed slave will have the option to remain in their current position either for a wage or for a stake in the business," Jason explained to John.

"A stake in the business?"

"Yes. They've put more into this place than I have. For years, they've labored here without compensation to make this ranch what it is. If they're willing to continue to throw their lot in with ours, they'll reap the benefits of it. The shares given to freed slaves will come from mine. If they decide they want to leave, they'll be paid a sum from my personal accounts."

"Fair enough." John nodded.

Jason pulled out the writs of manumission and set the stack on the table. He slid one to John. "I'd like you to fill them out while I talk to each slave and then pass it to me to sign. It's pretty straightforward. You just have to write in their name and then the last name they're adopting. I'm offering all of them the Wadsworth name if they want it. Of course they're free to choose whatever they like, but they're responsible for building what the Wadsworth name stands for and may lay claim to it."

Jason had discussed it with Kale. For some reason, he'd thought Kale would mind sharing their name with so many people. Nothing could be further from the truth. Kale was honored, not only by the name, but by the incredible man he shared it with.

"Do you have any questions?"

"Nope. Let's get started."

Kale opened the door to the dining room. A line had formed outside, and he admitted the first person to be freed.

◆ ◆ ◆

"Billy, do you understand what all this means? Even if you choose to be free, you'll still have a place here. We're not going to turn you out."

"Yes, Master."

"Do you want to be free?"

Billy nodded.

"All right then. What do you want your last name to be? You can pick anything you like, even Wadsworth."

"Like you?"

"Yes, Billy, just like me."

"That's what I want, Master."

"I'm not your master anymore."

"Yes, Ma—Mr. Wadsworth."

◆ ◆ ◆

"Darlene, do you want to keep working here? We'd love to have you."

"Child, if I left, the lot of you would starve within a week. What have I ever done to make you think I'd let people starve as long as there is breath in my body? Don't tell me you thought you were going to let anyone else in my kitchen without me there. And I'll be taking the last name Wadsworth as well."

◆ ◆ ◆

"Demetri?"

"I'll take my freedom, sir."

"Are you going to stay here?"

"With all due respect, I think it's time I make my own way. It's too hard being here. This was always the master's dream, not mine. There's too many memories. Everywhere I turn, I see him. I need to move forward."

"Do you know what you want to do?"

"Honestly, no. I tried not to think about it too much. I didn't want to get my hopes up if the law didn't pass."

"Well, you're welcome to stay here as long as you need."

"Thank you. I appreciate it."

"Do you know what last name you want?"

"Roberts. Demetri Roberts."

◆ ◆ ◆

They'd freed every single Wadsworth slave by lunchtime. It was the best day's work Kale had ever done.

They gathered in the study with John, Thomas, Ellen, and Demetri after lunch to enjoy a glass of champagne to celebrate their freedom. Soon, they would be going out to the family plot to unveil the monuments to Robert and Adele. They had arrived months ago, but Kale and Jason had decided to hold off returning until matters with the law were settled one way or the other.

"Jason, I have something I want to give you before we unveil the memorials."

"Why do I get a present?" Jason's bewilderment was so adorable that Kale couldn't resist kissing the tip of his nose.

"Because I want to give you one." Kale'd had John bring it into the study earlier, so it would be ready. He'd shipped it to the ranch before they left on their vacation. Kale opened the crate and withdrew the painting. He removed the packing material and examined it before turning it around so Jason could see. "And for making me and your father proud."

Jason gasped. "I don't know what to say. It's beautiful. I can't believe you could do something like this." Jason stood to get a closer look. Kale had painted a portrait of Jason as a man with his mother and father.

"It was simple. I know what you look like well enough, and I had a fresh memory of Robert. I used the painting you brought home of your mother as a model."

"No, you don't get to belittle your talent this time. This is really amazing, Kale."

"It is. I didn't know when you said you were an artist you meant like this. I thought you just did those sketches. We'll have to have you do our wedding portrait." Thomas wrapped his arm around a glowing Ellen.

"It's a perfect likeness of him."

"Thank you, Demetri. That means a lot coming from you." Demetri didn't speak much since Robert passed. Kale suspected Robert's death had hit him harder than any of them could imagine. Jason had told him that they had been lovers for a time.

"Thank you, Kale." Jason had misty eyes when he kissed him, but there was a smile on his face. Kale was amazed at how well Jason had recovered from his father's death. He had kept expecting him to break down, but he hadn't. Looking at him now, Kale saw a strength he didn't think Jason had been aware he possessed.

At four o'clock, Jason entwined his fingers with Kale's and walked with him outside to the family plot with the others following. They had bundled up in coats and scarves against the chill. Clouds threatened to obscure the sun, but there was still light for a while. Once everyone was gathered, John removed the canvas tarps that covered the monuments.

Kale stepped forward to run his hand along the granite of his mother's memorial, barely registering Jason's awestruck exclamation. Jason had let him choose anything. The only image he could remember clearly enough of his mother to replicate was her hands. They were vivid in his mind, so worn and yet so gentle. They were a perfect representation of the woman he had known. He had drawn detailed pictures of them cupped together, palms up, giving, open and supplied them to the mason. Before him was a perfect recreation of those hands, and under them was his mother's name, Adele, etched in stone, never to wear away or be forgotten.

"Thank you, Jason." Kale choked on the words.

"It's an honor to have her memory here." Jason placed a hand on Kale's shoulder.

Kale collected himself and wiped the tears from his eyes before he stood. Robert's memorial was a bust of him as he appeared in the family portrait painted when Jason was a toddler. "It looks just like him." Jason marveled. Demetri murmured his agreement.

John cleared his throat. "I took the liberty of having something else installed as well." He walked over to a large oak tree, and Kale saw another tarp. John lifted it to reveal a wooden bench with wrought iron arms and legs. "I thought it'd be nice for people to have a place to sit when they come to pay their respects or just to think."

"It's wonderful, John. Thank you."

"You're welcome."

Jason took Kale's hand and led him to the bench. Together, they sat as everyone else made their way back inside. They were each wrapped in their own thoughts, letting the silence go undisturbed. Little snowflakes began to fall, resting for a moment on the granite statues before melting. Kale didn't mind the cold. He could feel the warmth of Jason's hand through his glove. Kale gazed at Jason, admiring his profile. He was so damn lucky.

This was love. It wasn't the sex, or the good times laughing with friends. It was weathering the storms. Love wasn't passionate; it was peaceful. It was the peace of knowing at the end of the day, there was another man who understood him, who knew him, who would let him stand by himself and catch him if he stumbled and fell, someone with whom the word wrong had no meaning. Wrong would only be being apart. Whatever storm raged around them, they stood together in the eye, the peaceful center. Love wasn't freedom. Kale had no desire for freedom. He was bound to Jason, as surely as Jason was bound to him. Love was the peace of knowing that he was all right, the security that no matter how dark the world around him grew, Jason would always see him. It was the peace of knowing that, no matter how ludicrous and illogical, Kale was as perfect for Jason as Jason was for him. It was the peace of two flawed men, joining their lives together, to create their own joy. Kale had known lust, happiness, and passion with Jason. Now he knew peace, and it was the sweetest of all.

Thank you for reading *Measure of Peace.*

If you liked *Measure of Peace*, please consider telling your friends about it or leaving a review.

To learn more about the author and sign up to be notified of new releases, visit CaethesFaron.com/Newsletter.